THE POWER POTENTIAL

MARK R. RIVARD

The Reading Glass Books
1-888-420-3050
www.readingglassbooks.com
fulfillment@readingglassbooks.com

Contents

Thursday, May 17, 1990, New York City

No one that watched them dance had any idea Mr. and Ms. Perfect had only met a few days earlier; they appeared to fit together perfectly, as if they had known each other for a lifetime. It seemed that it was a match made in Heaven. This ideal couple floated around the floor as if one person. When they danced, when they laughed, and when they moved, they moved as one, it appeared as if they were truly soul mates. When one of them started a sentence, the other would finish it. They laughed each time this happened. They were obviously made for each other.

All eyes were on them-the beautiful couple as they left the dance floor. They certainly were the envy of all who beheld their presence. They were stars. Julia, so beautiful, was a very successful actress; she had it all, but there were two things she still needed to make her life feel whole. She lacked a major leading role opposite a Harrison, Mel or Sean. All of her movies so far were well made and money makers, but she was not a household name but everyone recognized her. Her other aspiration was to meet a man with whom she could spend the rest of her life. It didn't matter what walk of life he came from. This felt like the one. She had found Victor or rather Victor had found her and with Victor, she knew she had found the first of the missing parts.

Victor Madison was everything a woman could wish for: He was a handsome, strong, virile young man, and a self-made millionaire. He was funny, classy, athletic and fun to be with. He showed her respect, and brought passion to her life. How could a woman not fall in love with a man like he. She was in love. For the first time in her life, she was truly in love. There was no doubt about it this was nothing she had ever felt.

As they danced, as they walked from the floor, she spoke softly, "I love you, Victor, I love you," she cried, "I've never been so happy in my life." She was restless, she beamed, it was a special night in her life, and she wanted everyone to know it. The dinner atop the Paradise Hotel was exactly as she had imagined in her dreams. The dance floor was perfect. Their evening had been perfect, as one could only imagine. Everything was perfect. Life was finally good. No….life was finally great.

Victor looked in Julia's eyes, "I love you too, Julia," he breathed into her left ear, kissing her on the neck. "Why don't we sneak back to the hotel room? I have a surprise for you; a wonderful surprise." He put his arm around her, hugged her and stared into her eyes. "Such a wonderful surprise," he whispered.

Her mind raced, she imagined the surprise and shivered, her lips parted, her eyes closed, her head rolled back and tilted to the right. She sighed, and in a deep gravely voice said, "I have a surprise for you too…I have one for you too. Let's go." A sly smile came across her face; they had not yet made love.

They had only been dating for a month; she had been swept off her feet, but had not yet slept with him. She had been too afraid to spoil a good thing. This was just one of the things that impressed her about him so much. He seemed to know exactly what she wanted, everything she wanted. It was a consummate match. It was an answer to her prayers. He was perfect. Tonight was the night. She would make it a very special night.

They walked down the club's hallway to the elevator. Their room was in the old tower of the hotel, built in the early nineteen hundreds. The hotel was totally renovated but in its original style. They had to go down the elevator, from the thirty-second floor, walk through the lobby to the front of the old hotel, and take another elevator to the tenth floor, which overlooked a full city block park in the center of the city. The old rooms were an immense exhibition of decadence-old and beautiful. Room 1032 was on the top of the old twin towers. They were home; brass knobs on the dressers and credenza, brass hooks on the doors, and a rich oak trim highlighted the entire room. There were imported, custom carpets, antique chandeliers, a king size canopied bed, and antique furniture. It was old and romantic-the perfect setting for a young couple in love.

All was perfect. They had barely gotten into the room. Julia could not hold back. She swung around thrusting herself onto him, "I love you, Victor, I want you, make love to me, be in me, make love to me." She pulled on his tie, kissing him with every fiber of her body. She wanted him right away.

"I want you so badly, Julia." He pulled her hips towards him. He slid her shoulder straps down over her arms, pulling the dress over her hips. She stood gazing into his eyes while it fell to the floor. They kissed; her hands pulled on the back of his head from behind. He lifted her into his arms, and carried her to the bed, laid her down and looked quietly down at her. "This is going to be so right, so good Julia, forever good, forever and ever."

As he lay her down on her back, she reached up and helped him unbutton his shirt. Victor looked down with his knees straddling her hips. He supported his upper body weight with his hands on either side of her head. Gazing into her eyes for a moment, he said, "I do love you, and I wish it could be different, but I need to protect Daddy."

"What do you mean? Protect Daddy, your Daddy? What are you talking about?" She felt him pull his knees firmer against the side of her body. She looked up into his eyes, puzzled and half-laughing. Her lips parted. Her mouth opened. She looked up into his eyes, wanting to kiss him, wanting him to kiss her, she looked into his eyes but...she became frightened. She felt like screaming, but didn't. She was in a confused trance. Numb with fear and confusion.

"Victor squeezed his knees tighter, holding her still on the bed. He gazed blankly at her face, but appeared to see nothing. He said nothing more. He quickly picked up the pillow and pushed it down hard over her face, pushing down harder. "I'm sorry, but it can't be any other way." Victor held his knees tightly against the sides of her body.

Julia's arm reached up for Victor. She grabbed for something but could only feel the muscles in his arms and sides as he held the pillow down. She wriggled, she struggled, she tried to fight, but she had no power. She tried to scream, but the pillow only sucked into her mouth and aided the suffocation. He was too strong, she could not move. She was helpless. Her hands held his rib cage momentarily and began to slide lifelessly down his side.

A few minutes went by, he lost track of how long, but he could feel the life leaving her body. She was motionless, and in a few minutes it was over. He held the pillow in place for another minute and waited. He placed his finger across her neck and checked for a pulse. He felt no pulse, no blood pumping through her vein. There was nothing. She was dead. He sat for a minute near the window, and gazed down into the lit park. A drunkard staggered and almost fell into a couple. He asked for money. They ignored him. He looked up towards the hotel, shook his head and stumbled off.

"It's time to go," Victor thought. With Daddy's instruction, it had all worked out just as he had planned. He took his small bag from the closet, took out his own clothes and shoes, his traveling clothes. He left everything else. He only needed his most important multiple ID's and cash for his getaway. The rest of the stuff could not be traced. He had bought all of it with cash after he arrived. He could not be followed. The only time he had been fingerprinted was as at the age of twelve, ten years ago. That was just before he had been given to his Daddy. Daddy ensured him that they would never match those prints with his adult prints. They would never think to look. He picked up the phone next to the bed and dialed the front desk. "This is Victor Madison, in room 1032. My friend and I are very tired, could you please hold all calls and the maid service until late tomorrow afternoon. We really need our rest."

"Very well, Mr. Madison, room 1032, no calls, no maid service until late tomorrow afternoon. That is no problem, sir, happy to be of assistance, thank you, sir." He went to the closet and located his leather carry-on bag. He emptied the contents onto the bed, quickly changing into his traveling clothes. He had come to town with only the clothes on his back. He put on his Levi jeans, loafers, a white button-down, braided belt, and jockey shorts, and carried the camel blazer over his arm. He picked up his small bag, and headed for the door. He turned to have one last look at Julia. "Daddy says it was best this way, for our protection, I know it is hard for you to understand, I'm so sorry," he said out loud. He cracked the door open, and peeked down the hallway, being careful not to be seen. As he closed the door he pulled the 'Do Not Disturb' sign off the inside knob, hung it on the outside, and closed the door.

He was careful not to look anyone in the eye as he rode the elevator down to the lobby. He wore lightly shaded glasses, and had changed the way he combed his hair by messing it up with gel, rather than combing it neatly. Daddy had told him that small changes in his appearance would make it difficult for someone to recognize him. On his way down the hall and while riding the elevator, he encountered less than a dozen people, including employees. He was positive no one would remember him as the same guest in room 1032. Within a few minutes, he was on his way to the airport in a cab. As he rode to the airport, he glanced at his tickets. He was on a United flight 412, departing at 2 a.m. for Toronto, under the name of Jon Pederson. Once in Toronto, he would purchase a ticket to St. Louis, under the name of Albion Gant. From there he changed carriers again, and would be registered as James Fender when he landed in Tulsa. Then he would fly to San Diego as Peter Hampton. The last leg of the flight would be home to Atlanta as himself, Randy Curtis. His small duffel bag contained the ID's and cash, Daddy had thought of everything-every little detail. He studied the personnel profile provided by Daddy; he knew her hobbies, likes, dislikes, favorite food, flowers and animals.

By the time the body was discovered, almost sixteen hours later, he would have already been five different people, and have flown to four cities. The last leg of his trip, he returned home using his real identity. There was no way he could be traced back to Atlanta, absolutely no way. They could never find him, because he had never really existed. He had become the mysterious lover of this young beautiful woman and had disappeared into thin air. He had eliminated her without a trace.

He paid the cab driver, and walked into the terminal and directly to the men's room. He put on his blazer, combed his hair neatly, and then stowed his glasses in the bag. He then proceeded to the ticket counter. He had timed the arrival perfectly; he had about twenty minutes before the plane's departure, and held only carry-on luggage. Now, he was just another traveler among many.

* * * * *

Next: A Reflective Flight Home

Jon Pederson took his seat next to the window and laid his head back and closed his eyes for a few moments and took a deep breath and exhaled long and slowly. The stewardess offered him a pillow and he accepted. A moment later, the "Fasten Seat Belts" light came on; he lay back against the pillow, closed his eyes and quickly envisioned the past few hours. He was not happy with what he had done, but it was a must. Daddy had instructed him to help, and he always helped Daddy, he had been trained to be appreciative and gracious. His mind wandered back in time. He was so grateful that he had met Daddy; he was so happy that his prayers had been answered all those years ago as a twelve-year old boy in trouble. Daddy had given him direction; he had given him life. He had saved him from the courts, and from some terrible foster home. Daddy had personally tutored him so he could catch up to his age group in school. If he had to repay him, he could never have made things even. He could only do as Daddy asked repayment enough, Daddy had told him. Randy felt obligated. He felt indebted. He remembered….so well…almost as if it were yesterday… he recalled how he met Daddy…

… The judge asked, "Are your parents here yet?" He cast his stern look in Randy's direction.

Randy on the other hand looked around the room nervously. "It's only my mother, and she won't be here, she is busy, sir, she is always busy, she's never here."

The judge looked up over his bifocals at a neatly dressed, clean-cut, young man. He was actually a handsome young kid, kind of cute. He didn't look like the usual ethnic gangbanger the judge met in court. He was Caucasian, without an accent, and just did not look like a punk. "Young man, do you realize the seriousness of your crime?"

"Yee-up, I do-oo," the boy sort of sung the answer with an attitude. He wanted to get this over with.

"My God, at your age, what are you doing here in my court?"

"I wish I knew judge."

The judge peered over the top of his glasses again at Randy Curtis. He wondered how a twelve-year old could get to this point. Especially with this youngster, he didn't look the part. Either he was totally naive or one hell of an actor. "You have been charged with breaking and entering, grand theft, grand theft auto, and driving without a license. You were caught with Mr. Sorenson's television, stereo and some other items belonging to Mr. Sorenson in Mr. Sorenson's truck. That's a pretty gutsy move. You take all of the guy's stuff, put it in his truck and drive away. How does a twelve year old pick up a 30lb television. You're twelve years old and this is not the first time you have been in trouble. You've broken a lot of different laws and found trouble since you were nine years old, but this is real serious. You are a repeat offender. You are in trouble, young man. What do you think I should do with you? You got any ideas."

The young boy tried to act interested, but after all, he was a seasoned criminal. His early home life had begun as an abused youngster. But now, after two or three years of this stuff, he just wasn't sure if he cared. "I don't know judge; I guess you gotta do what you gotta do." He also knew they would not send him to jail, maybe a juvenile home of some kind. He would probably be free in nine months to a year.

"Mr. Curtis, on the suggestion of the District Attorney and the Juvenile Custody Division, we will remand you over to the Juvenile Psychiatric Clinic in Long Island. You will be tested and evaluated over the next thirty days. After that time, we will decide what to do with you; most likely you will be placed with a foster family. Your mother has proven that she cannot take care of you; she did not even bother to contact the courts. And it appears by your earlier records, she never has made an attempt to help. Bailiff, take Mr. Curtis into custody, someone from the clinic will be here this afternoon to pick him up. And try to find his mother."

* * * * *

Randy Curtis' mother was once a beautiful woman. She had dreamed of being a famous actress, but booze and drugs had gotten the best of her. Her reputation for bad work habits overpowered her beauty and talent, and she began to look for income from other sources. Prostitution paid the most for the least amount of work-in the beginning-high class stuff though, appointments and big money only. She had some pretty good connections, working mostly with film studio people when they visited from LA. She had married once, another abuser, Randy's father. During many of their drug and alcohol binges, they had fought violently. While Randy was very young, he had suffered serious emotional abuse, not to mention the physical abuse from both of them. Roger Curtis' favorite was to see how much pain Randy could endure from burning cigarettes before he would scream. He had numerous, small circular burn marks on various parts of his body. His mother had spanked him so hard that permanent bruises were left on his ass, but the serious mental scars were not as visible. He had learned to block out the physical pain, as well as the pain of reality at an early age; he had an invisible bubble surrounding himself. He had cultivated a grand imagination, and would just invent another thought to replace the real thing. A lot of kids do this without even thinking; just block it out. His mother's life kept going downhill. By the time he was ten, she was doing anybody who would pay.

Randy was expected to do men, women, two men, whatever paid the bills. He had been included in a one particular scenario; the man had offered her triple the regular price if she would include Randy in the deal. He was nine. He knew it was wrong, but he imagined he was in bed with a large teddy bear. It hurt him, but his mother needed his help, she said. Help to pay the bills. He learned to use his imagination to the fullest extent. He could put himself anywhere he wanted, anytime he needed to do something painful, he just traveled in his mind. He would imagine he was doing something else. He had gotten good at it. But now, he wanted to be away from her, away from the pain. There had to be something better, even jail would be better than what was going on at home. So, maybe he had to go to a clinic, and then to a foster home. He had thought he would never tell of his home life. He was afraid of what might happen if he told. Now, he did not care, he would tell, if it would help him get away. He wondered to himself what a psychiatric clinic was like.

* * * * *

Daydreaming and thinking of...

The stewardess' hand tapped him on the shoulder. "Excuse me sir, we are approaching the airport, could you please put your seat in the upright position, I'll take that pillow from you."

Within twenty minutes, the plane was on the ground, and Jon Pederson was on his way to the airline counter; he only stopped momentarily to stuff his blazer into the bag, and mess his hair up a little more. He put on his tinted glasses again; he wanted to change his appearance just a little. He did not want to be too cocky. Daddy had told him to do just the opposite at the next stop. He approached the counter, reached into a side pocket bag in his flight bag, and pulled out $400. He leaned over the counter slightly with the money in his hand. "I would like a one-way ticket to St. Louis, Missouri, please."

"Yes sir, that flight leaves in twenty minutes, the cost is one hundred thirty one dollars please. What is your name? Do you have any luggage?"

He looked around; this time of the morning there was no one around except the ticket people, and the man working one of the riding-type floor cleaners. "Jon Pederson." He handed her the money. "I just have this carry-on bag, quick business trip, you know?"

She pushed the computer buttons, handed him his change, and within moments a ticket was printed, and in is hand. "Confirmed flight, Mr. Pederson, Gate 33, 2:03 a.m. The flight is on schedule, have a good trip."

"Thank you very much." He didn't say much as he didn't want to draw attention to himself, even with a different name. Nothing he did should draw attention.

The ticket lady watched him as he walked away. She noticed how handsome and well proportioned he was. He had an easy relaxed walk, and a pleasant, peaceful look on his face. He was young and solid, and traveled light. A lot of these businessmen had more than one office with clothes waiting for them. Not unusual.

As the L-1011 reached twenty-seven thousand feet and leveled off, Randy dozed off again. He was in his half-day dream, half-asleep mode. As he gazed out of the window at the city lights, he recalled his first meeting with Daddy, some twelve years ago. The first time they met, there were eight other young boys in the room, seated in chairs arranged in a half moon, while the doctor sat on the floor, looking up at them. He later found out that the psychiatrist wanted to help these young boys feel more powerful, by having them look down at an authority figure. More powerful by being above, more powerful by not feeling inferior. It was necessary for them to feel more powerful than the doctor, so they felt better about themselves; it was part of the therapy to help them acquire more self-esteem. The doctor taught them that people with low self-esteem could not achieve control over their lives, and usually felt powerless to do anything about it. His therapy began with his greeting, and attitude toward them.

"Good morning, gentlemen." The psychiatrist spoke with confidence. He didn't treat the boys like the cops did. The cops seemed mad; this guy seemed friendlier. Yet, even as a nice guy, he could not be trusted. Most of the boys were already figuring out how to get over on this guy. They all knew the game; they acted sorry for what they did, and showed remorse. The smart ones went from arrogant to humble in a heartbeat. They knew that if they held the fake attitude together, they would be handed the easiest judgment available. They simply lied their way through the program, got through it, and got out. But Randy felt differently about this deal. Randy felt good about the doctor the moment he walked into the room.

"I've been told that the eight of you are here because you have made life difficult for your families, your friends, your victims and yourselves. I am here to see if I can help you. That's right. Help you! Help you figure out why you do the stupid things that get you into places like this--and worse. If you listen, be honest, follow directions, I can save you all from repeating these mistakes. You will learn the right way or the best way to do things-not the dumbest way. I only want to see you all once. When we are done with this series of classes, I don't want to see you in a future series. So, try to graduate.

* * * * *

My name is Eric Bright. I am a psychiatrist, a doctor of psychiatry. For those of you who may not know what that means, psychiatrists are regular doctors who look at brains, instead of legs or arms. I like brains. I like to look at them in pictures, out of the body and cut apart, and in books, but especially when they are still in a person, and causing a problem. While you are here I will be writing down all the problems, and how we fixed them. Your names won't be used, just your problems. In the future, students of psychology and psychiatry will use part of the work we do here as a textbook for their study. In other words, you guys will be the book. By being in this book you will be helping others learn from your mistakes. Some of you may feel very good about helping others, and some of you will not care. But beware, because part of my job is to help you care. The program is not easy, or short. We may be together for a couple of years, but I am here to help. I am your grandmother, and this program is like chicken soup for your brain. Are there any questions at this time?" No one spoke.

"Okay, no questions, let's get started and since we must start somewhere, you can begin by giving your first name, where you come from and why you are here." He looked up from his lotus position, and looked around the circle to the first boy on this left. "You can go first." The boy made a noise from his throat, and gestured as if he were going to hawk-tooey on the doctor. The other boys broke into laughter. The doctor formed his hands in his lap as if he were going to catch slime. The boys laughed even louder.

Maybe this won't be so bad, Randy thought. This guy's okay, the cops would have screamed and thought of some bullshit duty to pull.

"Now, may we proceed?" The doctor asked loudly.

The same boy introduced himself and began to speak. As his story of stealing and bullying came out- he had finally been caught in a TV store trying to steal two VCRs at the age of eleven, his fifth arrest - Randy tried to organize his thoughts. His turn was next, and it came soon enough.

Randy's story was similar- fights, arguments, lying, stealing, trouble with his mother, and abuse from his father. Each time he got into trouble, it was something bigger, something more expensive. The final straw came when he was caught in the pick-up truck with the owner's goods. Each one of the boys had a similar story. An hour later, Randy was back in his room-cell-in juvenile detention. He had been paired off with another young boy who was the same age, and had a similar background; the group would meet again in two days for another sit down discussion. They would have a chance to talk about the hell they had been through. When the doctor had enough information about the boys, he would meet with each one of them four hours a week for another ten weeks; their level of response would determine how long each child stayed in the program. Randy remembered one of his group sessions when he had been asked to recall the worst things that had happened to him. His first recollection of his abusive situation had been when he was three, maybe four years old.

"Tell me, Randy, do you remember anything when you were young that really hurt you? I don't mean just physically, but something that made you feel terrible inside. Tell me if there was anything that you felt you could not control, change, or do anything about. Tell me something that made you feel like you were worthless and useless."

Randy thought for a minute; he was very reluctant to tell or even try to remember some things. He began to speak slowly, one word at a time. "My… father… used… to… put… my food in… in … in a bowl on the floor next to the cat's food." His eyes began to well up with tears, but he held back the actual crying. "Then he would laugh hard from his beer belly; his head would fall back, he'd grab his stomach and laugh, and say, "It's easier to raise two pets at the same time.""

Then he would open a beer, and chug it down. He was gross." Randy began to get mad, and it showed on his face as a scowl. He could talk much more easily now that he was angry. "He was a total asshole, and he loved being that way. I mean he really enjoyed being an asshole." The others started to laugh, point and elbow each other, whispering amongst themselves. Randy's eyes darted around the room.

It was a terrible feeling, he felt like crap all over again. He stopped, he didn't want to share, and he was embarrassed. He stared at the blank wall; he was destroyed all over again. He felt as if he was back at square one.

The doctor broke in, "Randy, hey, my young friend, listen! The reason we're here is to talk about it. Why did you get here? How did you get here? It is not all your fault. Sure, you did the stuff, the stupid stuff. But, you are the victim. They did it to you; you are not to blame. You can learn to live differently. You don't have to continue your life doing to others as was done to you. You took the blame, and by robbing, stealing and hurting others, you made the wrong people pay. But, not any more."

The doctor grabbed Randy by the chin with his right thumb and forefinger. "Try looking at it this way. Everything done to us is connected to what we do at a later date. If Joe hits you, you hit back. Neither of you were right, but you had the chance to not hit. You had a choice. You didn't have to hit back. I will teach you to see the choices, and wait just a moment before you make the choice. I will help you make the correct choices. Sometimes, you get hit on Monday, but you don't do anything until Saturday. Sometimes you don't do anything until a year from Monday. You do have a choice. You don't have to hit back at all. Do you understand what I am saying?"

Randy nodded a 'yes.'

"You other guys understand what I'm saying? Anybody here have a question about this stuff?" There was a whir of 'yeah' and 'you got it, doc.' but the good doctor had his doubts. "Listen, guys, this stuff will help. We are all going to deal with this crap. All of you! Listen for just a minute…pay attention and listen. Some things that were done to you as small children have an effect on your lives. You act out, creating problems for everyone around you. Most of the youngsters in your situation are angry with their parents for things that they should have protected them from. Deep inside, you all want to get even, to punish someone. I am telling you that most of you are really pissed and fighting mad. If you don't deal with it now, if you don't try to fix that pain and anger now, you'll never get over it. It will be with you until you die. Get into it, solve it, hear it, live it again, and fix it. Your anger is your trouble. You are all rebels; you're mad, so you rebel against society in general. You take out all your hurt on everybody else. Your rebellion is nothing more than a need for attention, you are really just trying to say, "I didn't do it, they hurt me, they made me do it, I really didn't want to!" Well, guess what? You've got our attention, so talk!"

Randy tried to talk, but now he was embarrassed and angry. He could feel the anger building from deep within, like a whirlwind gaining power, growing larger and larger. He recognized what the doctor had said. It pissed him off; he didn't like being laughed at. But, he had this fire burning deep inside. He was pissed at his mother, his father, and her boyfriends, all of them. He was so pissed at so many things; he didn't even know what pissed him off the most. His reaction was street learned. "I can't say anymore, you guys are going to get into my shit, and then I'm going to have to kick some ass."

"You ain't kicking no ass, muthafucka, I be kickin' yo' ass." The big, black kid leaning back in the chair mouthed up. He was bigger than anybody in there. Randy's first thought was to look around the room for something to hit him with.

The doctor broke in, "We can have you handcuffed if you want trouble, knock off the bullshit."

"Muthafucka, I get your ass later."

"You better watch your own ass," Randy warned him.

Add a space here

"And I'll get both your asses." The doctor was getting a little short in the fuse department. "We've got work to do. Mr. Curtis, get on with your story." There was silence for about five minutes, and then Randy began again. He spoke hesitantly at first, but each time he went to the meetings, the sessions became easier for him. Soon it was as easy as telling a story.

* * * * *

Life Goes On

The group meetings were held daily, but it was in the individual sessions when the doctor would actually determine the patient's needs, and their treatments. It would be two to three weeks yet before Randy met the doctor one-on-one. Days passed, Randy finished his whole story, and talking became easier at each group meeting. Time went by fast, and Randy's first individual session came soon enough.

"Good morning Randy, how has your stay been so far?"

"I'm getting used to it, Doc."

As the screeching wheels touched down, he was brought sharply back to reality. His head bobbed forward and back as the brakes caught hold, and he stretched his arms upward, wriggling his shoulders free of tension. He then unbuckled his safety belt, reached down to pick up his small bag from under the seat, and glanced at his watch. The plane was on schedule; within forty-five minutes, James Fender would be on his way to Tulsa. In less than three hours he was already a second person, and her body had not even been found yet; no one even knew that a crime had been committed. This was too easy. He felt safe already, but would only feel totally secure once he was home. Approximately seven hours to go, get the new ID, cash, get his ticket, and get to the plane.................. so easy. His head lurched back as the plane climbed steadily. He felt himself sink back into another new seat-another new plane, another window, and another direction. He breathed a sigh of relief. He closed his eyes, gazed out the window and went back to his daydream.

.... "One of the stories you told us was about eating dinner with the cat, which was a pretty mean thing to do, don't you think?

How did you feel about that? Did that make you angry, sad, inferior to other children, inferior to your father? Did you feel like an animal?"

"I'm not sure, I didn't think about it much the first time it happened. I thought I was a bad kid, and was being punished. After a while though, I started to get pissed. I wanted to do something to get even with him."

"What did you want to do to get even with him?" Dr. Bright felt he might have to pull this out of him; some of these kids had suppressed things very deeply. They basically lied to themselves about what had happened, which was their own form of denial.

"Well, I really didn't know when most of the things were happening. I remembered them later. I wished he hadn't done those things to me."

"Were there other things that were as bad, or worse?"

"Shit, I don't know, I guess so." Randy seemed very reluctant to talk. He wasn't completely comfortable around the doctor yet. He liked him, but he couldn't talk as freely as the doctor expected him to. It was hard to explain a lot of it; he had just learned to deal with it. The doctor made Randy feel relaxed, safe, but not completely safe.

"You guess so? What does that mean? The guy treated you like an animal; he kicked the shit out of you. Maybe, you don't think those things are bad. I do! You MUST talk about it now, or it will resurface later in your life, and make you miserable. We need to get to the bottom of your feelings; you need to admit it all happened and that it was bad. We will not be able to make things better for you until we can do this work; it is called therapy, and it is the only way you will heal yourself. Now, do you want to talk more about the cat thing? Or would you rather talk about something else?"

"Something else."

"Like what?"

"I don't know, nothing."

"Nothing, nothing at all? You must have one story."

"Well, maybe my birthday," he said reluctantly.

"What happened? Which birthday was it?"

"Fourth. He had said he would teach me to swim; I had seen a swimmer on TV, and asked if it was hard to do. He told me he was a great swimmer, and could teach me easily. When he got home that afternoon, he was drunk. I didn't want to go with him because of the booze. He forced me to go, said he would beat my ass if I didn't go. We went to the community pool, and when we got there, he picked me up and carried me to edge of the pool. He threw me into the deep end, but I couldn't swim at all. He kept yelling at me to move my arms, and when I'd go under and then somehow get my head above water, he would reach that pole with the basket to me. I'd grab the end and he'd pull me to the side of the pool. When I climbed out, he'd push me back, and keep dunking my head under the water. He was screaming at me to swim, and I yelled back that I couldn't. I was crying and screaming for help; a lifeguard finally came down, and told my dad he was going to call the police. I was cold, I kept choking, and I was afraid he was going to kill me. When we got back to the apartment, he whipped me with a belt and locked me in my room. Then he came into my room, and ate cake in front of me and wouldn't let me have any. If he did those things to me now, I would kill him, fucking kill him. I don't take any shit from anybody who hurts me now." His eyes were wet; his face red with anger and hurt. His mouth tightened and the veins popped out on his neck. Randy had never told anybody these stories, but there were many, many more.

" Okay, Randy, I understand, it hurts. It's okay to cry if you want to, and if you don't want to, then don't. I'm going to show you how to calm down. Sit in this chair." The doctor pulled out a folding chair; Randy walked over and sat down. "Now, sit in the chair with your back straight, leaning as far back in the chair as you can. Look straight ahead, and place your palms facedown on each thigh. Put your feet flat on the floor, point them straight-ahead, and close your eyes. I want you to take a deep breath, and let the air out through your mouth and nose at the same time. Sit very still. Keep breathing deeply, air out from the nose and mouth at the same time. Now, listen to me, and try to make my words form a picture. These things that happened are in the past, a long time ago; it's all over. I want you to imagine a nicer place. Have you been to the beach?" Randy nodded his head 'yes.' "Did you like the beach, were the waves rolling over and over?" 'Yes,' again. "Now, I want you to imagine the waves, and keep breathing deeply. Do you remember the waves rolling in? Keep breathing; keep the picture in your mind. Waves rolling in, deep breath in, deep breath out. Keep the waves. Listen to your breathing. Feel the breathing; air deep into the lungs, air out. See the waves? In, out. Now, you are going to lie on the beach. On top of your stomach place the cat food dish, fill it with cat food. Can you see yourself with the bowl on your stomach?"

Randy nodded.

"Air in, air out. Waves in! Waves out! The air and the waves come in at the same time; the air and the waves pull out at the same time. The next wave barely touches your hand, and when it leaves it takes a little sand through your fingers. It makes your hand feel so good as it pulls you towards the ocean. The water cleans your hand; the wave cleans the shore when it leaves. All the things lying in the sand are gone when it leaves. Air Iiiiiiiiiinnnn. Air Ouuuwwt. Put a piece of cake on top of the cat food. The next wave laps over your arm, and out it goes, the water and sand pull you a little towards the ocean. The wave comes in over your arm and hits your rib cage, Ouuwwt. It feels great; it's so gentle. On top of the cake, let's balance a small stepfather. He is standing on the cake. The next wave comes in over your arm, over the cat's dish, over the food, over the cake, over the man. Ouwwt goes the wave. It's all gone. The wave has cleaned the mess off your stomach, taking all the bad things with it. Now, it is just you, the waves, and your breath - keep breathing, deeper, deeper breaths. You are clean; just lie there on the beach and keep cleansing yourself. Twenty-five more waves come in and out. Count them as they come in. Keep the picture going, I will be back in five minutes." The doctor left the room, but walked around the corner and watched Randy through the two-way mirror. Randy followed his directions perfectly. Five minutes went by, but it seemed like a lifetime to him.

When the doctor entered the room, he spoke softly. "Randy, can you hear me?" Randy nodded. "It is time to leave the beach, and return to the office. The waves are not reaching you anymore; they are receding. You stand up and walk away from the ocean. There is a wooden wall a few yards away from you, with a lone door in the middle of it. You open the door, walk through it into my office and sit in the chair. Open your eyes. You are back."

Randy opened his eyes, and looked around. He felt calm; he felt almost happy. He had never felt this way before.

"How do you feel, Randy?"

"I'm not sure, Doc, this is something way different than anything."

"Is it a good feeling?"

"Yes, it is. I feel clean, even though I have not taken a shower. I feel really clean. I feel good. That was neat."

"Randy, you just learned to meditate. Spend a half hour each day doing this; each time you go to the ocean, pile these things that have hurt you onto your stomach, actually your solar plexus, right here." Dr. Bright put the palm of his right hand on his solar plexus to show him. "Just above your stomach-this is your center-and wash them into the ocean. Soon, you will learn to live by this meditation, this cleansing. Do you have any questions?"

"Ah um, I don't know, it seems too easy." He felt the calmness wash over him once again, and he smiled.

"It will help you stay relaxed, and make you feel better about yourself. We'll talk again tomorrow, I'm sure you will have a question or two by then."

The next day, Randy went to the doctor's office.

"Good morning, Randy. How are you today?"

"Great, just great."

"Good. Today, I have a few questions, and then we'll do the meditation again. There are many details that need to be filled in. I'd like to get into this, and then meditate as soon as possible. Are you ready?"

"Yeah, I think so, yeah, let's go." Randy felt so good; he couldn't wait to get started.

"Let's get started!"

"OK, here we go. I want to talk a little about your mother, and her part in all of these things that were done to you. Where was your mother when all this happened?"

"She would take a nap, or take a walk, or hide in the bedroom. She worked at night, mostly. She seemed to always have a headache. She very often didn't feel good."

"Do you think she knew what was going on?"

"I don't know. She wasn't blind."

"What did she do when she found out?"

"Nothing."

"Nothing? Not anything?"

"Nope, sometimes she did stuff too."

"You mean she abused you?"

"Yeah, I guess so."

"What do you mean, you guess so? Do you want to talk about that?"

"Not really."

"Why not?"

"I never told anybody about those things."

"What things?"

"You are trying to trick me into talking about it, but maybe I don't want to talk about it."

"Why not, she isn't here to hurt you? It's all over, it won't happen again. Sometimes it helps to talk. Tell me how she got along with him."

"I don't know if she got along with anyone. When I was five, she kicked him out 'cause he was beating her up."

"Did he ever beat you up, I mean really hurt you so badly you had to go to the hospital?"

"Naw, not bad, but he did beat her bad, so she went to the hospital. That's when she went to court, and had him thrown out. She only kept him around cause he got free money, and she hated to work. But he started to hurt her."

"Free money?"

"Yeah, he was a fireman and got hurt. They paid him full pay `cause he couldn't work another job. That's why she let him stay."

"What kind of hurt?"

"Some kind of back deal."

"So she got help from the courts, kicked him out, and he never came back?"

"Nope, he never did."

"So then what did she do for money?"

"Well, the court said he had to pay her something, but it wasn't enough. So, she began selling it."

"Selling it?"

"Yeah, a hooker."

"Where did she work? On the street, in bars, hotels?"

"Mostly at home, the phone was always ringing, and there were quite a few guys around. She must be good at it because she always had some money. Sometimes she would hand me five and I had to leave. Then, a couple o' years ago she told me I had to get my own money. I could stay there, but she wasn't going to pay for my shit."

"So you started stealing stuff?"

"Yeah."

"What about the things she did to you?" Randy was startled, the lights suddenly came on, and he heard the captain's voice.

"We are now approaching Tulsa Airport, please fasten your seat belts, and put your seats in the upright position." Randy's thoughts were interrupted; he picked up his small flight bag, and searched for his money and 'Peter Hampton' identification; just in case they asked, he wanted to have his ID close at hand. So far, nobody had asked yet, but he wanted to be prepared. It had all worked so easily. Daddy was so clever; he had foreseen all the pitfalls, and things were working just fine. The next leg of the trip would take him to San Diego, and in just a few hours, Randy would be boarding a plane from San Diego to Atlanta, as himself.

* * * * *

Another Flight, another city, another person.

As Randy sat in seat 7c against the window, just in front of the wing, he strapped himself in, and immediately fell back into his trance, even before the small trucks backed the plane onto the tarmac. He was tired. Flying at night was good; there were very few people on these planes. As Daddy had said, with no one on the planes there would be no one to recognize him, and when he got to San Diego he would just be returning from a long business trip. Ever since he had left New York, he seemed to be in a semi-zombie state. Not asleep, and not awake. In this dazed state, he began to think; he had killed one person before. Just like this time, he had to protect himself and his home. This time he also had to protect Daddy; he wasn't about to let this woman destroy their relationship. He laid his head back, and began his daydream.

When you are ten years old, the idea of being with boys instead of girls seems okay, sometimes. Many boys go through that stage; his mom had told him that it was okay. "Now, honey, when this man comes in, be really nice to him, he likes you."

"Who is the man?"

"He is one of my regular clients, you'll recognize him. He really likes you; in fact he likes you more than he likes me. I told him that you liked him, and wanted to please him, so he is going to be with you instead of me. He is going to want you to help him, and he will pay us a lot of money for your help. So you be nice to him."

"What kind of help does he want?"

"He'll show you, remember he is giving us a lot of money. Every week he will give us a lot of money. You want to help mummy pay the bills, don't you?"

"Yes, I do, but............I'm not sure about this."

"Just do as he says, he will take care of us, okay, Randy? He's really going to take care of us. He will give us a lot of money. I'll be there in the beginning, and then you'll have to help him, just like I help him sometimes."

"Yes, mom, but what do I have to help him with?"

"I said he'd show you." She sounded angry, and in a hurry. "Just do what I say!"

Randy instinctively knew that there would be sex involved; he didn't know how, but he knew. He prepared himself; as this was not the first time he had had to be somewhere else when it got ugly. His father had hurt him in so many ways, but he had taught himself to travel to other places, and ignore the pain. He learned to picture different places; he learned to make the picture in his mind more important than anything else going on around him. Meditating was so similar; he knew he'd have to do it again.

He remembered the man helping him take off his clothes; he remembered his fat, ugly body, the smell of cigarettes, and him leaving an hour later. It was over. The next morning he remembered blood in the toilet, and he hurt. He hurt so much. He wished he could get even. For four months, every Wednesday night, he traveled. He used to go to the library, and look through the Encyclopedias at the pictures of tropical islands. Every Wednesday night he was gone, gone to one of those pictures. No one could find him when he left, not until he was ready to be found. He had taught himself to travel in his mind. When he began the journey for Daddy, he had ~~put~~ imagined himself in a perfect life with the perfect woman; he was there the night he had eliminated Julia, and would not be found until he arrived in Atlanta. Daddy told him it was okay to eliminate someone if they tried to hurt you, just like he did to the man who hurt him. It was okay; he just had to travel in his mind.

"I don't want you here tonight," his mother said.

"But, this is a good movie, it's a Charles Bronson movie. It's almost over."

"I said leave, I have a client. How else do you expect me to pay the bills?"

Randy left. Soon afterward four fire trucks showed up, Randy was on the front stoop about the same time his mom showed up on the porch.

"What happened, whose car is that?"

"It's his."

"Ralph's? What the hell happened?" His mother looked on in horror.

He had never heard his name before, "Ralph is gone, and I was in Hawaii." Randy mumbled to himself, and walked away.

"What did you say?" asked his mother.

"Nothin' mom, nothin'." As he walked down the porch steps, turning in the opposite direction from the fire, he thought, "Now he can't hurt me anymore."

Daddy had told him that although it was a terrible thing, sometimes, in self-defense, it might be something you have to do. When the adults around the child don't help, or won't help, it may be an acceptable out. "The man was hurting you, you were protecting yourself," he had told him many, many times.

He thought to himself if only Julia had not tried to hurt Daddy. She seemed very nice, and she was beautiful, like his mother. But in extreme cases, there was no other way. His mind wandered to the present, and his eyes opened. He looked out the window, as the plane circled out over the ocean, and headed back towards the airport. He guessed they had landed from the ocean side so if the plane crashed, it wouldn't wipe out a whole neighborhood.

Randy Curtis bought his ticket, and got a cup of coffee. He hadn't eaten or drunk anything since leaving New York. He wasn't even sure if he was hungry, but he ate a Danish anyway. Another five and half-hours and he would be home; he could go back to work as a freelance architect, and things would be normal again. He had been away on this 'project,' as Daddy had called it, for almost a month. He didn't like the project; at least the end of the project was distasteful, the first part was fun. "She shouldn't have tried to hurt us though," he thought. Daddy was his best friend. Daddy had taken care of him for ten years now; he had taken care of everything. But this time, Daddy had needed HIS help. He had made it so easy to seduce her; he had all the details- the right words, the right flowers, food, colors, car, cologne, dance-everything was made to be perfect. It was so easy to meet her, seduce her. His game plan was all laid out. Just like Daddy had told him, if you just give her everything she wants, she'll be yours. He was so smart. When she is yours, eliminate her, quietly. Smother her with a pillow; don't let go until you are sure she is gone. Now, they were both safe from a woman who could hurt them. "If you hurt Daddy, you hurt Randy." That was what Daddy had told him. Randy passed the time with breakfast, magazines, and music, and before he knew it, the plane had landed in Atlanta.

"Cab," he yelled, as he walked from the arriving flight's doorway. A yellow cab pulled up to the curb, and Randy Curtis threw his bag in the back seat and got in. "Pheasant Run Condos, out on Peachtree Lane, South Blvd, number 3045." The cab sped off.

"That will be eleven twenty, sir."

"Here's $15, keep it, thanks." He walked up the stairway and opened the door, making a beeline for the phone. "212.344.7009," he said out aloud as he hit the buttons. The phone rang at least a dozen times, but he let it ring. The phone was in Daddy's private office in the back, and it sometimes took him a few minutes to get there if he had a client; a little red light would go off in the front office, and he would excuse himself. The back office had a secret resting room with a bed, and music, so Daddy could rest when he was tired. It also had a secret elevator, behind the hardwood bookcase. It was fast and quiet, it took half the time to get to the office as a regular elevator, and it couldn't even be heard. It reminded him of a Dracula movie with special passageways. The elevator was so quiet it didn't even make a noise when it stopped and the doors opened. Daddy had made it like that so the SP's, Special People, could come and go without being noticed or heard. The SP's were assigned numbers to protect their privacy. Randy was SP1001; Julia had been SP1002. SP also meant Special Project. They were supposed to be in Daddy's next book. He would use these people to write the perfect book on learning to be powerful. Daddy thought that most people needed to learn how to feel powerful, and to use their power to become personally successful. He also needed these clients to be secret so no one could steal his ideas. Randy was learning to be powerful, Julia was also learning, but she got some strange ideas and had to be eliminated. She was going to tell everyone about Daddy's Special Project and ruin everything. He didn't have a choice; it had to be done.

"Hello," he answered.

"Daddy, it's done, there was no problem. I liked her, but she can't hurt us now. When can I see you?"

* * * * *

"Good afternoon, gentlemen. Who wants to fill me in?" The body had been discovered by the maid service, and the police called. Rudy Auggur, homicide detective, was assigned the case. He was twenty-seven, had been in blue for six years, and had applied for homicide detective and been promoted.

"Hey, Auggur, get your errands taken car of?" Sergeant Moleson, who usually partnered Auggur, had ridden over in a squad car. He was the first on the scene, and had started the preliminary report. "We've got a Caucasian female, early twenties, found in the bed, partially dressed in sexy lingerie, cause of death- she was smothered with a pillow."

"Who found her?"

"The maid service." It looks like the killer called the front desk last night, and asked not to be disturbed until late this afternoon. He already has an eighteen-hour head start.

"Did you establish the time of death?"

"Sometime between 10 p.m. and 2 a.m."

"Do we have a name and a description, whose room is this?"

"Guy's name is Victor Madison, 6' tall, athletic build, brown hair, early twenties; the room was in his name. Other than the body in the bed, everything in the room is clean. He even left his clothes. Good stuff, Saks, Nieman-Marcus-top of the line shit."

"How did he pay? Can we run a credit card check?"

"No good, he paid for everything in cash. We have an address for him in Ontario, Canada, town called Sarnia. We're checking it out now."

"I have a gut feeling on this one, there will be no leads, it is too neat. I mean, it was quiet, no mess, and an eighteen-hour head start; looks like it was well planned." Auggur's experience gave him an inclination on this one.

"Moleson, can you get me a history on this girl? Like for starters where she lives?"

Add a space here

" I have her purse and drivers license. She lives here in New York; I think this address is in Manhattan."

"That was quick, you don't mess around," he quipped.

"Here's an Actor's Guild membership card. It figures."

"It figures, what do you mean?" Rudy asked.

"Well, look how beautiful she is; she had to be a model, or an actress, or something like that."

Auggur agreed. "Yeah, she certainly is beautiful. How could someone this young and beautiful make someone else angry enough to murder her? Maybe she had a past, like she was a hooker or something. This makes no sense; I'm going to her home, and to talk to her friends. Call the Actor's Guild; find out what you can. Let's try to make some sense of this mess. Guys, listen up, let's dust this place, take the clothes in, and see what you can find out about this man. What's her address?"

"Actually, I think this address is in Washington Heights, 175th and Wadsworth, 17555 Wadsworth, apartment 3c. That's a pretty nice area."

Rudy Auggur and Mitch Moleson had been on a couple hundred cases together, but this was different; this was a real mystery. It just didn't make sense, what motive could there possibly be? They rode the elevator down to the lobby.

"What do you make of this one, Rudy?"

"So far, I'm pretty confused, Mitch. It's almost like reading a murder mystery. Handsome man kills beautiful girl, man disappears without a trace."

"Yeah, it feels kind of weird. It's too clean, like a conspiracy, why would anybody conspire to kill this innocent young girl? It makes no sense." The door opened, and Rudy and Mitch made a beeline for the front door, and their car. Mitch was the designated driver. They pulled away from the front of the hotel, and headed east on 48th Street to Broadway, and then headed north. The drive would take about thirty minutes.

Rudy picked up the hand mike, and called in. "Detective Auggur here, over."

"Go ahead, over."

"Have one of the officers at the Paradise Hotel ask around, see if this Victor Madison guy left the hotel in a rental car or cab, over. Have him interview people on the front desk, room service, and housekeeping. Let's see if this guy has left any kind of clues. Just have him put his report on my desk, ASAP, over."

"Right away, Rudy, anything else?" came the response.

"That will do it, out." Rudy hung up the handset.

"I really doubt if we will get anything on this guy, I mean, look at that room. Other than a messed up bed, and a dead body, there was nothing to see. This deal was really slick, nothing left to investigate."

The detective's unmarked car pulled up in front of the Henderson Apartments building. "Here we are, Rudy."

Rudy and Mitch walked up the twelve cement steps, and looked at the mailbox. "Manager is in 1a, Rudy." Mitch buzzed the apartment.

"Yeah, what do you want?"

"NYPD, Detectives Auggur and Moleson, we need to ask you a few questions."

The voice on the other end sounded cooperative all of a sudden, "Be right down, I'll buzz you in," the door opened, and Rudy pushed on it. From down the hall a large-waisted, 50-ish, balding, chubby, yet clean looking man strode toward them. "I'm Bill Kulver, the manager, what can I do for you guys?"

Rudy and Mitch pulled out their ID's. "We'd like to see Miss Phillips' apartment, 3c, please."

"That beautiful, nice girl, what's she done?" His voice sounded astonished. "Is she okay?"

"We'd rather not say at this time," Rudy offered.

"I think her roommate is still here, both of those girls worked nights when they couldn't find work in the theater," said Kulver.

"What is her name?

"Cynthia Warnow."

"Could you take us to the apartment?"

"You, bet. She really is a nice kid, I mean never made a sound, never any trouble, always helped the older people in the building with shopping, errands, that kind of stuff, you know? What'd she do?" He super-quizzed the detectives as they walked down the hall and up the stairs.

They ignored the questions, and continued walking up the stairs to the third floor. Rudy was in pretty good shape; Mitch was a different story. "I've got to lose a few, Rudy, I'm having trouble getting up these steps," he huffed.

"Lay off the donuts after breakfast, that'll take care of most of it," Rudy kidded.

Kulver spoke as they hit the third floor, "Two doors down on the right."

Rudy knocked.

"Yes, who is it?"

New York City Police, ma'am, we'd like to talk to you."

"Right away," the door opened, "What have I done, not pay my parking tickets?" She started to laugh.

"No Miss, I'm afraid this is about your roommate, Miss Phillips, may we come in? You'd better sit down."

"Oh my God, is she alright?" Cynthia sat on a bar stool at the kitchen counter, and offered the men a seat on the couch.

"Say, Kulver, why don't you wait in your room downstairs, we'll have a few questions for you before we leave?" The super had followed them in, expecting to get the whole story.

"Yeah, sure detectives, I'll wait down there." He left the room, closed the door, and put his ear to the panel to listen.

"Miss, I'm afraid we have some bad news for you, Julia Phillips is dead."

"Oh God, Oh God, how can that be?" Tears formed, and ran down her cheeks, and she almost collapsed. Rudy underhanded her forearm "How could this happen? What happened, was she hit by a car, what the hell happened?"

"Well, it looks as if she was murdered by a Victor Madison. All the evidence points to him, do you know him?" Rudy spoke.

"You've got to be kidding, that guy was wonderful. I mean he was handsome, nice-a cool guy. At least, it seemed that way but I really only met him a few times. Just to say hello." Cynthia had a look of disbelief on her face.

"What did Julia tell you about him?"

"Not much, she spent all of her time with him since they met. He came out of nowhere."

"All of her time? How did they meet?"

"She met him in the grocery store. She talked about him right away, which was unusual for her. So many men hit on her, but she kind of shied away from them; they had to be very special. She came home and said she had met this guy in the organic foods department; they had been talking about organic foods- those are foods that are grown only during the correct season, with no chemical or artificial additives to the soil- not many people know much about that stuff, but Julia was almost fanatical about it. She said he knew more about healthy food than she did, she was very impressed."

"So they went out right away?"

"No, not right away, she bumped into him again at 5:30 a.m. on her run in the park; she said that the hotel had suggested to him to run in the park. That's when she started seeing him. They met the next morning and the next, then they started going out in the evenings."

"So, she fell in love with him immediately, like love at first date, huh?"

"No, Julia was not like that. She was tough about that stuff, like I said, the guy had to be very special. She was very special herself. She had only slept with one guy, her college lover. She was really straight."

"How did she end up spending all her time with him?"

"Turns out this Victor guy loved old Charlie Chaplin movies, any old movies, Laurel and Hardy, that kind of stuff, so did Julia. I mean, she studied them, she was fanatical about old movies- and so was he. She found that out about the third or fourth time they went running together, and then they had dinner. She told me one night that they had so many things in common she was falling in love with him. That's why she was with him last night."

"What do you mean?"

"Well, she decided to sleep with him at his hotel... and he hadn't even asked her. He hadn't put any pressure on her to sleep with him. She was really impressed by him; she was ready to give it all up. God, she was so wonderful. How... how did she die?" Tears ran down her cheeks again. "I'm so sorry, we were really close, like sisters."

"Apparently he smothered her with a pillow. We haven't put together all the evidence, but that is what our initial investigation shows. It looks like they had dinner, danced, and she was dead within a few minutes after they returned to the hotel room. I have a few more reports to look at, but I'm afraid this guy planned the whole thing. It was too smooth, and there's no evidence." Rudy shook his head, and looked at the floor.

"May we look through her room and belongings, we want to see if there is anything we can link to his identity and whereabouts?"

"Sure, okay, her room is right over there. Help yourself."

Rudy and Mitch went through the room, closet, drawers under the mattress, hoping to find anything that might help, letters, cards. But nothing showed up. Nothing. There was not a clue connecting her with anybody else other than Victor Madison of the Paradise Hotel. He seemed to appear and disappear without a trace. They excused themselves and after getting even less from Kulver, they left the building, and headed back to the precinct.

When Rudy arrived, a preliminary report from Officer Parker was on his desk. He read through the one-page report; they had gotten the same information from the hotel staff that they got from the apartment manager, and Cynthia- nothing. There had been a cab trip that took Victor Madison to the airport, and his name was found on a flight manifest to Toronto, but after that, there had been no Victor Madison on any of the flights, no rental car, as he had probably been picked up at the airport, and then he had disappeared. They had a call in to the Toronto police, and the Mounties, but Rudy suspected that it would come up empty. Every lead he followed, fingerprints- zero, there was no credit card numbers, as he had paid for everything in cash. No phone calls, nothing that lead anywhere. After three weeks of exhaustive research, still nothing had turned up; Auggur felt quite worthless. "I just don't understand this, Mitch. This guy disappeared. He did a job, and disappeared. I wish I could do more, but I'm afraid this is going to be one of those unsolved mysteries. It's really too bad, this girl was a good one, great future, so pretty and bright; I'm putting her picture on my bulletin board to remind me of all the creeps out there, someday, something will happen, somehow this guy will screw up, he'll tell someone, and we will get this asshole. This son of a bitch can't hide forever."

Thursday, June 11, 1992, Denver, Colorado

Jon Pederson got off the plane in Denver, and walked through the concourse with one carry-on bag. He headed directly for the Dollar Rent-A-Car agency desk.

"Good morning sir, how may I help you?"

"I believe there is a Chrysler LaBaron convertible reserved under the name of Pederson, with a 'd.' I'll need the car for about a month."

"Yes, sir, our pleasure, I'll just need some information from you." She placed the application form on the counter in front of him. "Please make sure and sign here, here and here." She made X's in the appropriate places, "and I'll need to see a driver's license or passport."

He produced the ID's, and began to fill out the application form, he then asked, "Do you happen to have a steel blue one, it's my girlfriend's favorite color?"

"Well, we did have one, let's see." She perused the pages in front of her. "Yes we do, you're in lucky, it just came back this morning."

Pederson handed her the form, "Here you go, all finished."

"How would you like to pay, Mr. Pederson?"

"I'd like to pay cash. I understand you require a large deposit, is that correct?"

"Yes, sir, there is a $500 deposit."

"And you need it for thirty days?"

"Yes, that is correct."

"For that car, it will be $1690 including tax and insurances."

Jon Pederson pulled out a money clip, with a half-inch thick wad of $100 bills, and counted..."13,14,15, 16, 17... Thank you."

"Okay, Mr. Pederson, if you will just take this paperwork out to the curb, a van will be out in a moment to take you to your car." The young lady ripped off the last two pages, "The pink one goes to the attendant, and the green one is yours."

Jon waited at the curb, as the Dollar Rent-A-Car van pulled up. The side sliding door opened, and he stepped in, and sat back against the window. He put his leather carry-on bag on the bench-seat next to him, and gazed out the window as the van headed around the corner and out to the rental lot; soon he was in the LaBaron heading west towards the mountains on Martin Luther King Boulevard. The trip to a shopping center was about twenty blocks. He drove out of the airport, and made a left turn on Monaco, headed south, and then west on Leetsdale, to the Cherry Creek Shopping Center. All the directions were there for him, just as Daddy had said. He pulled into the parking lot outside the new Saks Fifth Avenue store. As he got out of the car he turned west, and could see the snow-capped mountains in the distance, about forty-five miles away. Even though it was June, it had been one of the best winters in recent Colorado history. He walked into the store and took the escalator to the fourth floor men's department.

"Yes sir, may we help you?"

"You sure can, the airline lost my luggage a few days ago, and I'm tired of waiting for them to find it. I'll be here for thirty days, I'll need everything." He glanced at her nametag. "Catherine?" He made sure that she was not wearing someone else's nametag.

"This is going to be fun." The young counter girl was happy to get one of these types. He would probably spend a couple of grand. "Where would you like to start, sir?"

Pederson immediately walked over to a rack and pulled off a dozen pairs of underwear, then headed for the socks. He pointed at the colognes in the glass case." Fahrenheit, and you pick one. I'll need two suits, three sport coats, some dress shirts, workout clothes and ties. Then we'll head for the shoe department."

Within two hours he was finished, $4100, paid in cash. "Could this be delivered to the downtown Radisson Hotel? My name is Jon Pederson." He wrote it down on a slip by the cash register.

"Yes, sir, and the suits and trousers will be ready in a few days."

"Could I at least get the gray trousers and black blazer by tonight, as well as with the things that fit?"

"We can do that, sir, about seven-ish?"

"That will be just fine." He handed the girl a $200 tip, "Thanks for your help, Catherine, have a nice one on me."

"Oh, Mr. Pederson, thank you so much, this is really not necessary." She started to hand the money back to him.

He cuffed her fist around the money, "You deserve it; you did a great job." He turned and headed out the main aisle towards the escalator.

"If I can be of service, please don't hesitate to call, for anything." Caught up in the excitement of the sale, she hadn't noticed how handsome the twenty-four year old was until now.

Jon turned around, with a sly, half-smile on his face, "I'll remember that, in case I do need a little something extra."

He turned west out of the parking lot, and took Spear Boulevard towards Moran, then headed north to Fifteenth Street, and the hotel. He pulled up under the canopy, and a doorman walked to the car. "Good afternoon sir, will you be staying with us?"

"Yes, my name is Jon Pederson, and I'll be here for about a month."

"May I help you with your luggage sir?"

"It was lost, but some things will be delivered later, would you bring them straight up? I want to go to the gym and work out at about 7:30, and my workout clothes are coming with the delivery." He handed the doorman a $20 bill. "I know you'll take care of everything, thanks."

He walked up the steps, through the door held by another doorman, said "Thank you," and went up to the front desk. "Jon Pederson, I requested a top floor penthouse."

"I have it right here, Mr. Pederson, you are from St Louis, Missouri, correct? How would you like to pay?"

"I'll pay cash, and I'll pay about every two or three days. I hope you understand, I'm on call to Europe, I may have to leave very quickly for business. I might be here as long as thirty days, or gone in a week." He made it sound very important. "What is the rate per day?"

"The Penthouse is $600 per night, Mr. Pederson."

"Well, here is $4800. When that is used up, let me know and I will give you more." He counted out sixty $100 bills. "I will be paying cash for everything; it is so much easier."

"As you wish, sir, I hope your business venture will be very lucrative for you, Mr Pederson."

"If the sale goes through, it will- a winery in Switzerland."

"That sounds wonderful, good luck."

"Thank you. By the way, isn't there a health club very close?"

"Why yes, in the Manhattan building, just two blocks west of here. You can pick up a pass here at the front desk on your way out. The hotel has use of the facility; the workout rooms are on the third floor facing the mountains, with a pool on the fourth floor. It is a very nice club. The Manhattan Cafe is a fine restaurant- a high class saloon."

"Great, will you make a 10 p.m. dinner reservations for me? Thank you very much for your help." He tipped, and grabbed the key, glancing at it- Penthouse I, sixteenth floor. He walked slowly to the elevator, and pushed the up arrow; within a few moments the elevator door opened. He stepped inside, turned around, and glanced at the row of buttons. He pushed the Penthouse I button. The door closed. The elevator was one of those express, fast moving ones, in just a few moments he was there. The elevator opened onto a large foyer. A sign directly in front of him pointed the way. Penthouse I, left. There were four units on the sixteenth, each one about one thousand square feet. He walked down the hall and around the corner. He put the key in the lock and turned it; the deadbolt and doorknob turned and opened at the same time. The Radisson was one of the finest hotels in Denver, if not the finest. The Penthouse could be compared to a townhouse; the main room was about 20' by 20' square, and took up half of the entire space. It contained the living room, wet bar, kitchen and dining area. To the right were three rooms. The first door off the dining area went into a large bathroom with a large, tinted, glassed- in shower, facing the city skyline. There was also a sunken hot tub and bathtub combination. Another set of double doors opened into a three hundred square foot bedroom, with a full dressing area and king size bed. There was another set of double doors leading back into the living area. Two single doors, one each from the bedroom and living area, led onto an office area, complete with a computer, fax machine, copier and phone with a speaker for conference calls. There was also a personal safe. Most of the better hotels had safes in the rooms instead of at the front desk. A large desk with four chairs surrounding it was in the center of the room. Jon looked around, and was pleased.

Pederson undressed and turned on the shower. He found a large, heavy, terry cloth robe with the Radisson logo on the right chest inside the closet. After his shower, he helped himself to a Johnny Walker Red on the rocks, and turned on the radio. It was already set to the classical station, and melodious sounds of a nineteenth century composer filled the room. It was 6:15 p.m. on June 11th. He was very relaxed; so far everything was perfect.

One scotch, and thirty minutes later, at 6:45, there was a knock on the door.

"Who is it?"

"Saks Fifth Avenue delivery, Mr. Pederson."

"Great, great, come on in." He opened the door to a young man, pushing a hotel luggage cart, holding twenty or so boxes. "I'll tell you what, here's $20, why don't you unpack all of this stuff for me? Put it wherever you think it should go. The bedroom is this way. But first, see if you can find the workout stuff and aerobic shoes, I want to go over to the health club" While the delivery boy unpacked, Jon went into the bedroom closet and located the safe. He changed the combination per the instructions on the inside of the safe door—sixty, two and eight, his birthday backwards, and put his travel bag into the safe.

The Mile High Health Club was just two blocks west. After picking up his club pass at the front desk, Jon Pederson walked down the steps across to Moran Street, then north to sixteenth, west again to Gibson, and then one half block north again to the Manhattan Building. He looked at the brass plaque on the outside of the building, which read; Health Club-third floor. This beautiful building had been through a refurbishing in the late 70's; the owner of the Manhattan Cafe had only thought he was going into the restaurant business, but when the health craze took over, he not only ended up with a health club and restaurant, he also bought the entire building, and changed the name. Jon took the elevator up to the club. The door opened, and Jon walked up to the desk. He presented his pass, and placed his gym bag on the floor in front of the counter.

A young, athletic woman in multi-color tights was working behind the counter. "Good evening, sir, would you sign in please?" She pushed a clipboard across the counter in his direction. "Is this your first time here?"

"Yes, yes it is. I'm visiting for about a month, staying at the Radisson."

"That's a beautiful hotel. Where are you from?"

"St Louis, Missouri."

"That's a nice town. I've only been there once, but I did have a good time. Would you like me to show you around the club, or are you familiar with Nautilus equipment?"

"Yes, I'm very familiar with it, you really don't need to show me, I belong to a club in St. Louis, so I'm sure I can find my way around. I would like a locker though, and also the aerobics schedule please."

"If you have any questions, don't hesitate to ask. Here is a key, locker #413. The men's locker room is the first door on the left in the hallway." She pointed to her left, down a hallway. "Here is a schedule, there's a class at 7:30, a step class, have you done step routines before?"

"Only a few times, but I like it, I need to work up a sweat. Do I have to sign up for that class?"

"Yes, you do, the sign-up sheet is at the end of the counter."

Jon took a pen and signed up for the 7:30 class, glancing down the list of names as if he were looking for someone in particular. At 7:30, Jon walked down the hall and into the locker room, found number 413, took off his warm ups, placed everything in the cubicle, locked the locker, and pinned the key to the inside of his workout shorts. He left the locker room, and walked down the hallway into a large, 30 by 40 carpeted room, with mirrors on all the walls. It filled up quickly, mostly with women, about four to every man. Great odds! Jon waited at the entrance to the room, looking around for a place that felt comfortable. When most everyone was in place, Jon walked over to the third row, fifth person, and took a place next to a tall woman, with beautiful, flaming red hair, freckles and a Raquel Welch look-alike face and body.

"Busy place, isn't it?" Jon said, while doing some stretching exercises on the floor.

"You talking to me?" The response was cold and inattentive.

"No, actually I was talking to myself and you interrupted." A wry smile came across his face.

"That's a good one, I've never heard that before, who writes your material?"

They looked at each other and laughed, "I'm Jon Pederson."

"Debra McMann." From a prone position, she extended her hand, and their eyes met at the same time as their hands. She felt the heat rush to her forehead; she was immediately attracted to him.

The aerobics instructor started, and led the class thru fifteen minutes of stretching movements, before beginning.

Between deep breaths Debra spoke, "You're new here, did you just join the club?"

Jon puffed a little as he stretched his right leg over his left, and touched his toe to the floor. "No, I'm here on business, staying at the Radisson."

"Oh really, what kind of business?"

"My partner and I buy wineries that are financially burdened, and turn them around."

"You're kidding? There aren't any wineries around here." Studying wine has been a passion of mine for years. I love good wine."

"You get right down to business, don't you?"

"I'm sorry, I don't mean to be nosy."

"I'm just teasing, I don't mind. We are using a Denver bank to buy a winery in Switzerland." The music started, and the instructor yelled out the steps.

Debra spoke. "You know, this is amazing, I love wine, in fact, wine is my passion." Now, she was even more interested. "I collect a few rare varieties; I wish I could afford to go to wine auctions, but I'm afraid I would raise my hand at the wrong time, and that would be the end of my life savings. I'm not keeping up, let's talk after class." They both went back to following the instructor. Debra's mind wandered; this is neat- a handsome man, interested in wine and aerobics, my kind of guy- here for a short time, he'll help me get my mind off of New York… "Right foot first…step up, cross toe-kick, return, both feet down-opposite, the same-left, step up, cross toe-kick.........." She caught Jon's eye, and smiled to herself. "He's neat," she thought.

"This is going to be easier than I had imagined," Jon thought to himself.

When class ended, Debra went up to the front of the class, and spoke with a few people. Jon waited at the back of the room.

After ten minutes, he headed for the weight room door. "Hey, wait, Jon, wait, I'll be right there." Debra hustled over to him. "I'm sorry, I didn't mean to be rude. Do you do weights?"

"Yes, I do, I'd like a short workout if you'd like to join me."

"I'd love to." She was happy to find a man that shared the same interests; and he was rich. Her favorite!

She led him up the stairs to the weight rooms. "Nautilus or free weights?"

"Free weights."

"You're reading my mind." They walked in, and looked around. "Today is the day for a mini- routine, I do full workouts every other day."

As they made their way over to the bench press Jon spoke. "So what is your line of work?"

"I work mostly as an actress and model, I usually work out of New York, but I grew up in Denver, so in between jobs I come back to Denver to relax. I'll go back to the City in two or three weeks for an audition in a new movie; I just finished a play that ran for sixteen weeks off Broadway."

"Where do you live?" Jon made sure to sound very interested in this young, beautiful, successful woman.

"Well to cut a long story short, a long time friend of mine from Vail, Jerry Wraung, opened the Manhattan Cafe in '76. He was so successful, that he bought this building, and then opened the Health Club. After that, he turned the old storage spaces and offices into thirty condo units. Last year I bought one on the top floor. Of course, as my old friend, he gave me a great deal."

"Well, everyone needs a good deal on real estate, it's also convenient for you to be able to work out, eat a good meal, and never have to cook or leave the building, all in your own backyard."

"Yeah, I love it. I don't have to mess around with traffic, and the mountains are so close. I can ski in the winter, hike in the summer. I couldn't ask for a better deal."

"Speaking of restaurants, why don't I go back to the hotel, clean up, and pick you up at about ten for a late night snack and some good wine? What time does the Manhattan Cafe stop serving?"

"Well, it closes at eleven; but I did sort of have plans tonight. Although this sounds like a much better deal, I can always change plans with my friend, she'll understand. Yeah, that would be wonderful. I'll meet you down there."

They finished their workout and walked down the steps.

"Listen, I have to pick up my bag in the men's locker room, I'll be back in a minute." He was in and out of the locker room in a few moments, as he walked by the desk, he tossed the key on the counter, and met Debra at the door. "I'll see you in about an hour." Jon opened the front door, and turned around, leaning on the glass for a moment and looking into Debra's eyes.

She felt the heat rush to her forehead again. "See you in about an hour." She turned, and walked toward the elevator, pushed the 'up' button, and watched Jon as he walked out the door and down the sidewalk. She thought about the meeting as the elevator rose. "This is great, he's handsome, athletic, I can't believe he's a wine lover, my passion, and he is so sexy. He's so perfect, but I just met him. Be careful, you've met Mr. Right before," she told herself.

Jon approached the hotel steps, and walked up to the front door. "Good evening, sir." The doorman held the door open as Jon entered. He walked to the front desk.

"I just made a call to my partner, I don't think I will be here as long as I thought. In fact, I may only be here a few days. I'll let you know, I'll probably have to leave on very short notice."

"Fine, Mr. Pederson, whenever you are ready, just come by and let us know, and we'll take care of you."

He took the elevator upstairs, and walked to the Penthouse. He thought to himself, "I've got to play this cool, take her out for at least a week before I make my move, I need her total confidence; it has to be a surprise."

He showered and changed his clothes. The gray trousers and blazer fit perfectly. White button- down shirt, and red club tie, he felt good in the new clothes. He took the elevator to the lobby, walked down the steps and made his way over to the Manhattan Cafe. It was 10:20 p.m. Debra was already waiting at the bar.

"You're here, already. I'm sorry; I'm a little late."

"I just walked in a few minutes ago, feel better after the shower and fresh clothes?"

"Yes, I feel great, how about you?"

"Just wonderful, I always feel rejuvenated after a workout, kind of like starting the day over. Meet my good friend, Joey, he's been bartending here since the place opened."

Jon extended his hand. "Nice to meet you, Joey, beautiful restaurant you've got here."

They shook hands. "My pleasure, Jon, any friend of Debra's… you know how that saying goes. What are you drinking?"

"How about a wine list?"

Joey gave him the list, and as Jon looked it over, Debra and Joey made small talk. "He's a really great guy, I just met him at the health club, a very successful wine entrepreneur, he's got wineries all over the world."

"Let's try the Napa Valley Frog's Leap Cabernet." It was number one on the list he got from Daddy, along with all her other favorites.

"That's one of my favorites, how did you guess?"

"Oh, just lucky I guess, most of my favorites are from the Napa Valley."

"Perfect choice," Joey said, uncorking the wine, and pouring a taste. He laid the cork on the bar, and Jon picked it up and read it. "Ribbit," he laughed. "I'd forgotten they put that on their corks."

Debra took a sip. "This is great, thank you. I heard they decided to do that one night after about two hundred glasses of wine. It makes a great conversation piece." Joey filled their glasses.

"Let's get a table, where's the maitre'd?" Jon asked.

"I've already talked with Alfred, he gave us the one over there in the corner, the small booth." They walked over and sat down.

"Great place..."

"I don't always..."

They both spoke at exactly the same moment.

"You go first," he said, nervously.

"I was trying to say that this kind of thing is not the norm for me. I mean, I am very cautious." She looked into his eyes as she spoke.

"I know what you mean, I try to stay more aloof myself. I am not usually so forward; I was just trying to be friendly and something in your smile said it was okay to let something more happen."

"I know exactly what you mean, kind of like it was meant to happen. Like fate." She reached across the table, and touched his hand. Her face flushed again when she gazed into his eyes.

Jon nervously cleared his throat. "What do you suggest, what is the best item on the menu? I'm not a vegetarian, but when I travel, I try not to eat fatty, high cholesterol items. I like to eat as healthily as I can."

"Well, I already know I'm going to have the avocado bisque and the pasta primavera, and you've already picked my favorite wine, so I'm happy."

For the rest of the evening they talked, shared experiences, past loves, and just enjoyed each other's company. It seemed a shame to Jon to have to take a life so vibrant, so happy, so seemingly together, but it had to be done; he had to protect Daddy at all costs. This beautiful young thing was trouble for their existence and she had to go; Debra was walking dead, and in a few days it would all be over. He must gain her complete confidence, and catch her off guard. Eight days went by amazingly fast; they had spent some time together every day. He had astonished her by always seeming to suggest things to do that she liked, or always agreeing with what she had chosen. He knew she was falling in love, and he was about to make his move.

The phone rang. "Good morning, Debra here," she sang into the phone.

"Good morning, my love, I've got an idea." Why don't we drive up to the mountains, find a great little spot, and spend a few days hiking and relaxing?"

"God, that sounds like a great idea, I know a great place up in Evergreen. It's only about thirty minutes from here. There are small cabins, patios, river, and beautiful views, I have never been there, but I have always wanted to spend time in one of those cute, little cottages. How does that sound?"

"Perfect, why don't you call and make the reservations, do you want to go right away, or wait until tomorrow?"

"Today is good, let me call and see if the cottage is clear, should I book it for two nights?" Debra was excited. "It's a two bedroom- I know I can trust you." Debra was really happy.

"Two nights will be perfect, I'll be back in my room in a couple of hours, just let me know when you're ready, and I'll pick you up. By the way, I am very trustworthy."

As Debra hung up, she smiled to herself. "This is so incredible, I am the luckiest girl in the world. Thank you, Lord."

He put the phone down and called United Airlines. "What time tomorrow evening can I get a one- way flight to Toronto? Midnight? That's perfect. My name is Jamie Fender. No, no credit card. I'll come out and pay you in cash in a few hours." He held the receiver button down, and called the front desk. "Would you connect me with the Manhattan Cafe please? Hello, good morning, this is Jon Pederson; I am staying at the Radisson Hotel. I had a wonderful dinner last night with Debra McMann, one of your regulars…Yeah, that's me; so nice of you guys to remember. Listen, I wonder if you could do me a big favor? I would like a picnic basket with two-pasta primavera, two-avocado bisque, a bottle of Beringer Reserve Chardonnay, French bread, and that special olive oil with the crushed red peppers and garlic. I'll pick it up between 1:30 and 2:00 p.m. Great, thanks very much; I appreciate your help. I'll be there. Thanks again."

He quickly held the receiver button down, and pushed another for the front desk.

"Good morning, Mr. Pederson, may I help you?"

"As a matter of fact, you may. I will be gone a few days, and I just want to make sure I have paid all my bills in case an emergency keeps me away longer. But, I expect to be back on by Monday."

"You are current, Mr. Pederson, is there anything else we can do for you?"

"No. Thank you, though, I'm all set."

He opened the safe, and pulled out his duffel bag, careful to leave the safe open as the directions on the door stated. He quickly inventoried its contents, $20,000, 1-2-3-4-5 sets of ID-okay. He took out Jamie Fender's wallet, put seven one hundred dollar bills inside, and placed the wallet into his inside jacket pocket.

He put together a second duffel bag with hiking boots, lightweight rain gear, sweats, and running shoes, and headed for the elevator. He put his personal duffel in the trunk; it included the money, his toiletry bag, camel blazer, blue western shirt, Levis and aerobic shoes- the same clothes he had worn when he arrived in Denver. He placed duffel #2 on the back seat.

The trip to the airport was very short. He parked and picked up his ticket, one-way to Toronto, in cash, in the name of Jamie Fender. Once in the car, he placed the ID along with the plane ticket, into the duffel bag in the trunk. He was back at the hotel within an hour and a half, ready to go.

Jon parked his car in front of the Manhattan Building at 1:45 p.m. and went down to the cafe to pick up the picnic basket. He went out to the car, and placed it in the trunk. He then buzzed upstairs for Debra, and they were on they way by 2 p.m. The drive up to Evergreen was easy; they took the highway part of the way there and then off on Old Highway Six into Evergreen- she showed him the turn off- and down through a beautiful valley of one hundred-fifty foot pine trees and old-moss covered cedars. The road wound its way through the valley alongside the river. Forty-five minutes out of Denver and they had arrived. He drove into the horseshoe-shaped driveway, and up to the main house. The driveway continued, and exited back onto the small trunk line some five to or six hundred yards down the river.

Debra leapt from the car, throwing her arms skyward, taking deep breaths, "Isn't it lovely? It is just so beautiful. I can't stand it. The air is so clean and listen, no cars, no noises. It's too bad we have to live on cement." She looked over at Jon, "I know, I know, we have to make a living, I can't help it if I am a Romantic." She skipped back to the driver's side of the car, reached over and hugged him, smiled and kissed him gently on the lips. "I love it."

Jon parked the car and got out. "Okay, lets see if we have a two-bedroom cottage on the river. There don't seem to be many cars here, I am sure there is lots of room." They walked towards the office and yelled "Hello, hello, anybody there?"

The manager walked around from the garage to the front of the building. Debra checked them in, while Jon parked the car. He gave them the largest cottage on the creek, which just happened to be the furthest from the office and nearest the driveway. "We just love that rushing water sound, it will get us away from the traffic sounds we are so used to, and drown out any passing cars on the road fifty yards away."

"You won't hear any cars on this road after 8:30 p.m. and you'll be all by yourselves down at #9, The Southwest Cottage. You won't hear a thing, guaranteed." The manager was quite serious about how quiet this cottage was.

The two bedrooms faced the creek, and were separated by a large fireplace in the wall, with opposing side-by-side fire pits that allowed fires in both bedrooms. The bedrooms both had large 8 by 10 glass doorways leading to the deck, overlooking the creek and rapids. The doors were bi-fold, old style wooden ones with the one-foot square windowpanes, and because of the position of the fireplace could be left open all night. The owner had explained how cozy the cabin was- his best. It was the second to last before the bridge, and exit to the highway. He found out from the owner that he need only take one right turn, and he would be taken back to highway 70 in a few minutes. They arrived on the two-lane back road into the complex. When he bought the tickets he found that the I-70 from the mountains went around Denver and directly to the airport. He could be at the airport in about an hour and fifteen minutes.

"Jon, let's get our grubbies on and hike down the river, I want to show you some great views." His thoughts were interrupted by Debra's desire to get busy doing something.

As they walked along, Jon thought of how he was going to do this. It had to be peaceful; she had to be happier than she had ever been. It must be a complete surprise; he would catch her off guard. "It sure is the most beautiful scenery in the world, Debra." It was 3:30, they would walk for a couple of hours, make love? Maybe not, maybe she was really hard to get, but he should try, make a good attempt. Why not? He had not made love with Julia; Daddy said if he had he may lose his nerve, he may not want to finish his task. He could make love, then- no don't! The voice in him said 'no.' It would not work if he made love to her, he would lose his nerve, get attached, not be able to help Daddy. He must stick to his plan- hike for three hours, clean up, present her with the picnic basket, start a fire, a big roaring fire in the fireplace, and eat a perfect dinner. Then at 8:30, start the seduction, get her to bed, and be gone by 9:30/9:45 p.m., drive out very slowly, no lights, he didn't want to bring attention to a car leaving after it had arrived so soon. He'd be at the airport by 11:00, and gone by twelve. Leave all the clothes; take only the clothes you wore into Denver. They would find her body in the morning, and he would be home. Daddy's plans were so perfect, so detailed- but she was so pretty and so nice.

* * * * *

As the plane roared out of Denver, Randy gazed out of the window. "Why did these women want to hurt Daddy?" First Julia two years ago, and now Debra. They seemed like nice girls, so why would they want to ruin our lives? Why would they want to tell everyone of Daddy's success? Why would they give others all his information, his life's work, before he was ready to tell the world? They were so stupid, couldn't they see how nice a man he was? He was so helpful, look at all he's done for me," he thought.

Half-dozing off he thought of his early teen years with Daddy…

He was fourteen and a half, and had been with the group for two years when the court granted Dr. Eric Bright custody of him. This was not something that was normally done, but Dr. Bright had such a good reputation as a psychiatrist. Randy had been in the children's program, and his attitude toward life and people had improved so dramatically that the good doctor was considered a good choice as a foster parent. He had also hired a full-time nanny and housekeeper.

When he first moved into the doctor's home, he was given a school placement test, and found to have the equivalent formal education of a nine-year-old. The doctor convinced the court that he could catch him up with his peers by the time he turned sixteen. Dr. Bright hired tutors to teach Randy nothing more than reading, writing and arithmetic. Each night when Eric came home, he would test Randy by having him write a short story about going into a business, sports, or just his day's activities-anything as long as he included arithmetic, and his use of the English language was correct. Eric would then correct the story, and Randy would rewrite it. This he would do on his own computer. He was also given piano lessons, dance lessons, and lessons on proper social etiquette. He was given the best clothes, and his own personal trainer, who worked with him at a local gym. He received the best of everything; Dr. Bright believed that children were a product of their environment, and if he controlled the environment, he could change the child.

By the time Randy was sixteen, he was a new person, he had been reborn. He was in school, he was a good student, and he had friends. He played sports, and was viewed by other students as the son of a famous psychiatrist in New York City. He began to call Eric, Daddy. He felt like he had a family. For the first time is his life, he had a real family, and was treated as a human being. He learned well, he liked everything they told him to do; it was a dream come true.

Only once did his mother contact him. She asked for money, and he never talked to her again; he blocked her out. He did not tell Daddy about the contact.

............His daydream ended with the sound of the bell, the "Fasten Seat Belts" sign went on, and the plane started its descent. Randy pulled his bag out from under the seat. He unzipped the leather duffel bag, and looked inside. He took another seven $100 bills out of a wad, and placed them in the wallet with the ID of Peter Hampton. He then exchanged Jamie Fender for Peter Hampton, placed the new wallet in the inside pocket of camel blazer and waited patiently for the plane to touch down.

He didn't have any real direction to fly, as long as he flew to another city as another person. As soon as the plane landed, he would look for a screen of flights available and get the next flight to anywhere under another name, and leave as soon as possible.

It would be impossible for the authorities to follow him, he didn't even know where he was going, and he was always another person. He never used the name he used when he met the girls.

Walking off the plane, he found a screen immediately; he chose to fly to Little Rock. The flight was departing in forty-five minutes; he headed for the ticket counter. Shortly thereafter, he boarded the plane, and found his seat. Once seated, and with his bag tucked neatly under the seat, he began to relax and listen to classical greats over the headset. He let his head fall back naturally once the plane was at cruising altitude.

After high school with Dr. Bright's help, Randy was able to get into Columbia University, and began his study as an architect. He was an exemplary student with a 3.5 grade point average, and graduated within three years by attending summer school. The first time he was called to help Daddy; he had been out of school for two years. He had been working out of his own home in Atlanta, subsidized by the good doctor when work was thin. He had actually not needed his help more than a few times in the beginning, he was good at his trade and a pleasant person to be around. During his high school and college years, even though he lived with the doctor, he continued to play the role of SP1001, and visited the secret back office weekly. It was during these visits that he started to develop his unflappable loyalty to Dr. Eric Bright.

Eric used hypnosis, and regression trips to help his clients attain their highest level of power. By dealing with the worst of their nightmares, he was able to find solutions to real problems, current problems and deal with the real, not the past. It was during one of these sessions that a bond of protection for each other developed. Randy began to feel like it was not only protection, but also self-preservation, no one was going to get in between them, no one was going to ruin this new life he had. He deserved it; he had been tortured so much in his young life. He was now twenty-two years old, his whole life had changed over the last twelve years and nothing, and nobody would ruin it. Nothing!

"Do you remember eating cat food out of a dish on the kitchen floor?" Eric wanted Randy to deal with his most nightmarish recollections.

"Yes, I do."

"Tell me about it."

"There were so many times."

"Let's concentrate on one particular time, one time that sticks out more than the others."

"I guess it was the first time, `cause after that I was able to block out most everything I didn't like." So many abusive things were done to him as a child that most of his childhood was blocked out.

"How old were you?"

"I guess I was about four or five."

"Tell me about it."

"My dad came home drunk, and I was just sitting down to eat at the kitchen table. My mom had cooked me some beenie-weenies, you know those hotdog and beans together, like a hotdog bean soup. It was good with chips or crackers." His eyes were closed, and his speech was labored. The hypnosis calmed him, and slowed him down. He had trouble getting the words out; he was trying to recall what happened.

Dr. Bright helped, "Just try to visualize and tell the picture, take your time."

"He...he had a beer can in his hand, and a cigarette hanging out of his mouth. My mom put the bowl down in front of me. I was just about to put my spoon in, when he put his cigarette out in my food. He yelled real loud, "Eat that, you little fart."

"He laughed, and spat on the floor."

"Leave him alone, Roger."

"Sometimes my mom tried to help, but he was so mean, if she disagreed with him, he would hit her. So she didn't say anymore."

"Shaddup, you dumb cunt, I'm just having some fun with the little prick. Maybe I ought to have fun with you instead, bet you'd like that." He warned her, and she left the kitchen fast.

"Then he took my food, spilled it on the table, and told me to lick it off the table, because I wasn't good enough to use silverware. Then he pushed my face into the beans on the table, and smushed it around the table with my nose. I couldn't do nothin'"

He started to cry; and his body shook.

"It's okay, Randy, it's okay, it already happened, it's not ever going to happen again. You are strong; you are powerful; you can handle any situation. Breathe deeply; sit back, as far in the chair as you can. Let your muscles gain weight; make yourself feel heavy, so heavy. You are part of the couch. That's it; nothing can hurt you. We can stop if you want to, would you like to stop?"

Randy's body tension relaxed and his breathing became slow and soft.

"Did you feel you wanted to get even?"

"Yes, but I didn't know how. I wanted to kill him; I really wanted to kill him."

"But you were too small."

"Yes, he was too big."

"What happened next?"

"The cat jumped up on the table, and started nibbling on one of the hot dogs."

He started yelling at me. "You are no better than the cat, not as good as the fucking cat."

"Then he grabbed me by the back of the shirt, put me on the floor, and pushed my face into the cat's dish. He grabbed the cat, and pushed his head into my dish on the table. He told me that from now on I had to eat cat food, and drink from a dish on the floor. I got up and ran for the front door. He just laughed, and called me his shitty, little dog."

"You shitty, little dog, you are no better than an alley dog, you piece of shit." He would do this once or twice a month, until mom finally had him thrown out."

"How do feel about it now?"

"I'd still kill him, if I could get away with it."

"Do you really mean kill, or just protect yourself?"

"I really mean kill. I got away with it a few years later when Ralph hurt me."

"But don't you think killing is wrong?"

"Yeah, it's wrong, but sometimes it has to be right, like in a war, if people are bad, and others need protection, then they have to be killed. Maybe sometimes, other people are really bad and a person has to kill someone for protection. Maybe sometimes people hurt you over and over, and the only way to help yourself is to kill them, get rid of them."

The doctor thought for a moment. "Let's try another word. What if people were eliminated because they tried to interfere or ruin your life? Eliminate is a better word than kill."

"My life is so good now, I would kill to save the life I have now." He said it so matter of factly. He meant what he said, and Eric did not try to change his mind. He only tried to change his use of the word 'kill.'

"You mean eliminate? You mean eliminate a person trying to hurt you, take away what is yours? Is that what you mean?"

"Yes, I would eliminate them. That's the word you want me to use. I would eliminate them if they interfered with my life."

It was on April 10th, 1990 when the first call came, and Randy learned that he must eliminate to protect. Little did he suspect that he would be called again and again to eliminate problems in the good doctor's world?

* * * * *

July 1ˢᵗ, 1994

The phone rang, and Randy answered it. "Hello, Daddy, yes, yes, I am fine. Life is good. I have a big project I'm working on… Yeah, I know I promised I'd help, but, but…yeah, yeah, I understand, I understand… okay, I'll be there tomorrow." He hung up, thought for a moment, looked through his phone/address book, located the name, and dialed a local number. "Jack Porter, please. Hi, Jack, this is Randy Curtis. Listen, I hate to bother you, but I need your help on something. Something came up; can you give me three weeks extension on the project? Yeah, I've got a family emergency, need to get to New York. Is that okay? Thanks, I owe you one, I'll call you when I return…. Promise, twenty-four hours a day…I'll still be done by November 15th. Thanks Jack, I really appreciate you being so understanding."

He didn't bother calling the airport; there were so many flights from Atlanta to New York on various airlines, so he knew he wouldn't have any problem getting there on short notice.

The way Daddy had phrased his message Randy knew what he wanted. "We need protection, can you come right away?" Randy knew that a woman, another SP was trying to break them up. She wanted to tell everyone about his research. Daddy sounded very worried, very threatened.

The cab let him out at the service entrance of the thirty-story building, not too far from Rockefeller center. Randy used his personal key to enter the building, and walked down a long corridor, where all the personal and freight elevators were located. He took the elevator marked twenty-second to thirtieth floor Penthouses; this elevator serviced twelve private offices and businesses. He put another special key into the elevator to activate the code; his code allowed him to go to Daddy's office only. The office holders and special guests of the office holders used this elevator, Daddy liked it because it allowed his SP's to come and go unnoticed. He had told Randy that many of them were very wealthy, well known, successful people, and they wanted privacy from prying eyes; no one needed to know they were seeing a psychiatrist. The elevator car moved very fast, and very quietly. When it docked at the office entrance, it was if it landed in a huge down pillow, it made no noticeable noise. The silence of this machine amazed him. He entered the office, turned right, and took four or five steps inside before Daddy noticed him, and looked up from his notes on the desk.

"Randy, hello my son, I didn't hear you come in. How are you?" He stood up and walked around the desk, hugging Randy and patting him on the back. "You look great, have you been working hard?" They hugged each other as a father and son would.

"As a matter of fact I have, I am designing a large wing to a home out at the Georgia Country Club. The man wants an arboretum, library/office combination. It faces the thirteenth green, looking down from the second floor. It's going to be beautiful. I'll be glad to get back and finish it; this could bring me a lot of work."

"It sounds like it will be a fun project, but we have a lot to talk about, why don't you have a seat?" Daddy took his usual seat in the large high back leather chair, and Randy took his place on the contoured couch. It was specially made of leather, and was down filled to mold to a person's body shape.

Within five minutes, Randy was in his hypnotic state, and Daddy spoke. "The spirit that has been trying to ruin our lives has surfaced again; this time it has taken the form of a woman in New Orleans. Her name is Brandy Bennett. I have asked her not to tell of our sessions, my Special Project. She refuses to listen; she says she will tell everyone. I have invested so much time and energy, I can't afford to lose it all now; we can't afford to lose it all now. I wish there were another way, but there seems to be only one way. She must be eliminated. She wants to hurt us; she wants our wonderful life to be stopped. Are you able to understand how this spirit must be dealt with?"

"Yes, I understand, but why does this spirit hate you?" Randy questioned.

"We all have spirits surrounding us, some good, some bad. We all have past lives. In one of my past lives, I dealt a blow to a bad person, and the spirit of that person is following me through my lives. This bad spirit finds his way into these SP's, these beautiful women and then finds me. It takes me some time to figure out what has happened. I don't know if this spirit will ever leave us alone until I am gone. Luckily, I recognize them and stop them before they can stop us; together we are powerful enough to deal with the situation. I just hope that this spirit will give up, and go away, finding us too strong. But, for now we must find her, and eliminate her."

"How do you know this is the spirit?" This was Randy's third encounter with one of the doctor's women; he was beginning to question the necessity of elimination.

"My experience tells me that she is, the questions she asks, her need to know too much- much more than I am willing to give. She wants information that only I need to know. It is time for you to awaken now and go, and I will leave you with the information you need to find her. Count to one hundred, then open your eyes, I will talk with you soon."

After the count, Randy awoke and found the file on the table in front of him. Daddy had gone to his front office. He picked up the file and placed it on the desk. He then walked over to the Chemakian Oil known as 'Still Life With Knife,' hanging on the wall. He took hold of the painting and pulled at the lower right hand corner. The picture swung open to the left revealing a wall safe; he turned the dial quickly. He opened the safe, and pulled out the small leather duffel bag. Next to the duffel were about a hundred wads of $100 bills, each totalling $5000. He counted out five packets, $25,000. He opened the duffel to check its contents; it contained five wallets with the ID's of five different people. He then sat down at the desk, and studied the portfolio of the 'devil spirit' he was about to eliminate.

* * * * *

Friday, July 25, 1994

Brandy Bennett was twenty-seven years old, another one of the many actresses who was looking for her big break. She spent much of her time in New York working off-Broadway; she also worked small improv clubs, and had done numerous small parts in big movies. She made her home in the French Quarter of New Orleans. She had grown up as the daughter of a wealthy attorney, who also owned an offshore oil company. She was a beautiful young woman, not necessarily athletic, more artistic, into meditation, horses, and small animals. She wore very little make-up, had no boyfriend, and a very small nucleus of friends. Everything he needed to know was there, including her photo, address, phone number, car, and license plate number. The file also mentioned her favorite wines, flower, music, actress, actor, movie-everything he needed to know to entice her into thinking he was Mr. Right. He just had to study the file for a few hours before heading to the airport. This time he would fly out of New York as Albion Gant, and introduce himself as Peter Hampton once he made contact.

Including his own ID, he could be any one of six people. He really only used his own ID on the last leg of his trip- the return to Atlanta. Part of his trip was used to study his intended victims. When he arrived in New Orleans, he immediately took a cab to the French Quarter, and as always checked into a small medium-priced hotel, this time as Albion Gant. For the next three days, he would walk around Brandy's neighborhood. He would watch her, find out her favorite places to go, learn as many details as possible about her; he needed to know her habits. He must be careful not to attract any attention to himself. As he always did, he bought jeans, a t-shirt, jacket, and running shoes, and wore those clothes as he collected information. He would not shave for those few days, and wore an inconspicuous baseball-style cap. He did not want to be recognized by anyone when he re-appeared. Daddy had always told him to be casual, and not to do anything that would draw attention to him. He must blend in until he was sure of his character, and familiar with the victim, and the area. Within a few days, he had collected enough information and added to the other information he had gotten from her file, he felt confident that he could convince her to love him, just as he had done before. He knew that it was necessary, or his life would change. That was something he didn't think he could accept.

He took a cab to the airport and as Albion Gant, rented a car to Baton Rouge. It was important that he could not be traced; he must appear from nowhere, and vanish into the same place. He drove the eighty miles to the Baton Rouge airport in a couple of hours. He shaved in the airport bathroom, changed into his travel clothes, a camel blazer and trousers; he then stuffed his jeans and sweatshirt into the trash bin in the bathroom. Peter Hampton boarded a Southern Airlines flight to New Orleans at 9:00 a.m. on Friday, July 25, 1994? .

A close neighbor found Brandy Bennett's body on July 26, 12:05 p.m. The headlines read, "NEW ORLEANS SOCIALITE STRANGLED BY LOVER, KILLER DISAPPEARS!" The article read, "The body of socialite, actress, and model, twenty-seven year old Brandy Bennett, daughter of New Orleans attorney and oil magnate Robert Joseph Bennett was found in her French Quarter flat at noon today. The apparent cause of death was suffocation. Police are looking for a recent love interest, although his current whereabouts are unknown. The article went on to tell the details of the whirlwind affair, and the absence of clues of his identity and whereabouts.

Because of the importance of the family involved, national news picked up the story. Rudy Auggur, the New York detective who covered the murder of Julia Phillips five years earlier in New York was up late the same night watching CNN.

"Goddamn, Goddamit, Go-o-o-ddamit, I'll be a son of a bitch! He did another one, I knew he would do it again, it's the same guy, I know it." Rudy picked up the phone, and dialed quickly. "Chief, you sleepin'? Sorry to get you up so late, yeah, I know, I know what time it is. It's really important, though. Clear your head and listen to this. I need to go to New Orleans, yeah, right now, it can't wait! Remember, back in '90, spring of '90? There was this beautiful young actress found smothered in her hotel room. Her lover disappeared; we never found a clue. Yeah, yeah, that's the one, the one on my bulletin board, yeah, vanished into thin air. Well, I was just watching CNN, and another girl was found exactly the same way. Smothered by her lover, whirlwind affair, guy disappeared, nobody knows him, nothing about him, exact same scenario. I'd like to leave in the morning. Great, thanks, I'll save all the receipts. What do you mean, don't save 'em? Right!"

Rudy had called ahead, and asked permission to exchange information on the case. A police escort would be waiting for him at the airport. When the plane set down he was escorted off, and immediately down an employee stairway to the tarmac. A blue suit was waiting and took him immediately to the police station. He had already talked with the detectives on the case by phone, and had stopped off to get his personal file from the office. Now all he had to do was compare the information for similarities; this guy had to leave some sort of trail.

Rudy had left a picture of this young, beautiful girl on the bulletin board above his desk, a reminder to him of all of the crazies out there. The murder of Julia Phillips had been one of his first cases as a detective and he had gotten nowhere, so he vowed never to give up on the case.

His stay in New Orleans was short; there were no leads, nothing to go on. The cases seemed identical, his description of size, weight, hair color, everything the same, except he was older. The lover swept them off their feet in a few short days, lured them into bed, and smothered them. He had two different names; he disappeared quickly without a trace. The time between the two cases was almost exactly five years. Rudy thanked the New Orleans police, and returned to New York the next day. On the way back, Rudy thought, "Maybe there had been others, maybe these were just two of twenty, or fifty, God forbid!" He made a promise to himself to send out information flyers to all major cities in the country. He would continue to send them out monthly for two or three years, whatever it took. If this guy had killed more than twice, maybe somewhere he made a mistake, somewhere somebody knew something that would help them find the killer.

A year and eight months had passed, and Rudy had continued to send out fliers. Every six months he sent out new ones to twenty-five major U.S. cities, and a few cities in Canada. He knew that most of the offices threw them away after a couple of months, but he kept sending them out anyway. He was determined not to give up on these two murders. On Friday, December 15th, 1989 (Shouldn't this be 1999 since the first murder only took place in 1990?), Rudy walked into his office. "Hey Rudy, call this guy in Denver, something to do with your girls." Detective Potacki waived a piece of paper in the air wildly.

Rudy grabbed it as he ran by, "Thanks, Polish. This could be it, this could be the answer my girls need." He looked at the corner of his bulletin board, where he had hung pictures of Julia and Brandy.

"God, I hope this is the break, Auggur." Potacki sounded genuine. "I think this is a third, I just talked to the guy for a few minutes; he said to call him right away. It's good news, and bad news, if you know what I mean?"

"Yeah, I know what you mean. Did he say if it was a new one or an old one? When did it happen?"

"Hell, I didn't get a date. I think it was an old one though just by the way he sounded, I don't think it was very recent."

Rudy immediately got on the phone to Denver. "Detective Taylor please, this is long distance, from the New York City Police Department.... yes, I'll hold."

A few moments passed. "Taylor here, to whom am I speaking?"

"Taylor, this is Rudy Auggur from the NYPD, I'm returning your call about the murdered girl." Rudy was really anxious.

Taylor spoke, "I saw your flier on the murdered girls, and I may have something here. In June of 84 (shouldn't this be '92?), there was a young woman's body found in a cabin in the mountains of Evergreen, Co. She had been smothered to death, and the only possible killer was her boyfriend. She had only met him a few weeks before. She was a beautiful kid, an actress and model, home on vacation from a stage production in New York. She was twenty-five years old, and a redhead. The guy disappeared without a trace. I mean, we could not find anything to go on, no clues at all, and he left all his clothes. He just vanished. What do you think? Sound familiar? Is this what you are looking for?"

"Well, it sure sounds familiar. Say, what was the guy's name?"

"Ah, let's see, here it is, Jon Pederson. If this is what you want, I could send you a copy of my file."

"Well, it's kind of hard to tell, since there were no clues at either murder scene. I mean, the only thing we have to compare are the girls, a new, fast love affair, the way he murdered them, and the fact that there are no clues. But, yeah, Taylor, It does sound like the same guy; you'd better send me your file. I sure wish there was more information."

"Yeah, me too, but there is nothing, I mean nothing, and we had no more after two weeks of investigating than we did after twenty-four hours. This guy seems to have planned it; I mean, really thought it out. I'm completely baffled."

"Listen, when I get your file, I'll match it up with the two others here, one from New York, and one from New Orleans. There has got to be something to tie these things together. That asshole has to have made a mistake somewhere. Thanks for your help, I sure hope we can get this guy." Rudy hung up, and looked at the detective who gave him the note. "I think we found another one."

* * * * *

Auggur put all three files in front of him on the desk. He had put a sketch board up on the wall, and began to compare the murders. He drew a line down the middle of the page. At the top of the left column he wrote in capital letters: HER, and listed on different lines the following; actresses, New York, reddish hair, young, beautiful, smart, talented, single, never married, clean living, not currently working. They all fell madly in love with someone they just met.

On the other half of the page he wrote: HIM, and listed: handsome, young, athletic, in town on business, all the right answers, and his name was Victor Madison, Jon Pederson and Peter Hampton and??????? "How could women with all these wonderful qualities fall for this mystery man? These women were known as very special, careful women."

Rudy was extremely puzzled by all of this, as far as he could tell; there was no real connection. The women had things in common such as working in New York as actresses, being redheads, and were all beautiful, good, upcoming actresses, but not well known. Probably could have played the same characters, in essence, they were the same girl. But other than that, checks into their type of work, friends in New York, that sort of thing, they had nothing in common- except for the circumstances surrounding their murders. Rudy typed the list, and placed it on the wall with the three pictures. He stared at the display for a few minutes. "How long can this guy go on before he makes a mistake? These murders seem perfectly choreographed; I wonder if he has an alternate plan if things get screwed up? What does he plan on doing if something goes wrong? Goddamit, these three murders are perfect, he did nothing wrong, no fuck-ups. There has to be something there. I'm going to look at the list every day, every day, there must be an answer there somewhere," he vowed out loud, shaking his head.

* * * * *

Thursday, October 22, 1996

Another beautiful sunrise on the beach as Tygre began her morning meditation. The thing she liked best about the Florida beach was the sunrise. A Japanese gentleman friend, Shimizu, told her that each sunrise was different; each sunrise had its own meaning and if we studied them, we could learn their meaning. Today's sunrise was brilliantly clear, with perfect definition; the glowing, orange sphere's edges were free from defect, as if someone had traced it on a background. It rose from the ocean's edge into a fireball that balanced on a disappearing floor of water. Tygre sat on the beach towel with her legs crossed; feet tucked up near her hips. Her head was held high, tilted slightly back so she could feel the sun on her face and throat, her eyes were closed. She could see the outline of the sun through her eyelids. As the round glow came through, and the warmth of the sun began to cover her body, she contemplated. She saw her imaginary tail grounding with the earth's hot, fiery core. The core sent this pure clean energy to the surface, and connected to the first chakra at the base of the spine. This energy connected with the other chakras; cleansing as it moved throughout the body. Chakra # two, the sexual chakra, # three, the solar plexus or seat of personality, onto # four, near the heart, the chakra dealing with compassion and healing, to # five, the throat chakra which enables communication. The last two and most important are the sixth and seventh chakras. They are the mind's eye or clarity, and the crown or top of the head. The crown connects directly to the sun, then shines back to the earth's surface, and is absorbed into the earth and down to the core. From the core to the base chakra, this circle brings the sunlight back to the earth, and is absorbed to the earth's core again and again.

This spectrum of life circulated through the chakras of her body, and as she continued to assist this circle by remaining whole, she felt her body cleanse itself as the light circulated through her chakras. She continued this cleansing process for nearly an hour, as she had done daily for the past year. Tygre had been living with her secret for fifteen years. Since she was a young teenager, she had been unable to tell anyone, not even her therapist in New York; he had hit on her, and now she needed a break. Meditation seemed to be the answer; it gave her strength. She felt that soon she would be able to use her inner strength to find true freedom. She would be able to admit her secret to everyone, and get on with her life. Once on with her personal life, she could truly focus on her career as a serious actress. She collected her things from the beach, and headed towards her car, and breakfast with a friend.

"Good morning, Janice, how are you this fine morning?" Tygre leaned over and gave Janice a peck on the cheek, and sat down at the table and picked up a menu. "God was great this morning, he gave me another perfect sunrise to begin my life with...I feel so full of energy, good, positive energy. I feel like doing something different today. What do you want to do today?"

"Hi, babe, I'm fine, just a little sleepy, that's all. I only have one important thing to do; I have to take Bob to the vet, the fat, old guy needs his shots. He is the best cat in the world, I got to take care of him, you know? After noon I'll be free for whatever. What have you got in mind?"

"What are you going to have this morning, Tygre? The waitress broke in; she had already taken Janice's order.

"Just a bowl of mixed fruit, and an onion bagel with a dash of jalapeno cream cheese. I'll also have a double latte without chocolate. There's that guy again." Tygre's voice had a tone of frustration.

"What guy?" Janice wanted to know.

"The hottie at the table in the corner, he just sat down." Tygre sort of tilted her head, and let her eyes point in his direction.

"You mean the guy in the jeans, white shirt and vest?" Janice picked him out.

"Yeah, that's him," Tygre affirmed.

"So what's the big deal?" Janice wanted to know.

"I met him on the beach, he's a big sunrise guy too. He's been hitting on me for the last few days. He's really nice, but he wants the big 'R.'"

"The big 'R,' you mean Romance? Why don't you just come out and tell him? He'll leave in a heartbeat. Shit, I'll tell him." Janice was assertive.

"You know how hard it is for me to tell anyone about it; you're the only one who knows for sure. I mean I spent almost two years in therapy just so I could learn to deal with it, and I couldn't even tell my therapist! I left him because he hit on me. What a jerk! I ought to report him; I think it's some sort of ethics violation, or something like that. At least I didn't have to pay him; he gave me a freebie for some book he was writing. Has a number of us he documented, says he can help us become famous, great actors."

"He's waving, he wants to join us." Janice covered her eyes, and grimaced slightly. "What do you want to do?"

"Oh hell, let's be nice, I'll wave him over." Tygre smiled and gestured him to the table.

"You're too nice, that's your problem, you are too fucking nice, you've got to tell him before he gets the wrong idea. Tell him this morning," Janice warned Tygre as she quickly smiled, and looked up just in time to meet the stranger.

"Hi, Jamie, this is my friend, Janice Hackett, Janice, Jamie Fender." They shook hands.

"So, Jamie, what brings you to Daytona Beach?" Janice thought she would be the first to ask.

"Business. I work for a Micro Brewery in Minnesota; I'm here to do a promotion with a local distributor. We want to get our beer onto the market before the kids come down for the spring."

"Well, this is the place to sell beer. There will be a million kids here from February to May, they'll drink more beer here during that time than anywhere in the world. That's when Tygre and I leave. It's a nice town when the kids aren't partying up a storm, and they party all the time when it's the season, I mean the kids that visit party all the time …the kids living here don't party…. Well they party, but not all the time…only when they party…but I like to party sometimes with them…the kids that are here…not the kids that visit…except some of them…they are cool to party with…and I like it here…most of the time… I'm sorry, I don't mean to say that it's not a nice town, I mean, it's a nice town------help me out, Tygre." Janice was taking the conversation in a large circle, and confusing herself…something that wasn't that hard to do anyway…

"That's okay, Janice, she just means to say, we like it here because of the perfect beach, the good weather, not because it's a party town. Basically, it's a country town except for the kids. It's quiet and relaxing most of the time." Tygre was good at bailing her out; Janice had a habit of getting her foot where her words ought to be. "What is the name of your beer?

"It's called Timber Wolf Lager. It's a sweet beer brewed using an old Scandinavian recipe; I'll have some here in about ten days, so I can give you a taste. "He knew that he could always lie later about bad shipping, or some complication if they really asked for some. He wasn't worried.

The waitress had put all the food on the table, including Jamie's order, and they all took turns making small talk and eating. Jamie paid for all of them when the checks came.

"So, what's on the agenda today?" Jamie asked both of them at the same time.

"Well, we were just discussing what to do with our afternoon when we saw you. We really haven't decided. But, I'm sure we'll figure out something," Tygre offered.

"Tell you what, I'll take both of you to dinner, then we'll hit the Amphitheater for some late night dancing, treats are on the brewery." Jamie figured if he couldn't get close to Tygre alone, maybe if he forged a friendship with the two of them, he'd be able to get to her.

"I'm not sure about that. What do you think, Janice?" Tygre did not want to be the one to make the decision for both of them.

Jamie jumped in, "What's the harm, new guy in town, show me around, help me get the feel for the area, won't cost you a dime, limo if you like? Come on. Let's do it." Jamie tried to put a little pressure on them, and it worked.

Janice blurted out. "That's a great idea, have the limo pick us up at my house at 9:00 p.m., here's the address, I'll call for reservations at the Angelino, the little Italian place upstairs, down the street from the Amphitheater." She wrote the number down on a napkin, and handed it to Jamie.

"See you at 9:00 tonight." Janice smiled triumphantly.

"Yeah, see you at 9:00." Tygre leaned over to Jamie, and kissed him on the cheek. She felt confused.

As Jamie walked away, Janice yelled out, "Thanks for breakfast, see you at 9:00."

"What the hell was that all about, you cretin?" Tygre was pissed. "I've been trying to avoid going out with the guy for two weeks because of YOU, and YOU make a date for the both of us… godammit." Tygre was completely frustrated.

"Here's the deal, tonight is the night. You tell him your secret tonight, but after he spends a whole bunch of money on us, he'll be the first one you tell. After him, it will be easy. Whoa, I'm running late, I have to take Bob to the vet, I will call you when I am done, we will go shopping for some great outfits to wear. Love you." Janice kissed Tygre on the cheek, pulled her car keys from her jeans pocket, and ran to her VW Rabbit convertible. Waving as she drove off, she yelled, "It'll be fine, trust me."

Jamie went back to the hotel after shopping for a few items. He decided to try a different approach: Cowboy boots, jeans, a stylish T-shirt, and a vest. Maybe if he projected a model look, an actor look, or an LA look, something a little different than the usual. What was he doing wrong? How could Daddy have misled him? He had done everything, just as before. He used the doctor's file to try to seduce her; it had worked each time before. He met her casually, asked her to lunch, accidentally mentioned her favorite flowers, her favorite wine, her favorite plant, poetry, clothes, movies, everything, but nothing worked. He was supposed to be her perfect match. He hadn't even gotten her to go out on a late night date alone. Tonight was going to be different; he was going to try to feel this one out on his own, be more natural, and enjoy himself. He called for a limo, tried his clothes on, and called the drycleaner to make them perfect. Always perfect!

After Bob's trip to the vet, the girls met at Tygre 's apartment. Janice showed up with a snack, and brought her new outfit. "Wait 'til you see this getup, I'm in leather, leather everywhere, leather pants, leather vest, boots, look at the silver toe clips, baby spurs with chains around the ankle. I am way too cool. Wait 'til you see how tight these pants fit."

"I'm sure you will look great, Janice was tall with a great body, not a beautiful face, but she was impressive to look at, standing 5'10".

We'll need some music, and how about some wine, let's have a pre-party, party?"

"I still have that bottle of Tattinger in the fridge, put on some Bob Marley." Tygre was getting into this little game.

As the Reggae beat started, 'Wake up and live now' began, "Wake up, live life, wake up and live, life is one big road with lots of signs..." As Tygre 's body began to sway with the beat...don't complicate your mind. Yee, mighty people...there's work to be done..." She thought, "Here is the sign, this guy has come here to help me free myself, he is the sign. No more lies." She began to free up, and flow with the music. "Wake and live life, wake up and live…………"

Janice walked into the living room with the bottle of champagne; she began to writhe in time with the music. She held the champagne high, and twisted the wire holder free from the bottle and let the cork go. "Bang!" She shrieked, and watched as the juice shot out of the bottle. "Eeeeiiiii!" She drank from the bottle, and handed it to Tygre.

They both danced and drank. The champagne worked fast, they both giggled. They faced each other, and moved simultaneously to the music, as they moved closer and closer to each other, "We are the children of the Rasta man...Africa unite." They both sang, and drank, and laughed.

As the next song started, they moved in unison, slow motion almost, their bodies moving as one, as they got closer and closer. Janice put the champagne down on the table, as she wrapped her arms around Tygre, her large hands moved up and down, and across Tygre's back and shoulders, while her pelvis moved perfectly to Tygre's. Perfect unison; they were one. Janice put her hands on Tygre's ass, and pulled her close, Tygre tilted her head back, and stared into Janice' eyes. They kissed. All the time, they kissed and moved with the music. After a few moments, Tygre spoke.

"What do you think he will say when I tell him?"

"So, who gives a fuck? You are free, you can finally tell the world you are a lesbian, and you love it." Janice let go and walked to the kitchen to get the crystal champagne glasses. She walked back into the room and poured champagne into each glass, turned the music down a notch, and sat on the couch.

"I don't want to tell the world yet, I just want Jamie to know this was a test; it was a little test.-Remember that I had to find someone to tell; I went to therapy with the express purpose of helping me come out of the closet. I know I should have told him, but he didn't seem like the right person to tell; I never felt good about that doctor, something was weird about him. Then he hit on me, and I just walked out of his office. I couldn't believe it; he was there to help me, and instead he stares at my tits, and wants to get into my pants. There must be a law against that…maybe I should tell somebody about that weirdo. He shouldn't be allowed to help people. As far as you picking Jamie as my test, I think you were right to do this Janice, this guy is new in town, and he will leave in a few days. He is the guinea pig. First him, then another, then another, one-step at a time. Don't you go and blow it by telling everyone; the way you do things, you'd probably like to put a banner up, and hire a band. Let me do it, it's my deal, okay!" She was firm about it; they had talked it over for a couple of months. It had taken her years to get to this point, and it was almost over.

Tygre poured them both another glass of Tattinger, and sat down next to Janice on the couch. She laid her head on Janice's left shoulder. "You won't fuck it up for me, will you, Let me do it, okay? Okay?"

Janice caressed Tygre's shoulder. "Okay, I will, I promise. It was just easier for me, I guess. I just don't remember it being such a big deal, but then nothing I have ever done seemed like a big deal. You are the biggest deal that has ever happened to me, Tygre." Janice pulled Tygre to her, and kissed her on the forehead. They looked into each other's eyes; Tygre's lips parted, and they kissed passionately. Janice caressed Tygre's hair above her ear, and slowly worked her neck. She unbuttoned her blouse, and began to caress her shoulder, and then another button and slid her bra strap over her shoulder, and kissed the soft skin about her breast. She slowly moved her hand down to Tygre's left breast, and finding the nipple she sucked it, and began to rub the inside of Tygre's right thigh. Tygre responded. They were a couple.

9 p.m. came fast enough for the two of them. The limo pulled up, and Jamie checked his napkin for the address. This was the place. "Honk the horn, Jimmy."

"Eeeiiiiyyyah, look at us, we are ready." Janice yelled from the porch. She ran down the eight steps to the driveway, and up to Jamie. She gave him a kiss on the cheek. "Great car, come on, babe, let's get this show on the road. Tygre, let's go," she yelled at the top of her lungs as she bounced around like a cheerleader.

Tygre was next; she came down to the car much slower than Janice, and she looked marvelous. Tight Levi's, molded, fit like only could a young, tight, perfect ass. Black Tony Lama's, stiff starched white tuxedo shirt with gold studs, and gold cuff links. She had put three gold studs in the lobe of each ear. Three different sized gold ear loops above the left lobe, appearing as if they were coming out of the same hole. Her red hair was slicked down, straight back, wide avenues between the thick wall strands of hair-something not seen very often, unless one happened to be a regular at the runway shows promoting new women's fashion. She was devastatingly beautiful.

Jamie was stopped cold, he had not seen her with this look before, and he was pleased. "You look marvelous, absolutely marvelous." He had stupidly assumed she had dressed this way for him. Little did he know?

Jamie and Tygre got into the limo with Janice, all three sitting in the back seat, Jamie in between the two of them. Janice was all giggly and happy, while Tygre seemed happy but a little distant, staring out the window for a moment.

"Is everything all right? Jamie asked.

"Yes, Yes, everything is just fine. I'm just not used to this kind of treatment, and I was thinking a little too much." Tygre smiled, and gave Jamie a little elbow to the rib cage, and faked a tickle to his side while smiling. "This is going to be great. Tell this driver to take us to Cafe Angelino on Beach Street, that's where we're going to eat."

Jimmy the driver overheard and answered. "I know the place, we'll be there in about five minutes."

As the limo rolled down along the river on Halifax Avenue, Jamie thought to himself, "Look at these two beauties, godammit; this could really get to be fun." They seemed to be different, wilder than the others, he thought. Maybe they will both get naked, and have a little fun. Then I can do the job and leave. It is going to be hard, though. How am I going to get Tygre away from Janice, they seem to be attached at the hip?

"Ladies, Ladies, lets toast something-how about-Saturday night, a limo, champagne and fun?" The bottle popped, and Jamie poured, while the two girls laughed loudly.

Janice seemed more playful than Tygre, as she placed her left arm around Jamie. "You are such a good looking guy, you must have beautiful ladies chasing you all around Montana?

"Minnesota," Jamie blurted out.

"Whatever, I knew it was one of those 'M' states, where it's cold and up there." She pointed toward the sky. "Let's open the skylight.

Janice looked around for the button. She found it on a small console in front of them. She pushed the button and stood up in the middle of the car, putting her ass right in Jamie's face. "God, what a view." Janice laughed, looked down and back at Jamie. Jamie agreed.

Tygre became a little unnerved, and also stood up next to Janice. "Stop with the bullshit, if you tease him it will make things worse."

"But you know how I am, I love to run everything to the edge, right to the edge. Besides, I want this guy to suffer. He'll be whacking off in the back of the car on the way home tonight."

Tygre did not like the way Janice was acting, and gave her a look.

Jamie wedged his way in between them, and poured more champagne. "Come on you two, stop fighting over me, there is plenty to go around."

The girls looked at each other, and laughed.

"Angelino's straight ahead," Jimmy yelled out. "Time for dinner."

The three got out, and headed for the front door.

"Good evening, dining with us tonight?" The hostess at the front door asked.

"Yeah, the reservation is under Fender, three people upstairs on the deck. 9 p.m."

The hostess grabbed some menus and led the way up the stairs. "Follow me."

As they reached the top, Janice asked. "Can we sit near the edge, so we can see the Waterway without being blocked by other people?

"No problem," the girl responded, and seated them next to the wrought iron railing, placing the menus on the table. "Here is the wine list."

"Just bring us a bottle of Dom, I believe there should be a couple bottles reserved for me." Jamie had thought to order the best when he made the reservation. "Spare no expense for these beautiful ladies. This is a special occasion. In fact, I asked the chef earlier to prepare a special meal. He said just to tell you we were the Jamie party, and he would do the rest."

"Somebody's birthday?" the waitress asked, as she returned with the twisted metal cage from the neck, and the cork of the champagne.

"No, just Saturday night on the town, a great reason, and I am sure it is somebody's birthday, somewhere." Jamie giggled, as he tasted the Dom Perignon. "Just great, God, that's great stuff."

The girls both drank, and agreed. "This is so much better than the stuff we drink, I think, after twenty or thirty glasses, it is so hard to tell if Heineken is better than Miller." Tygre laughed at Janice's joke, as they downed their glasses.

"Do either of you dislike spicy food, I've ordered a special dish, so I hope it is okay?

Janice and Tygre both agreed that spicy was good.

"The chef is making us Lobster Fra Diavlo, with a homemade pasta and live Maine lobster. He is also making a special salad and dressing, more á la California style, with a mixture of greens, sun-dried tomatoes, apples and who knows what else? All he told me was that it was not from the regular menu."

"You are doing all this just to get a piece or two of ass? Wow, I feel honored; how do you feel, Tygre? Pretty neat, huh. All this is just for sex? Well, I've got some news for you." Janice was acting drunk all of a sudden.

"Don't mind her, Jamie, Janice has the weirdest, sarcastic sense of humor when she drinks too much. And we did polish off a bottle of Tattinger earlier this evening."

"Fuck you, fuck you, and fuck you again. I am not drunk; I am here to help you tell this man what's what. I am not, not drunk. Fuck you. Am I going to screw up something for you, Tygre? Oh, I forgot, I'm supposed to let you tell, that's right, I can't help. This is your deal. You can tell, well, tell him." Janice was beginning to sound angry, and drunk.

The bread and salad arrived, and the waitress ground the fresh peppercorns. "Let's not talk now, Janice, eat some food, and you'll start to feel better."

"What do you mean feel better? I feel fine. You are the one who is not feeling well. I mean, tell him, or I will."

Tygre stood up, and grabbed her by the arm. "Please come to the bathroom with me, I need to have a short talk with you." "I'm sorry, Jamie, give me a few minutes with her alone, I need to help her get her head screwed on straight. We'll be back in just a few minutes, okay? I'm sorry, Jamie."

"I understand, Tygre, take all the time you need, I'll just sit here and relax with the wine. I'll get the waitress to slow down the meal; don't worry about a thing." Jamie gave her the thumbs up sign.

Janice looked at Tygre, and after a few seconds of cross-eyed staring, nodded her head. "Okay, okay, yeah, lead the way, okay." Janice stood up, and the two walked off and down the stairs, Janice was bouncing off the walls as they walked away.

Instead of walking to the bathroom, Tygre led Janice down the stairs, and out the door to the sidewalk to get some fresh air. "You promised you would not do this, you promised to let me do this my way, in my own time, please straighten up, and fly right. Look, let's just enjoy this dinner, then I'll tell him, and we'll have him take us home and it'll be all over with. Okay?"

Janice stared off into the sky. "Okay, I'm sorry, but I just get jealous-jealous and insecure, because nobody knows I exist as your lover. I'm just your friend, they don't know, and I get scared that I may lose you. When I drink too much, it just comes out. I just love you so much."

"I know, me too, I love you too, Janice and I know it's hard. But in a few short hours, it will be over, no more hiding, no more lies. I just want you to relax, and enjoy this time, and let me do things my way. Okay?

"Okay," Janice hugged Tygre. "Okay, I'm sorry, forgive me. I know you're right; you need to do this on your own. After dinner, I'm going to get a cab home, and I'll meet you later at your house. "

"Oh, Gawd.... You are so melodramatic. Jesus Christ, can't you just tag along, and let me do my thing for once?" Tygre sounded exasperated.

"No, no, no, you've got me all wrong honey. You know as well as I do, that when I'm drinking, I get jealous, I get insecure, I need help. You should be alone to do this. Just do it my way, I'll go home, you come out of the closet, all is well in lesbian land. Just forgive me for almost making a mess, I'll take a cab home, grab some clothes and meet you about midnight, okay? Please?

Tygre thought for a minute, put her arms out, gave her a hug and kiss, and looked straight into her eyes. "You're forgiven, but that's it for the booze, no more to drink for you." They headed back into the restaurant, and up the stairs arm-in-arm.

"No problem, my darling, no problem, I won't drink a drop more, I'll just sip a few sips to be polite." Janice gave her a wry smile.

Tygre led the way as they walked up to the table. "Jamie, I'm so sorry about the interruption, we're ready to eat now. Janice has decided not to drink anymore this evening." Tygre tried to smooth things over.

"Okay, let's relax, and eat." Jamie was confused as to what was going on, but he was not about to butt in; he had his mission to concentrate on.

The waitress brought fresh salad, and hot bread, and they all dug in. "Great salad," Jamie broke the ice.

"Yeah, the food is perfect," Janice seemed better now. "If the meal is as good as the greens, it'll be out of this world." In fact, she seemed to have sobered up, and was actually being slightly nice; she acted as if nothing had happened.

Throughout the rest of the dinner, they made small talk about the weather, the beach, and the beer business. Jamie noticed that the two girls seemed to be distracted, and not into the night out as much as it had seemed earlier that day. The waitress carried a large tray to the table's edge. A silver cap covered each plate. She removed each cap as she placed the gold leafed-edged china in front of each one of them. "Lobster Diavlo," she announced, as she took the covers off one-by-one.

"God, this smells so good," Janice was the first to proclaim, and Tygre chimed in, "Look at the size of this lobster." The chef had served the entire lobster with the top half of the claws cut away, so that the meat was exposed; the tail had been split on the sides, and the meat was free from sticking to the shell. The split sides allowed them to just lift the shell up, exposing the meat. There was a portion of saffron risotto under the lobster meat, and bright green asparagus spears lying with their points facing outward to the edge of the plate, forming a green sunburst around the centerpiece. A light drizzle of drawn butter covered the lobster meat, and a small bowl of Diavlo sauce was placed in the middle of the table. It was a beautiful, special presentation.

"Ladies, I have a few things to say. I've been very lucky so far with my choices; I hope you are into soufflés. The chef has suggested a bailey's and chocolate combo for dessert. I had also ordered a Chateau d'Yquiem, but I think I will cancel that, since we all have already had quite a bit too much to drink. Is everyone agreeable to that?"

Tygre answered first. "Sounds good to me, I'd rather have a double espresso with dessert, how about you Janice?" She glanced in Janice's direction.

Janice chimed in. "I think that is the way to go, count me in."

The soufflés and espressos arrived, and they all dug in. "God, this is so divoooooone," Tygre giggled out the words. "If I ate this way all the time, I'd be as big as a Volkswagen."

"Yeah, me too," both Janice and Jamie said at the same time. The three of them laughed together honestly, for the first time the entire evening.

"Well, ladies, let me take care of this check, and then we can get on with our evening." Jamie knew that the best thing he could do was get them partying, and hopefully, Janice would get more drunk and she would have to be dropped off at her house, then he could get Tygre alone, and take care of her at her house. It would not be that hard to get rid of the limo and driver, and get out of town before anyone found her body. His plane did not leave until 5 a.m. But, first he had to get them separated. The waitress brought the check and Jamie paid, leaving her $600, including a $150 tip. "This was a great meal and great service, give my thanks to the chef; it was one of the best meals I've ever had."

The girls added their congratulations." It was perfect, everything was perfect, thank you so much."

"Okay, ladies let's boogie, next door we go, to the Coliseum." Jamie put himself between the two, and started down the sidewalk.

Janice pulled away. "I'm really not feeling so well, Jamie, why don't you take Tygre and the two of you have a good time. I've already had too much to drink; I've been a pain in the ass. It's only 11:30, and there is plenty of time for you guys to still have a good time." Janice hugged Tygre.

This was exactly what Jamie had wanted; they would be separated. He was in charge now; he could enjoy himself, and have the freedom to take care of her, and get out of town. "Janice, there's no need to leave, stay, have some fun, the restaurant deal was nothing. Please stay!" He tried to sound sincere, although his mind was racing through another scenario.

"No, no, I think she is right. We talked it over earlier. She wants to go, and I think she is right," Tygre added.

"See, Jamie, it's okay," Janice agreed.

Jamie smiled, and hugged Janice. "Jimmy, why don't you give Janice a lift home, while Tygre and I dance, then we'll meet you here in front of the Coliseum, okay?" Jamie motioned to him to open the passenger door of the car.

Jimmy had stepped out of the limo, and was listening in to their conversation. "That's fine with me, boss. Anything you say."

"Yeah, that would be great, thanks for everything, Jamie." Janice hugged him again, then hugged Tygre, and headed for the limo. She turned and waved. "You guys have a killer time."

Jamie thought about it and snickered, "We certainly will, we certainly will. "Jimmy, we'll meet you here in front of the Coliseum, okay?"

"Back where we started, Miss, or do we need to make a stop or two?" Jimmy asked for directions.

"No, No, no stops, just take me back to where you picked us up."

Jimmy headed the limo back to Janice's house. It was a twenty-minute round trip. "Sorry you're not feeling well, Miss."

"Oh, I'm feeling okay, Jimmy, Tygre and I just thought it would be better if she and Jamie spent the rest of the evening alone together; this is just fine with me."

The limo made a sharp right turn, and came to a halt. "We're here, Miss."

"Thanks for the ride, darling, see you around."

"Have you come to this place often, Tygre?" Jamie made small talk.

"Naw, since I met Janice, we stay away from the meat markets; we hang out a lot together." Tygre knew she would have to tell him soon, but she was avoiding talk about her personal life. "What are we drinking?" She felt really confused; the champagne was starting to take its toll, and she felt a little drunk. One part of here wanted to be nice, and get this over with quickly. A few drinks, a few dances, tell him the truth and it would be over. Another part of her kind of liked the attention she was getting from Jamie. She liked him; she felt attracted to him, and she wondered if she was making a big mistake by coming out. Was this the right thing to do? She had to wait a little while longer; maybe a few more glasses of something would loosen her tongue. Maybe a few more glasses of something would help her say the right thing.

"Miss, please bring us a bottle of Dom," Jamie said to the bartender.

"No, no, not a whole bottle. How about a nice Chardonnay?" Tygre asked. "I've really had more to drink than any normal human being. I'm feeling drunk; well, not drunk, but a little dizzy." The booze was confusing her thoughts.

"Okay, two Chardonnays then." The bartender poured a couple of glasses of wine. "Let's dance." Jamie wanted to get things going in the direction of his plan.

"Can we not dance and talk instead Jamie? I really don't feel like dancing right now; I have something to tell you, something that is going to surprise you, and it's really important to me, and to Janice, and to you." She seemed quiet and uninviting all of a sudden.

"This has really changed into something serious." Jamie was confused. "What is so important that our night out has to be reduced to this kind of conversation?"

"Let's just say that this serious conversation is something I've needed to talk about for a long time; something that has been on my mind, that I've been meaning to tell everyone, and you just happen to be the first. The reason Janice has acted so goofy is because she is a little more than my friend, she's my girlfriend, and my lover. I am gay; I am a lesbian. I might be bi. I like girls more than guys."

"G…Gay?" Jamie stuttered. "Well, shit…I'm…" Tygre cut him off abruptly.

"Please hear me out, you are the first man I've ever told this to. I've done everything a good young woman is supposed to do. Everything that is, except be true to myself. I've been living with this on my mind since I was thirteen years old. Even then I knew that something was different. I tried to be straight, but I couldn't. Maybe I am bi- but I am not sure, but I know I feel better with women, and it takes a special man to make me feel like that. So here I am. With you, telling you, and I feel good. Janice was right; she said I would feel good when the truth came out. There, I said it, what do you think? I feel good; I feel great. Wow! Janice was right."

"Well, I never…I mean…you know, I just never thought you were one, I mean…you are gay. Man, I never suspected." Jamie's mind raced. Does this change anything? Should I call Daddy? Should I still eliminate her? What the hell? He was lost in thought, and started to space out.

"Jamie, Jamie? Are you alive? Hello in there." Tygre had trouble getting his attention. "This really affected you much more than I thought. I mean I didn't expect it to put you into a catatonic state. Are you okay? Hello!"

Jamie had been staring straight ahead, not seeing anything. "I'm sorry, I'm sorry. You just caught me off guard, that's all. I don't know what to do, I mean, what to say." Jamie had been thinking about the near future, and was now totally confused.

"Is this hard for you to accept? Are you still going to give me a ride home?" Tygre tried to lighten things up a little.

"No, no, it's okay. I'm glad for you; I know this has been difficult for you. And, of course, I'll still give you a ride home. Forgive me if my reaction was…let's say…different than you expected. I suppose you want to go home right away?" Jamie was at a loss for words. But, Tygre was not.

"Well, let's have one more cocktail to celebrate my coming out… bartender, bartender…. Two double shots of Jose Cuervo 1800, and don't forget the limes." The bartender brought over two shot glasses, and filled them from the Cuervo bottle. Tygre pushed one glass, a napkin, two limes and a saltshaker to her left, and looked at Jamie. "Bottoms up, you hunk."

The two of them drank the shots in one gulp. Tygre motioned for another as she stuck a lime wedge in her mouth. "Keep 'em comin' bartender." Two more shots were poured. "Just one more," Tygre yelled out, immediately after chugging her second. Then she chugged a third.

"Whoa darlin'. You're going to pass out at that speed; slow down. Try an empty one this time around." Jamie thought for a moment. If she is really drunk, this could be easier. "Never mind, bartender, let's have one more." The bartender poured another shot. "This is our last one," Jamie slurred jokingly.

Tygre did not feel drunk anymore, she was loose but she figured it might be time to go. "Jamie, how about giving me a ride home? I think it's time to go now; it's almost 1 a.m. I think my coming out party is about over." Tygre looked at Jamie, and smiled as she ran her fingers though the hair above his left ear. "I'm sorry if this ruined your evening, you've been so nice, so understanding. I wish there was something I could do for you, but it's just not in my chemical makeup, although I suppose I could fake it once more for old time's sake." A wry smile spread across her face, as she looked at Jamie. She did the last shooter, smiled, and motioned towards the door. "I'm ready to go, how about you?"

"Let's go." Jamie put his right arm around Tygre's waist, and directed her towards the door. Once outside, he looked for Jimmy and the limo.

Jimmy was standing by the black caddie fifty yards south of the main entrance of the Coliseum. He waved and called out, "Mr. Fender, Mr. Fender, over here, folks, over here."

Jamie waved back. "Jimmy, how are you doing? Look's like you're going to have an early evening; Tygre is tired and ready to go home. Did you get Janice back home safely?" Jamie needed to know where Janice was so he could plan his attack for later in the evening.

"Yes, sir, I did, she's back at her house, back where we started." Jimmy assured Jamie that the coast was clear at Tygre's house. He closed the back door of the limo, walked to the front and got in behind the wheel. "Where to now sir?"

Jamie glanced at Tygre as she spoke. "My little house is on the other side of the river. We have to head north, and go across the new bridge at Seabreeze Avenue, then go north on Halifax almost till we get to Ormond Beach. I have the upstairs in a boathouse; it's on the property of one of those big houses on the Inter-Coastal Waterway; 822 North Halifax. It has a big double driveway; mine is on the left of the house. It goes straight back to the water. It's kind of a neat little place and I can get to the ocean in a few minutes." Tygre snuggled in close to Jamie, as she looked into his eyes, "You have been so good to me. I really like you, and I feel like I owe you something for being so nice.

Jamie started to feel a little guilty, like a normal human should, but he had work to do. They started kissing and groping each other and Tygre She was actually enjoying this and she was very good at it. As she did her thing, Jamie flashed on killing her. Daddy had told him not to get sexually involved. If he did, he took the chance on not finishing the job he there to do. He felt a tinge of guilt, but at this moment he also felt incredible pleasure.

"Are we there yet, Jimmy?" "We've been there for ten minutes boss." Jamie and Tygre laughed, and looked at each other.

"I guess it's time for me to say goodbye, Jamie. Thanks for the most wonderful evening. Thanks so much, and if I ever decide that I am not gay, you'll be the first to know," she laughed.

Jamie pulled on the door handle, and got out of the car. He turned around and helped her out of the car. "I'll walk you to the door, it's only the gentlemanly thing to do." He put his arm around her, and walked her to the step that climbed up the side of the building to the second floor.

"Do you want to come in for a while?" Tygre had promised him more.

"I would love to Tygre, but I think everything has been great so far, and I don't want you to get more confused; you have been wonderful." Jamie was on a time schedule. They kissed, and he turned and walked towards the car.

"Well then, this is it. It has been wonderful. Thanks again, Jamie." She watched him turn, and walk back to the car, and felt her attraction towards him, a physical attraction. She also felt very confused. What now? She walked to the front door, let herself in, and turned and waved just at the exact time Jamie turned and waved.

"You're very welcome," he said to her, "Very, very welcome. I had a great time." He waved again. "Adios, amiga, adios." He turned, and got back into the car. "Jimmy, could you take me back to my hotel?"

"Yes, sir, Mr. Fender, sir." He drove out of the driveway, made a left, and then a right turn towards the beach. In a few minutes he would be back at the Plaza Inn.

Tygre watched as the limo pulled out of the driveway; she walked to the refrigerator and reached for an open a bottle of wine. She glanced at the clock; it was 2:30 a.m. She walked to the kitchen counter, the blinking light on the answering machine got her attention, and she pushed the play button. "Hey 'T', just walked in, I am tired, drunk and going to take a nap. Call me when you get home." Her words were slurred.

"Janice needs to sober up, and I need time to relax and clean up," she thought. "Time for a shower, and I'll call her later." She put some music on, turned up the volume, undressed, and headed for the shower. Once finished, she changed into some shorts and a tee shirt, sipped her wine, and cranked the volume up some more. She felt very relaxed and happy, but a little confused; mostly she was glad about the night's happenings.

Jimmy pulled the limo up to the side door of the hotel, and Jamie got out. He quickly handed Jimmy $300 and thanked him. "It's only $200, Mr. Fender."

"Keep it, my man, you were great, thanks a lot, see you next time. I've got your number." Jamie walked into the hotel's side entrance, made a beeline for the elevator, and went up to his room on the fourteenth floor. He always avoided being seen by the front desk during his stay; he wanted the staff to only see him as a businessman and only in a certain way. He walked over to the room safe and dialed the combination. He opened the door, and pulled out his duffel bag; it was the all-important duffel bag. It was small, but big enough to hold the needed cash, different ID's and the few pieces of clothing he needed for his return. He laid out his return clothes, chained the door, showered and shaved. He then carefully glued on a mustache, put some water on his hair, ruffled it, and put a little goop on to make it look stylishly messy. He then took a pair of non-prescription glasses out of his duffel, and put them on. This is the way he had looked when he checked in, and this is the way he was going to look when he checked out, and drove off in his rental car. All of the other trips he had made from the hotel side entrance in the limo. No employee had even said hello to him and there was no doorman, as there would be in a large, major city hotel. He had successfully stayed incognito; each time he made one of these trips for Daddy, he had bought all his clothes locally in cash, and had left the clothes in the hotel when he checked out.

"I'd like to close out my bill, Fender, room 1453." Jamie stood at the front desk with a handful of hundred dollar bills.

"Here you go, Mr. Fender, four nights, no phone calls, no extras, that will be $985.20 including tax please." The desk attendant took the cash, and gave him his change. "I hope you had a nice stay, and please come visit us again."

"It was really nice, I'm sure I will be back." He tried to make it short and sweet, bringing no attention to himself, as he always did.

As he walked down to the parking garage, he examined his plane tickets; he had to drive to the Orlando airport, about ninety minutes away, and get to his plane by 5 a.m. The Daytona airport was way too small; he would surely be noticed there.

Now, he must get to Tygre's house and take care of business. He drove north on the beach drive, and made a left on Highway 40, then another left on the river road. When he approached the driveway, he decided to drive a few houses past and park in front of a house that already had three cars parked on the street. He could then walk back across the dark yards and up to the house.

He could see the lights of Tygre's apartment in the distance, and the stairs were lit for easy nighttime access. He pulled the mustache off, and carefully placed it and the glasses on the dash console. He left the jacket and shirt in the back seat; pulled a sweatshirt out of the duffel bag, and put it on. He was wearing topsiders and Levis. He locked the car door behind him, and headed down the street toward Tygre's house. As he neared the stairs, he thought to himself, "I must catch her off guard." He thought for a moment. "Maybe if I just walk up and ring the bell, and she answers, we talk, and then I end it, just like the other ones?"

He walked up the stairs. There were a few lights on. He put his finger on the doorbell as he glanced at his watch and noticed it was about 2:45 a.m.

Tygre came to the door. "Hey, Jamie, what are you doing here?"

"I just stopped by to say goodbye again. When I got back to the hotel, there was a message for me to come home immediately; my brother was seriously injured in a car accident. So I came by to say goodbye, and maybe take you up on your offer. Even though I will be back in a few weeks. Got anything to drink?" He needed an excuse to get into the house.

She laughed out loud. "So you want to take me up on my offer, huh? Well, I guess we could talk about it?" She had a devilish smile on her face, as she let him into the front room with a kiss. "I'm so sorry about your brother. Is it serious?" She sounded concerned. She opened the refrigerator and grabbed a beer, opening it with the wine key from the counter. "Here you go-glass?"

"Thanks," he responded. "Nah, no glass." He took the bottle from her hand and took a swig. "Got a few minutes to talk?" He started for the couch; he needed to get close to her so he could easily get his hands on her. He didn't have to worry about noise; the boathouse was fifty yards from the main house, and close to the noise of the river shoreline.

"Talk, huh, I thought you might have something else on your mind." Again, she showed that same devilish smile. "All, I was going to do was stay up late with my music and then sleep in late tomorrow." She put in a CD, and headed for the couch. They sat down next to each other. She found herself sitting close to him, and realised just how attracted she was to him. She was also confused although she now knew for certain that she liked both men and women. She took a sip of her wine, and placed the glass on the table. She didn't expect Janice to arrive for at least another hour or more…she still had to call her. She placed her hand on the inside of Jamie's thigh, looked at his face and gazed into his eyes. She felt her lips moving naturally closer to his. They kissed, her hand moving up his thigh to his groin. She rubbed him. "Oh Jamie, I think I like it both ways. I want to make love to you so badly." She grabbed at his belt.

He reached inside her tee shirt, and began to caress her breast; her nipples had become hard. She unzipped his pants and grabbed him. He was already excited. She fondled him.

"Let's go to the bedroom." Jamie wanted to get her in a position that would help him get the job done easily.

"Okay, Jamie." She answered. "Follow me." Tygre stood up, took his hand, and led him to the bedroom. Once there, she stood in front of him and pulled her tee shirt off. Her firm, perfectly round breasts were pointing directly at Jamie; her inviting eyes begged him to come closer, and he did. He held her in his arms and kissed her, reached down and stroked, then kissed her left breast. "Oh, Jamie, that feels so good." She pulled him towards the mattress. They went down together with Jamie on top. He started alternating breasts with his kissing and sucking. She tried to pull his pants down, and expected him to help, but at the same time she wanted him to pull his shirt up. When his shirt was off, she stared at his bare, muscular body, putting both hands on his chest. "Oh, Jamie, sometimes I wish I was only one way, instead of liking girls too. Tonight is one of those nights."

Jamie smiled. "You are so beautiful, I could make love to you forever."

"Do it, Jamie, do it." She began to pull her shorts down. "I want you to make love to me." She was so hot.

Jamie glanced at the bedside clock. He began to think, "It's almost 3 a.m. I don't have time. I have to get this done now." He looked at her, and his eyes filled with tears; this had never happened before. He grabbed a pillow with his left hand, quickly put it over her face, straddled her body and pushed. Tygre fought as Jamie cried. He cried hard, sobbed. What was going on? Why the tears. She kicked; she tried rolling back and forth. She was dead within five minutes. He was still crying as he pulled his pants up, he cried as he put his sweatshirt on, as he wiped the fingerprints off the bottle and glass, and as he wiped the doorbell clean. He cried as he glanced back at her body, as he checked her pulse. He cried as he left the house, and walked quickly to his car. He cried as he drove to the highway, and headed toward Interstate-4 and the Orlando airport.

It's 3:45 a.m. and the phone rings, Tygre's answering machine picks up after four rings. "Hey 'A', where are you? This is Janice; pick up. You sleeping? I'm coming over right now; I'll be there in fifteen minutes. Are you there? Anyway, I'm on my way. See you in a few."

Jamie had no way of knowing that the cops were at Tygre's house less than forty minutes after he had left; they had no way of knowing that he was on a plane bound for Oklahoma City a little more than an hour after they found the body.

* * * * *

Sunday, August 2, 1998

She had waited for this moment for three weeks; three weeks of constant companionship, and they had not yet slept together. How many times had she made that mistake before? She had slept her way through New York, and Los Angeles, in her younger, hungrier days, but she had learnt the hard way; she couldn't screw her way into the good parts. Fortunately, she woke up, and tried acting for the job. The wrong attitude had cost many young beauties their careers, but not Jeanna; she had woken up.

This was no audition; this was the real thing, the right man. Her hands felt his muscular frame, ran down across his buttocks, and pulled him against her. His long, strong fingers made their way across her brow, down her cheeks, and along her neck. He worked his fingertips across her forehead and eyebrows, ever so lightly, barely touching her. She shivered. Her eyes were closed to everything, her mind's eye seeing an imaginary light. Bright! Pure! They kissed, her tongue searching the darkness for passion. Serpentine fingers worked their way across her cheeks, onto her lips. She licked her lips seductively. Her back arched, her breasts rounded upward. With her head back, she sucked his fingers, one at a time slowly savoring the moment, waiting. God, she wanted him so badly. She felt weak, strong, and full of life, breathless. She was aware of her entire body, her neck, her breasts, her nipples, almost without touching them, she felt him caressing their outline. So lightly, his hands slowly followed the outline of her body. Down her sides, around her waist, she was so ready. She writhed, and felt the orgasm building in her. He touched her, and she felt a gush of wetness. She wanted it to gush, wanted his tongue inside her. She could only breathe out, gasping. Groping for him, her own strong hands worked her breasts.

"Touch me, kiss me, make love to me." She loved the feeling of him, his smell. His body fit perfectly against hers; she grabbed his strong frame and pulled him toward her. She could be with Albion for the rest of her life. Their thighs worked in unison, as he got closer to penetration, their bodies becoming one. She kissed and licked his neck, filling his ear with her hot saliva.

"Love me, make love to me."

He gasped in her ear. "Darling Jeanna, I've waited for this moment, I'm so happy I found you, I love you," he said. "I want you, you are mine."

"Yes, yes, I'm yours." She was ready for him to be inside her."

"I loved you the most." There was sadness in his voice, and he was distant. "I found you the hardest to part with." He resisted her pulling, pushed her legs together, straddled them, reached for a pillow, and placed it firmly across her face, pressing down hard, while holding her in place.

"Goodbye, Jeanna." He pushed harder.

"Albion, Albion, what are you doing? Stop it, stop screwing around, and let me get up." She tried to push him off of her, pushing against his arms. He did not relax and let her go; he held his place more firmly. She pushed harder. His knees squeezed her sides, and the pillow started to close in on her nose. She realized there was no air, yet she tried to scream, which only allowed the pillow to get into her mouth, and begin to choke her. She could make no noise. She flashed. "I'm being killed; it's all over." She instinctively began to fight, but he was too strong.

He responded to her panic, and pushed harder.

She tried hitting him, swinging her arms wildly, but it was no good; she had no leverage. Her screams, muffled by the pillow, went unheard. She reached for the night table, needing a weapon. She found the phone, and a picture f the portable phone flashed in her mind. She grabbed it, swinging it in the direction of where his breathing was coming from. She hit something solid, felt him relax his grip on the pillow. She swung again and again, each time hitting something solid. After a while, she heard a thud.

The phone had broken his nose, and knocked him partially unconscious. She felt his body relax, and rise upward. His grip on her loosened, freeing her, and she pulled her knees up to her chin with her feet above his chest. She pushed her feet upward, and he felt a solid hit to the jaw; her feet had found their way to his chest, and sent him reeling off the bed.

He fell to the floor, half holding his face, groaning. Blood was running out of his nose, and there was a gash on his nose and forehead; the phone had done some real damage.

She jumped off the bed, grabbing the covers as she did so, and covering him with them. Then she scrambled for the door. Albion reached one arm out from under the blanket, searching for her. Her ankle was caught in the snare, and she fell over, hitting the floor hard.

He pulled at her foot, grabbed her ankle, and was then able to get both hands around her calf. She rolled over onto her back, and with one foot began kicking what she thought was his head under the blanket. With her other foot, she made a direct hit to his face. Blood gushed out of his nose and mouth, as his head snapped back. She kicked again. She was sure she was kicking his nose, again, and again. There was blood everywhere, and he let go of her calf. She must get to the door, and out into the darkness before he could get himself untangled from the blankets. She was afraid that once he collected his senses, he would get to her again. She had to find help. "Scream," she thought.

"Help me! Help me! Somebody, please help me!" She scrambled through the kitchen door, around the porch railing, and across the elevated yard. The girl next door had parked her car in the driveway so the top of her Honda was even with the yard. "Help me! Help me!" she cried. She ran across the car as if it were part of the yard, down the trunk, and onto the street. She felt something tear the skin on her foot, and a warm rush of blood ran out. It didn't matter; she had to get away from him.

Screaming and running, she headed for the steps, the hundred twenty-one steps. She had run these steps so many times she could run them in the dark, with her eyes closed. She could get away. Her head snapped back, as he pulled her by the hair on the back of her head.

"I've got you now, you can't get away. It won't be as neat this time, but it will get done." He had caught her. How the hell had he caught up to her? One strong arm wrapped around her throat, his other hand covered her mouth. She felt a finger between her lips. Her mouth opened, and instinctively she bit down hard. She could taste the blood.

"Arrggh!" he screamed, and let go of her hair and her.

She ran further down the steps.

He was close to her; so close she could almost feel his breath. She was taking three steps at a time now. Suddenly, she heard a thud; he had fallen. She had a slight reprieve. She knew these steps, he didn't.

She ran down the third section of about twenty-five steps, and into the straightaway; her cut foot throbbing. She knew she couldn't outrun him, and then she had a flashback of herself playing touch football with her brothers, and thought, "Maybe if I just tried. Take the offensive! Like in self-defense training. Surprise the enemy." She turned and stopped, waited.

He was running down the steps, closing in on her, down the steep sidewalk connecting the third and fourth section of the steps. She stood next to the railing, holding on with her left hand, waiting for the timing to be just right. She saw him as he ran down the steps, bent down and readied herself. He got closer, twenty feet, and moving toward her. She waited. She needed to time it just right. He was close. As he approached her, she lowered her head and ran toward him screaming.

"Now it's your turn to hurt, son-of-a-bitch," she came at him low, just a few steps, piercing her head into his middle, and then quickly straightening up. It had worked! Just like in touch football, it had worked. His own momentum carried both of the backward against the railing throwing his body up, and over the railing. He bounced off the rock and moss slope, and landed on the moss paving stone work, twenty-five feet below. She could see him from the light of the street lamp as he landed on his back; there was no movement. She stood and watched, thinking, "What if he was just dazed? Where were the police? God, my foot hurts. What the hell did I hook it on?"

He didn't move. "He must be dead," she thought. Where was the help? She began to cry. She looked again, through her tears; he still wasn't moving. She cried harder, and started up the steps, clad only in her unsnapped teddy, which was pulled down off her shoulders, her breasts bared. She pulled it up, and covered herself. She heard the sirens; the police were on their way. She cried even harder, and screamed again.

"Somebody, anybody, help me, please help me!" She slumped down near the top section of steps, and sobbed.

"This is the police, who's down there? Identify yourself." The police were already at the top of the steps. Not knowing what had happened, they had approached the top of the steps with extreme caution, guns drawn. One of the cops had already been to the apartment at Five Josephine, and followed bloodstains across the white car, the street, and down the steps. A second police car pulled up.

Sitting near the top section of the steps, Jeanna sobbed, shaking, "Please help me, he tried to kill me."

One glance at her, clad in only a teddy, crotch unsnapped, shivering, the officer grabbed a blanket from the trunk, and hustled down the steps to her. He recognized her from her many years around town, and her morning runs; she was one of the most visible townies in Sausalito.

"Here's a blanket." He wrapped it around her shoulders, helped her up, and walked her to the top step.

"Thank you." The tears started to slowly flow from both eyes. "I can't believe this, I can't believe he did this to me."

"You're the actress who runs all the time, aren't you? Are you hurt? Look at that foot."

"Call an ambulance," he yelled to one of the other cops. "What happened? Who tried to kill you? What's your name?"

"The ambulance is on the way," came the response from one of the other officers.

"My name is Jeanna Vitelli, my boyfriend tried to kill me." She was exhausted. "I…. I guess I'm all right, except that my foot is killing me.

"There's a lot of blood. It's a big gash; it may need stitches. We've called an ambulance. It'll be here any minute." Officer Milligan looked down the steps below her. "Where is the guy?"

"He's down there." She pointed down the steps. "He fell over the railing, he wasn't moving. He was just lying there below the rocks under the light."

"Who's down there? What's his name? Does he have a weapon?"

"My boyfriend, EX boy friend, his name is Albion Gant. He doesn't have a weapon, he's still half-dressed."

Officer Milligan yelled down to another officer, there were now police cars at both the top and bottom of the steps. The flashing lights from the car were visible through the trees. "Johnson, can you see a body, is he down there somewhere?"

"No body down here," came the reply from out of the darkness.

"He's over the railing, on the tiles," she managed to cry out. "It just happened a few minutes ago, how could he have gotten away?" She was really frightened now.

Gun drawn, Officer Milligan walked back down the steps, and looked over the railing, while another officer comforted Jeanna. There was a lot of blood near the base of the railing, but there was no body. "Johnson, get the flashlight and check around the bushes, be careful, you got somebody with you?"

"Yeah, I've got help."

"Search around down at the bottom on the sidewalk, see what you can find. Be careful, he tried to kill her."

By this time there was a fire truck, an ambulance, and another unmarked police vehicle at the top of the steps. A crowd of neighbors had also gathered. She had plenty of help now, but it was all over. The other officer helped her to the ambulance, and a paramedic tended to her foot.

"I think you'll need stitches, we are going to have to take you to the hospital." He cleaned the wound with antiseptic, and put a four-by-four temporary bandage on the side of her foot. "Lie down here," he said. He gave her another blanket, and strapped her into the gurney in the back of the ambulance.

The officer stuck his head in. "I have to ask you a couple of questions, I hope you understand; the sooner we get some information, the sooner we can catch him."

"Yes, sure, that's okay, I understand." She wanted to help as much as possible.

"How well did you know this guy?"

"We had been dating for about a month."

"What is his name, where does he live?"

"I'm sorry...Albion Gant, and he is staying at the Alta Mira Hotel, but he's from Minneapolis, he's here on business," she said apologetically.

"Excuse me, Jeanna." Officer Milligan yelled out to another officer, "Get a few men over to the Alta Mira Hotel, and put a guard on this guy's room until we can get over there with a search team, don't go in or touch anything, understand? Move it. Wait, hold it a minute."

"Did he have a car?"

"Yes, he was renting a 1965 red Mustang convertible. I thought he parked it up on the ramp above the house?"

"You heard that, check the hotel parking lot for his car, and check out all rental agencies renting specialty cars. Although, I know it will be morning before we can find out anything about that car. Put out a bulletin for every police department within a two hour drive to look out for that car." Almost an hour had lapsed since he went over the railing.

"Yes sir!" The young uniformed officer left in a hurry.

"Sorry about that, Jeanna, but if we are going to catch this guy, we have to get moving fast."

"Yes, I understand, I feel better now, what did you want to know?"

"Did he rape you, or was this a fight, a lover's quarrel?"

"No, he didn't rape me, we had a nice dinner, went back to my house, and things started to happen, you know... we were making love, when all of a sudden he tried to smother me. I thought he was kidding around. It came out of nowhere; he didn't give me any warning." She began to cry.

"Well, try to relax and get some rest, and don't worry, we'll find him."

"Why don't you get her to the hospital?" he asked the paramedic. The officer realized he had enough information for now, and Jeanna was still bleeding.

"We'll follow you to the hospital and get the rest of the story, Detectives Bonner and Burns will find you. This is Officer Jayne Jones, she will pick up some clothes from your apartment," Officer Milligan said.

"Thank you, you're very kind, my sweats are in the bathroom, running shoes are on the floor, and socks and underwear are in the top drawer." She spoke weakly, but with a relieved tone in her voice. She was tired, exhausted, and she just wanted to lie down.

A second paramedic climbed into the ambulance, sat down, and closed the door.

Officer Jones went up the steps to the apartment as the ambulance pulled away, sirens blaring, heading up through the winding streets toward the highway, and Marin General. There were already a half dozen policemen and detectives in the room. There was a lot of blood, all Gant's, "He lost a lot of blood, he must be weak."

The policeman's handset blared out, "There is a trail of blood going across the street, heading North along Bridgeway. We're going to follow the trail, over."

New Paragraph

"They'll find him soon. He won't get far in underwear, bleeding," said Officer Jones.

"Excuse me, gentlemen, I have to get some things for Miss Vitelli, and get up to Marin General. The ambulance has left already."

In the ambulance the paramedic comforted her, kept her company. "You just rest and try to calm down, the cops will get your story when you are patched up, dressed and feel better. Don't feel like you have to say anything, there will be too many questions soon enough. Just rest and try to relax, you've been through a lot."

The ambulance sped along Bridgeway, and onto Highway 101 North, sirens blaring, and Jeanna began to realize the reality of what had happened. He was going to marry me; he was the perfect man, the man of my dreams. He was perfect! And he tried to kill me! She closed her eyes and wept. As she half-dozed, she reflected on the path that had gotten her to this point in her life.

* * * * *

A Relaxed, Quiet Existence

All children want to be movie stars at one time or another.

"I am going to Hollywood," Jeanna would say.

"Not me, I'm going to have six kids, and raise horses and have a big ranch in the middle of nowhere, so I can ride all over the place," another girl said.

She had wanted to be an actress ever since she could remember. As a youngster, growing up in Fresno, she was the only girl, other than her mom, out of eight children. With four older brothers, she was naturally raised as a tomboy, playing baseball, football, and basketball with the boys. She was the fifth sibling out of eight. She was a good hitter, had a great pair of hands. She was the girl next door; everybody loved her, and somehow, with all the time spent doing boy stuff, she still managed to go to ballet, tap, and karate, all the way through high school. She had made third degree black belt by the time she was sixteen, and was Valedictorian in her senior year. She did it all, and with a smile and wit that was unmatchable. She just always put in one hundred percent effort, learning that competitive edge from her brothers. No one could ever say she didn't give it her best shot. She hadn't changed as an adult either, and still always gave of her best. In relationships, although not very successful, she gave her best. But even now she was trying to find out why she could not have a successful relationship. She was in therapy with one of the top therapists in the world. She was going to make one work if it killed her, and it almost did.

After leaving Fresno, she had made the choice to study theater at UCLA. She finished her four years with a degree, and turned to

American Conservatory Theater, ACT, in San Francisco to study stage acting and comedy, before unleashing herself on New York. She had found this great little studio apartment in Sausalito; it was only a two-minute drive to the Golden Gate Bridge, and a total of fifteen minutes downtown to school. She worked as a part-time waitress at the famous old hotel, the Alta Mira. The combination of lax management, and their love for her, allowed her the freedom to come and go as she pleased for nearly five years. Between commercials, modeling and waiting tables, she had managed to pay the bills and save a little. Those days were her fondest, she had kept the same apartment during those fourteen years. She loved it there, and felt like part of the community and didn't want to lose the connection, even after she had become reasonably successful on the stage and in movies.

She had never quite become the star she had expected to, but she would not give up trying. She had made enough, invested enough, so that she could concentrate on success in two specific areas-her career and love. Her success in the film industry had allowed her to set up accounts, which would allow her to live modestly for the rest of her life. She had heard of too many who had squandered it all away, and now could not find work. She lived quietly, and worked at improving her acting skills. She would come back to Sausalito when she was tired, burned out from a hard shoot, or when she just needed an injection of relaxation, and a familiar face. Of course, there were always those trips back to Fresno, although only on major holidays, and other special occasions, but Sausalito was her real home. It was there that she felt the most comfortable; like the previous month when she had returned for a rest. She had flown in from New York late on a Monday evening, and taken a cab all the way from San Francisco International Airport to Sausalito, very expensive, but she didn't care. She had been through a very serious psychological upheaval, and she needed rest.

She took a shower and tucked herself into bed about midnight. She slept hard, so hard all she remembered was going to bed. She got up about daylight, and went for the same run she had taken for fourteen years. She would run down the hundred twenty-one steps.

Half asleep, she stretched a little, too excited to go through her normal routine. She ran out the door, down the steps, turned left, and headed down the hundred twenty-one steps to Bridgeway, the main street in Sausalito. She turned left, crossed Bridgeway, heading north on the sidewalk along the ocean. As she always did, she noticed the cloudlike rock formations, guarding the walkway from the big waves. She jogged her way north on Bridgeway, past the Bridgeway cafe, waving to the owner, Fred and his daughter, Roya. She began to wake up, running a little faster now. As she worked her way down Bridgeway, she made a right turn at Jean Hiller Men's Wear, and ran toward the Ferry Landing, waving at city workers who were cleaning up the parking lot, and emptying the garbage cans. Down along the waterfront, out to Spinnaker restaurant on the pier, back up the boardwalk where workmen worked on the hull of an old boat. They whistled, and yelled something like "Hey-BEAUTIFUL." She laughed and waved back- they had seen her before. Many of these people had worked there for the same amount of years Jeanna had made her run. She made a right turn at the guard/bait house, and headed north on the boardwalk, past the beautiful boats- the ninety-five foot sailboat, Pursuit, and the hundred-foot pleasure boat, Defiance. Those boats had been there a long time. Soon, she passed the Cafe Trieste, where a lot of 90's hippies, 50's beatnik types, and Europeans hung around eating pizza, croissants or pastries, and drinking beer or cappuccino. The service was bad, but it was a good place to relax in the early morning or late evening. She sprinted faster, across Bridgeway Street, and took the diagonal cutoff passing by the local police station, where the officers filed out and asked her if she needed personal protection; she knew some of them by name. She laughed, and did a couple of running 180's, clowning around and faking a near fall, which got their attention. As she ran down Caledonia Street, Water Street, as the locals knew it, a few shopkeepers appeared, and gave her high-five hellos, and friendly gestures as they prepared for the day's business. She made her way down Water Street to the civic center, and angled north on Bridgeway again, until she turned left at Fred's Breakfast spot, 'The cholesterol capital of Northern California,' as it was once called on the Today Show. Up Spring Street, and left to the ridge, where magnificent homes overlooked the boatyards, and

Angel Island. At the top of the ridge, familiar people appeared, walking their dogs, getting the morning paper. They recognized her, and there were more friendly hellos. Up and down past the homes, up the steep hill past the church, down the straightaway, past the beautiful Alta Mira Hotel and Restaurant, in existence for forty years. Some of the South Americans that worked in the kitchen were talking and smoking at the back of the building, Jeanna recognized one of her co-workers, and shouted "Buenos dias." Catcalls and whistles were returned to her.

"Hola Gorge, Como estas, you still working here I see."

"Hola, beautiful, I'll be here until my children finish college, another twenty years." He laughed; Gorge was an educated draftsman in Mexico, but could not use his education in the U.S., yet living here was still better.

It was only a few hundred yards more home; down a few gentle hills, and onto Harrison Street, with a steep finish down Josephine Street, and she would be home-all in all-the total run was four and one-half miles in all, a good solid forty-minute run. The next day she would run the opposite direction, through the hills first, which was more difficult. She would count her way up the steps, and never go the same direction two days in a row, careful not to become a creature of too many habits, and work a different set of muscles each day.

Before doing anything she headed for the Golden Gate Market, down on Second Street. Irv, the owner, was there again this morning; he almost always opened his own store. Espresso beans, fruit, cereal, muffins, and the paper were all she needed.

"Good morning, Irv, how are you and the family?"

"We're all the same, as always, when did you get here and how long are you staying?" He was still fiddling with the cash drawer, and getting things ready, she had been his first customer that morning.

"Last night, not sure how long I'll stay, I guess I'll stay until I feel like I am relaxed enough to leave. No definite plans! I am just going to hang around and enjoy myself, as always." She signed a charge slip, and walked out, up the dead-end Second Street, and another set of steps to North Street. Sausalito should be called the city of stairs, she thought.

Arriving home, she opened the bag of coffee, and thought. "The coffee beans smell really good this morning, better than usual, fresh beans, mmmm, that smell is so good, I'll make it a little stronger than usual, with the espresso beans." She ground the coffee, put the grind in the filter, filled the pot with bottled water, and turned on the coffee machine. She then turned on the shower and got undressed; it still took a good five minutes for the hot water to get to her bathroom in the old house. Slipping out of her running clothes, her solid athletic body cast a shadow on the bathroom wall. She checked the tightness of her thigh muscles with a pounding fist, and smirked at herself in the mirror. Fifteen years of exercising and running had paid off; it had kept her sexy body in the same shape as it was fourteen years earlier when she entered the theater as a twenty-one year old. Her career was not over yet, and she was about to prove it, if only the right role showed up. She clenched her fist in the mirror, and said to an imaginary movie director. "I'll show you, just give me a chance to prove it, dammit! Just give me the chance." She came back to reality when she realized that having taken so much time, not only was the coffee ready but also the shower was too hot.

While lathering up she planned her day. She decided that after breakfast she would hit some golf balls; hitting golf balls for a couple of hours in the morning was always fun and relaxing. When she had first moved to Sausalito, her neighbor was a golf pro, who wrote some instruction manuals, and used her as the guinea pig. She had learned to hit the ball well, and now people commented on her natural swing and ability, even though she rarely played. She never told anyone she had been taught, but rather let them think she had done it all on her own. She would hit balls at the Coast Guard station parade ground, down under the Golden Gate Bridge; no one ever used that space. After the golf balls she would try her hand at some surfcasting down on Bridgeway.

Being in Sausalito made Jeanna happy, under any circumstances. She had always felt good there- happy, safe, strong, powerful, sane, and loving all of it. If only she had a healthy relationship to share her totality here, she thought, as she gazed out the window. Angela Bonnelli had been staring in at her for almost a minute; Jeanna had momentarily forgotten her regular Tuesday morning breakfast bull session. She began to think about the circumstances that had caused her to come back to Sausalito. "Why? Why? Why? Why did he have to do that? I trusted him, and all he wanted to do was get into my pants." She felt like she was being watched, and looked up over her shoulder. "Oh, oh, oh, hi Angela, you caught me off guard, come in, come in. I was lost for a moment; caught up in my daydream. It's so good to see you, I miss you so much." Her voice took on a happy, gay sound. She sounded like a cheerleader in her high pitch. She walked over to the kitchen door, one of those cafe doors, cut in half, and went out onto the porch, and gave Mrs. Bonnelli a big hug and kiss.

"Well, I guess you were, must be some serious man in your life to cause that kind of concentration. What's his name?"

"Oh Angela, you are so perceptive, so smart. Yeah, it is a man. But not love, something else. I'll tell you later. There is so much more important stuff to talk about."

She set the table on the porch with bananas, strawberries, raspberries, whipped cream, some sort of health cereal she had taken out of the box, and put into a Tupperware canister, and freshly-ground coffee. She enjoyed Angela Bonnelli; this old gal had outlived three husbands, and had run the show for each one of them. They all made tons of money, and she was still around to spend it. She seemed to have a good solid grasp on reality. Jeanna was sometimes envious of her life. Wouldn't it be nice to have been through all of that and still have such a great attitude? She just seemed so young at seventy.

"Coffee smells better than usual, Jeanna. It is so good to see you child, I hope you can stay longer this time then you usually do." They hugged and kissed again, as a mother and daughter might, and Angela sat down at the table.

Jeanna threw all her answers back at her guest the way they had been thrown at her. "I don't know how long I'm going to stay, I ground some fresh espresso beans, made it a little stronger than usual, thanks for noticing. And it's not a lover, I've almost given up on one of those, but it is a man. Some serious life issues going on these days Angela," Her voiced rose in exasperation at the end.

"You young, beautiful, talented woman, you think the perfect man is going to ride in on his white horse, save your life? Ha-when he does, the horse will belong to somebody else, and he'll probably have had plastic surgery and an implant, the man not the horse."

"You're so bad, Angela Bonnelli."

"That's why I've lived so long, don't take any shit, and treat them mean-keep laughing though, never take them seriously." Angela laughed as she spoke.

"Give me a break, this is serious. It's about my shrink in New York, the famous Dr. Eric Bright; he is a very well known psychiatrist, a real big shot in the psychiatric world. I don't think I've ever told you about him, because he asked me not to tell anybody about our sessions. I started seeing him about eighteen months ago, went to him because he was the best, and he came highly recommended. He made me a special project, and gave me the number SP1007. The 'SP' stands for either Special Person or Special Project; the phrases are interchangeable. He has written three books on different treatments, and is going to use me as a case study in his next book, so I won't have to pay for the treatment. No one is supposed to know what is being studied; it's a secret. He even lets me use the private entrance to his office." She made it sound very important and hush-hush.

"For eighteen months we have been working on my attitude, self esteem, and ability to project myself and my quote, "Power Potential," who I can be, and who I see myself as. SP1007, Special Person, that's me, a Special Person 1007. He had other people he was using too. I know I can trust you not to ever tell anybody about this SP thing," she said sarcastically. She looked at Angela, who had a look on her face as if to say, okay, child, what is the rest of the story?

Jeanna reacted with a sad, confused look; an almost childlike look came across her face. After a deep sigh, she spoke. "Okay, Angela, here's what happened. The Doctor and I formed a close bond, a really close father-and-daughter relationship. To me it seems when a relationship is working for a long time, any relationship, love, friendship or even business, trust and respect become the two most important aspects of that relationship. Those factors are at the top of the list, and are of equal importance." She gazed over her friend's shoulder. "At that level in our relationship, it became so easy to talk, to be myself, to tell the truth, and to tell all the details with no hesitation, but Eric Bright destroyed it all in just a few moments; the entire eighteen months gone in one sentence. I thought he was my doctor, and my dear friend, but it turned out he was like so many others, only after my body. I just didn't believe he could even think like that; he is supposed to be a professional. He's respected, he's written books on these subjects. He deals with core issues. I… I… I don't know if I can ever trust him again. I am also thinking he should be reported. To hell with Special People, to hell with Power, to hell with Potential."

"Well, what the hell did he do to you?" Mrs. Bonnelli asked.

"During one of our sessions he asked me if I had ever had sexual fantasies about him, and if I would sleep with him. Then another session, he hypnotized me. I remember most of what he asked me to say and do. But, something happened during the session, and I woke up right in the middle of things; I couldn't believe what was going on. That sick bastard." Jeanna looked pissed at the thought of what had happened.

"Well, what was it? What did he do?" Mrs. Bonnelli was excited to know.

"When I opened my eyes, his pants were down and he was leaning back on the edge of the desk maturbating. My shirt was open, and my bra was unclasped in the front, and my boobs were out. My shorts were unzipped, and pulled down to my thighs; I was totally naked from my thighs to my neck. Unreal. Damn unreal." Jeanna was totally pissed.

"He tried to tell me that it was okay; he tried to tell me that people under hypnosis only did the things that they wanted to do, that if I didn't really want to see him like that I wouldn't have, and if I didn't want him to touch me, I wouldn't have let him, even under hypnosis. What a bunch of bullshit."

"Maybe he's right, do you find him attractive? I have heard that people will only do what they really want to do under hypnosis, too." Mrs. Bonnelli was trying to make her feel better.

"Are you kidding? I see him like my father. He's even built like my father, only shorter. He is very short, got kind of a monks style haircut, he's heavy for his height. He's my shrink, friend and confidant. I thought he was there to help me; he really caught me off guard. Then he tried to cover it up, saying it was part of the therapy to get a reaction from the patient. But I knew what he was really doing. I looked in his face when he spoke." She shook her head up and down, and squinted, knowingly. "I can tell when a man means it, and he meant it. I just wonder how many other girls he has done this to. He's a sicko!"

"What did you do then?" Mrs. Bonnelli asked.

"I just left his office, told him I needed to be alone for a while, sort things out. I'm so glad I'm here; it's always like coming home. I just needed some time to myself, to sort through this, exercise, work out, do some fishing, you know, enjoy Sausalito. But there are other things going on too. Good things! We can talk about him later. Listen to this. I've got some auditions coming up in a couple months. Could be my big break, Mrs. Bonnelli …... who knows? I could still be somebody, there's still time."

Jeanna really wanted to talk about something else.

"You are somebody to me darling, you are a beautiful, talented, tender, caring, young woman. You are doing just fine. What you need in your life is a man. You find a man and everything else will fall into place."

"I know, I know, you're right. But in my business, they're all actors; they don't even know who they are for sure. One week they are cab drivers, the next week they are kings, then murderers, then policemen, and then both. I don't think they ever get out of their last character until they get a new part. What I need is a doctor, or a lawyer, or an Indian chief-a real person, in my life. God does that sound desperate or what? I would really like to meet somebody who's not in the business; San Francisco is really not the right kind of town to find an eligible bachelor, if you know what I mean. Maybe I'll meet someone here in

Sausalito. You never know? I'm ready. Well, enough of that, it's time for me to go hit some golf balls down at the Coast Guard station. Then fishing, I'm going down on Bridgeway to throw a line into the surf, listen to some good classical music, and relax the day away. It's time for me to go, but I always love it when you come over for breakfast. It's a wonderful way to start the day, because I know I can really talk to you. You are my second mother, my other mother. See you next Tuesday."

They hugged. "Thank you, Jeanna, I always enjoy my breakfast with you too, you are good for my energy levels, you get me pumped up. You make me feel young; it's so nice to have you back again. Maybe I'll go visit Mr. Avery, he always has a lot of energy in the mornings," she said with a mischievous look.

"You are nuts, you beautiful, goofy, old lady. Now go and enjoy Mr. Avery."

"Takes one to know one, beautiful." She headed down the front steps, and then west up the hill on North Street toward Mr. Avery's.

Jeanna grabbed a few of her golf clubs, and an old bowling ball bag half full of golf balls, and headed down the steps for the second time that day. Those one hundred twenty-one steps were her friends; she had known them for fourteen years, 1,2,3,4,5,6, 7,8,9-27, she counted as she looked out over the Bay toward Alcatraz, and the San Francisco skyline, 28, 29, 30-71 she could see the bay over the tree tops that were cut off the trees growing from 35 feet below.

Skipping down the steep straightaway sidewalk to step 72-through the tunnel created by the overhanging limbs, 118-and yelled at the top of her lungs, "121." She was so familiar with them that she was sure she could run them in her sleep. Many times she had actually run sections of the steps with her eyes closed. Some mornings, after a late night shooting pool at Smitty's, she probably did. She turned right on Bridgeway, and walked briskly back south toward the Golden Gate Bridge. It was a one-mile walk down to the Coast Guard station under the Bridge. She thought about the basics of her golf swing as she had been taught.

It was surprising how well she hit the golf ball even when she only got to swing a dozen times a year or so; San Francisco didn't have too many driving ranges. Once in a while she got time while on location, but mostly it was down by the Coast Guard station with her own balls. Her golf pro friend had written books, and developed a way of teaching that just seemed to make sense. She could always remember how to swing and what was important, and it only took a few practice swings to get the correct feeling. "Hold the club, don't squeeze it to death, back to the target, turn my belly button to the target, arms fall, watch the ball, easy rhythm." She pulled a couple of balls over with the head of the club, and took a peak at the ball with her left eye. Forward press with the right knee, go! She thought, while she swung to a rhythmic count of one, two, three, four. The five-iron sailed out about one hundred sixty-five yards with that little professional type draw to the left near the end of its flight. She only managed to hit one or two good shots out of ten, not a bad percentage for someone who hardly ever got a chance to play, or even practice. Her thoughts wandered.

I wonder what Dr. Bright is thinking about? Will he try to call me and apologize? Does he feel bad? Will he expect me to come back and see him? God, why did this have to happen to me? I felt so good; I felt like I was getting somewhere, making progress. Now I'll have to start over. She lost her concentration, and hit the ball completely to the right, and into the parking lot.

"Whoa," she called out loudly. Her rhythm returned immediately; 1-2-3-4-. Another pretty good shot. Nice thing about hitting golf balls, it takes total concentration, and a golfer cannot let his mind wander. You really have to take your mind off of things and forget everything else; the old brain has to go blank in order to do well.

Forty-five minutes and sixty balls went by quickly, and it was still only 9:50 a.m. She took the sand wedge, and started out toward center field and the Flagpole. This part was fun. Holding the grip end of the club in one hand, she got the clubface under the ball, and flipped it up into the air, catching it with the bag. I hit the ball pretty damn straight today, and it was fun. I'll be surf casting by 11:00 am, she thought.

* * * * *

Reality Sets In

For a moment she had forgotten she was riding in an ambulance, the change in sounds having startled her. The gurney wheels made a rattling, squeaky noise as the attendants pushed her down the hallway. Emergency was not too busy tonight. Marin County was not like the city; there was not much late-night violence. And it didn't take long to get to the hospital. There wasn't much traffic, a California first. She recognized two of the Sausalito policemen. Jones was new to her, but she recognized the others.

"You'll be fine," one of them said.

"Couple of stitches, and you'll be back on the track," said another.

They rolled the gurney into a curtained off area to see the doctor. "This doesn't look too bad, a couple of stitches, a few days on crutches, and you'll be fine. The officer told me you did it on cement. Nice clean cut, you're lucky; won't even leave a scar. These other scratches are no more than surface cuts; you'll be healed up sooner than you think. You'll need a tetanus shot, though, that may hurt a little."

"Give it to me quick, before I wake up and figure out what is going on." She still maintained a little sense of humor in spite of what had happened.

"This is going to hurt, look at something out the window." The doctor pushed the needle in the fatty part of her hip. "There you go, now, let's deaden the area around the cut with a little Prolocaine, just like filling a cavity." He put a small amount of liquid into the skin on each side of the wound, about halfway between her little toe and the heel of her left foot. "I'm going to put in four small sutures, they'll be in for about a week, take two of these if you feel nauseous," he said, handing her a small bottle of pills. "The police are here to talk to you, but you don't have to answer their questions tonight, you can wait until morning if you like." The doctor knew he could tell the police to stay away if she didn't want to see them.

"I think I'd like to get this over with tonight. What a nightmare! Let them in, they need to find this guy."

Chief of Police Pentwell, and detective Burns entered the cubicle, Officer Jones followed with a notebook and tape recorder. "How are you feeling, Miss Vitelli, you've had a rough night? Are feeling strong enough to answer some questions?"

"I think so. I'd just like to get this over with, I'm so confused about everything."

Jeanna was beginning to put the events of the evening together in her head, and nothing made sense. "Yes, yes, let's get going, I'm as anxious as you are to find out what this was all about."

"Detective Burns will handle the questions, while Jones tapes everything, is that okay with you, Miss Vitelli?"

"Yes, that's fine, and please, call me Jeanna."

Jones continued with her machine, "Saturday, May 2, 1992, 12:56 am, interview with Miss Jeanna Vitelli regarding a physical attack on her, and her attempted murder by a white male suspect on the location known as North Street steps, Sausalito, Ca.

"Hello, Jeanna, I'm Detective Roger Burns with the Sausalito police department. I'll try to be as brief as possible, I know this has been a frightening night and you're hurt and tired. The first few questions will be for identification then we will get to this evening's incident. What is your address?" Burns had a very gentle nature about him, more like a father figure than a detective.

Jeanna responded, "5 Josephine #4, Sausalito, Ca."

"Your height, weight, hair color, eyes?"

"5'7", 125 lbs, reddish, green," she said as she pulled her hair back, "Does anybody have a rubber band, I'd like to get this hair out of the way?" Jones found a band from the desk nurse in the hallway; Jeanna worked her hair into a ponytail.

"Would you tell us of the events leading up to this evening?"

"I met Albion about a month ago."

Burns interrupted, "What is his full name? Where does he live?"

"Albion Gant, he is from Minneapolis, but he lives at the Alta Mira Hotel. At least, he used to live there, I would guess he is not at the hotel waiting to meet you guys."

Burns chuckled briefly, and began again, "So you met him a month ago, and..."

"Do you want to know everything? What kind of information do you want?" Jeanna was a little confused."

"Tell me in your own words the story leading up to the events of this evening, don't leave anything out, you never know how any of this fits into the story later." The detective had never been involved in this kind of a case before. Sausalito had never had a murder, or attempted murder. He didn't want to screw things up; he wanted to do things by the book.

"Okay, here we go. This shouldn't be too hard, 'cause I had to make these plans to get here. Okay, I left New York on July 2nd, and spent a couple days in Fresno with my family over the 4th. Then I came to Sausalito on the 5th, and met Albion on the 6th. I didn't have breakfast with Angela my first Tuesday in town, but I did meet Albion. I remember because the play I was in closed on June 30th, and then I saw my shrink on July 2nd. I did some shopping, straightened up my apartment before I left, and jumped on a plane and flew into Fresno. After leaving Fresno, I flew to the San Francisco airport. I had breakfast with Angela the next Tuesday, and told her all about my new boyfriend. Then we dated for about twenty-five days until yesterday. When I had breakfast with Angela again, like I do almost every Tuesday when I am in Sausalito."

"Where does Mrs. Bonnelli live?"

"She lives in the little house right across from me, 213 North Street. North and Josephine meet at my house. She has lived there for forty years. I've known her since I first came to Sausalito in 1984."

"So you had breakfast with her and then what?"

"Well, actually I ran first. Then went to Mrs. Bonnelli's to have breakfast with her. Then I hit some practice golf balls down by the Coast Guard station, and then went down to Horizons and fished off the pier, that's when I met Albion. I have always enjoyed fishing, my father used to take me trout fishing when I was upset; it always calmed me down. I always maintained this apartment in Sausalito even after I started making more money. I felt good in this town, I felt at home. So anyway, I ran early in the morning, had breakfast with Mrs. Bonnelli, hit some golf balls, and went fishing."

"And that's when you met Mr. Gant?"

"Yes, I had been fishing for a while, listening to music on my headphones, when I hooked a fish. It was a big fish, a two-foot baby shark, I mean. I was trying to land this fish, but it was a real fighter, and I didn't know if I had enough strength to outlast him. I never would have landed him without help."

"So, what happened?"

"Well, the fish was big and very strong, and I was beginning to think that maybe he would outfight me. Albion just appeared out of nowhere, and helped me. I was impressed because he let me do most of the work. That made me feel comfortable, that he didn't take the rod out of my hands, and make me feel like the weakling. He helped by pulling back on the rod, and wound the real. Then he climbed onto the other side of the railing, and was able to grab the fish with my net. We landed the thing together. He didn't know it, but he did exactly the right thing if he had wanted to impress me. He always seemed to know exactly what to do to impress me."

"How was that?"

"He let me do most of the work, and just always seemed to know what was the right thing to do, like he was reading my mind. That's why I fell in love with him; he was perfect. Handsome, intelligent, gentle, everything a woman could wish for." A tear streamed down her cheek, then another, and another. She began to cry, sob, she was gasping for air. The shock was setting in.

"Just a few more questions; about this evening? In as few words as possible, we'll be done in a moment." The officer handed her a box of tissues from the table, and Officer Jones gave her a hug.

"Hey guys, maybe you should wait until tomorrow?" The doctor broke in.

"It's okay, doctor, I'll talk to them; I can handle it. After we met, he never pressed the issue of sex. If he had, that would have been the end real quick; somehow he understood that, and gave me plenty of space. We went to dinner, dancing, movies, quiet walks, ran together, biking, all good physical stuff. I finally decided after a couple of weeks of this that I would make the move. I decided that after we had a nice quiet dinner at my apartment, I would let things happen. I did, and we were making love, almost making love, in the process of making love. We were just into heavy petting on the bed. He was over me. He was on top. He straddled me with his knees on the sides of my hips, and tried to smother me with a pillow. I thought he was just kidding at first, but he wouldn't stop. I wrestled around a little first, but he was too strong. I kept reaching to the bedside table, and found the portable phone. Then I grabbed the handset, and swung wildly. I guess I hit him just right because he went limp, and I got away. I am pretty sure I broke his nose. When we were on the floor, I landed a real solid kick with the heel of my foot, and felt something change shape. That's when I got away. He chased me down the steps and he fell once, which gave me a chance to think for a moment. I didn't think I could outrun him, and my foot was killing me. I stopped at the railing where the steps turn, and spun around. I waited for him to come running down the steps, then I bent over and ran toward him, rammed my head into his stomach as he was coming down the steps, and then stood up and flipped him over the handrail. I learned that stuff fooling around with my brothers." She began to cry. Her knight in shining armor had tried to kill her. Mrs. Bonnelli had been right on target about that.

The doctor put his arm around her, "Gentleman, I think this lady needs her rest, she's been through hell, why don't you give her until tomorrow, give her a good night's rest? I'm sure you have enough to go on for now."

I'm going to give you a sedative, you can stay here if you like," he said to Jeanna.

"I'll take you up on the sedative, but I think I'd rather stay at home." As she wiped the tears away, she felt the need for friendly surroundings.

Chief Pentwell broke in, "I'm afraid that your apartment is being combed over at the moment, but Mrs. Bonnelli has offered a room in her house, she even went over and got some of your personal things."

"That's my angel, my other mother, I'll be fine with her. Thank you guys so much. You've been great."

"You're welcome, Miss Vitelli. We are also going to leave a guard outside Mrs. Bonnelli's house, and outside your house when you move back in," the chief said.

* * * * *

At 5:38 a.m., sunlight shone through the bedroom window; she always awoke before 6:00 a.m. when she was home in Sausalito, regardless of the amount of sleep she'd had, because it was so beautiful, and there was plenty to do. She didn't always get up, but she woke up. This morning she felt as if she had lost the fight, but had won the war; although she had some new battle scars. The whole thing seemed like a bad dream.

Angela Bonnelli was also an early riser; she stuck her head in the door. "How are you feeling?"

"I don't remember coming here last night. Tell me I drank too much, have a hangover, had a nightmare, and now everything is okay." Wishful thinking was not going to change the events of the previous evening, but she could hope. "What a mess. How could I not see, am I that blind? My God, the man tried to murder me."

"They gave you a sedative, and the police delivered you here about 3:00 a.m. They're going to let you back into your apartment later this afternoon." Mrs. Bonnelli filled her in on what she had missed. "I know, dear, it's an awful thing to have happened, maybe the police will figure out what happened to him, why he snapped. That Mr. Gant sure did seem wonderful."

"Yeah, too wonderful, what a mess," she repeated.

"Why don't you take a long, hot shower? I brought down some fresh clothes for you, they're laid out in the bathroom. After that I'll make you a nice breakfast, you'll need your strength to talk to the police."

"That sounds good, give me about thirty minutes, I'll meet you in the kitchen. Ouch!" She had forgotten about her foot as she stood up. She limped to the door, grabbed a robe and made her way down the hall to the bathroom. As she turned on the shower and climbed in, she sighed and her eyes teared up, "Why me, why me?"

It was 8:00 a.m. when she finally appeared in the kitchen. Mrs. Bonnelli had the table all set with her favorite fruit and cereal. She actually didn't feel much like eating, but surprised herself with the volume of food she consumed. "I didn't think I could eat much, I guess I needed food more than I thought." she said sheepishly.

"Well, baby, you've got to keep your strength up, by the way, the police already called this morning, they don't want to talk to you until about five this evening. They said that there is another detective coming from New York to interview you. I've got his name written down here, Rudy Auggur. That is a strange last name isn't it, Auggur? Anyway, that detective Burns, and Auggur will be coming to see you at five this evening. Maybe you ought to think about taking a nap sometime today, a couple extra hours of rest couldn't hurt."

"Yeah, maybe that's a good idea; I'll try to fit that rest in. But I just don't understand this whole deal. Do the cops think he stalked me? It seems like it, but I am so confused. I wonder what that is all about, I mean, because I spend a lot of time in New York, and so little time here. Albion was from Minneapolis, and he tried to kill me here in Sausalito." Jeanna thought she was confused before, but now she was really lost. She shrugged, "I guess they know what they're doing." She hugged Mrs. Bonnelli, hoping some of the pain would go away. "After breakfast, will you keep me company while I clean my house?" Her voice was seemingly drained of any enthusiasm.

Mrs. Bonnelli put her arms around Jeanna and agreed to help, "I'll do anything you like, my dear, anything." She felt helpless, but this was not a normal situation, one that came up every day. "Just don't hesitate to ask."

* * * * *

The Connection is Made

Kill this beautiful woman! It didn't make any sense; there had to be a story here that made sense, Burns thought to himself, as he finished the last of his paperwork. Some-thing really bothered him about the whole affair. It was 4:45 a.m., and he should be tired, but he felt as if this story was repeating itself, as if he had heard it before. He wasn't ready to leave yet. Why did he know this whole scenario? He felt like he had seen the move. Déjà vu! He went back to his desk, and shuffled some paperwork. Something told him that he shouldn't go home yet. All the puzzle pieces seemed too familiar; the lover smothering the girl friend, the red hair, the actress, the perfect man gone mad and vanishing into thin air. It was all too familiar. He kept shuffling papers, he decided to listen to the tape of his interview with Jeanna; maybe it would fill in some blanks. He turned the recorder on, and within a few sentences he heard it. It hit him immediately, "I left New York on..." That was it, New York! He hurriedly looked through the papers on his desk; he was looking for the flyers that continually come through police departments. Often the police were looking for similar crimes committed by people in other states and cities; detectives in other places were always looking for clues, or information, or people. There it was. Detective Rudy Auggur, NYPD, was invesigating four previous murders. These murders appeared to be apparent serial killings. The first, ten years earlier in New York, had involved a beautiful young redheaded actress. In a whirlwind affair, she had apparently fallen in love with a handsome young man. He had smothered her in a hotel bed, disappeared, leaving no trace of his identity. This exact crime occurred three more times since then, only in different cities in the

"

country, the last one, two years earlier in Daytona Beach, Fl. No clues to the man's identity, or where he had come from had turned up. He just had arrived, committed the murder, and vanished from the scene with no clues. The women had a number of things in common. They had all been relatively successful actresses in New York, and were all young and beautiful. Burns got on the phone, and called Auggur.

* * * * *

Through the dirty office windows in a New York Police Department, you could see the newsprint and pictures hanging on the wall. The first one had been there for ten years. It was the highest one on the wall, and the first one on the left. It was more faded than the others.

Thursday, May 17, 1992, Julia Phillips, NYC, aspiring twenty-two year-old actress was found murdered in her own bed. Cause of death, strangulation by smothering!

Thursday, June 11, 1992, Deborah McMann, Gross Point, Michigan, twenty-five years old, redhead, extremely intelligent, beautiful, talented, headed for stardom, found murdered by her lover, smothered, in Evergreen, Co.

Monday July, 25, 1994, Brandy Bennett, twenty-eight, auburn haired, tall slender, and a dancer, successful in Off-Broadway productions, found smothered in her winter home, New Orleans.

Tuesday, October 22, 1996, Tygre Gates, twenty-six, model, actress, smothered by unknown lover, Daytona Beach, Fl.

Rudy had just arrived and sat down, when the phone rang. It had been two years since there had been a smothered, beautiful girlfriend, and he had wondered if there would be another. He had been the original investigator on the first murder, and had no solution when he ran across the second. He had found these similar murders in the fliers that came across his desk over the years. They were all so similar, but so far apart in location and time. His gut told him they were all related, but how? The common thread was that they had all been in New York a few months before their deaths, and had all fallen for a handsome man they had just met. All of them spent most of their time in New York, and none of them knew each other; they didn't even hang out in the same circles. The murders were almost exactly two years apart.

"This is Auggur." He answered the phone, and swung around in his chair looking up at the pictures, a habit he had developed over the years. It didn't take him long to answer, "I'll be there on the first flight out of La Guardia, someone will call you, and let you know the flight number and arrival time."

The flight was right on schedule, landing at 3:28 p.m., San Francisco time. Detective Burns, with his handwritten sign held high in the air, met Rudy at the gate. They shook hands; this case was the biggest of his Burns' career, and he felt a little insecure. After all, Sausalito was a pretty quiet little community. There wasn't much going on in this town. Oh sure, a few burglaries, a couple of fights once in a while, but the attempted murder of a beautiful, local actress in a quiet neighborhood was considered spectacular. This was the big time. Burns was a pretty regular guy of average height, full round face, and full head of dark wavy hair. He had a strong physical presence, and you could tell that he had been an athlete- he was just solid looking. He dressed better than most policemen, actually more like an attorney. He had to get his clothes tailored because of his build. Consequently, they looked good. He also had acquired a taste in designer clothes, and he was from Sausalito. He was a detail man; neat and orderly. That's why he had seen the flyer from New York while others overlooked it. Most guys throw those things away. He was good at his job and he liked the work. No one else in the office had even noticed it. This investigation was going somewhere because he had noticed a detail. He was pretty damn proud of that fact. He had done his job. He was also excited at the possibility of working with Rudy, a New York detective.

Rudy was actually a shorter version of Burns, but didn't have the same taste in clothes. But, he appeared bigger than his actual size. He was broad from shoulders through the hips, built more like a middle line backer. He had no neck to speak of, nor any real noticeable stomach; he was just broad and thick. Neither handsome nor homely, he had more friendly features. He had a good feeling about most people, and did not possess the jaded view of society that many would suspect a New Yorker to possess, especially a New York cop.

Burns was standing outside the ramp holding out his police badge, along with the handwritten sign. "Rudy Auggur, Rudy Auggur?" He yelled as the people walked out of the tunnel from the plane.

Rudy raised his hand and acknowledged. "I'm Auggur."

"Hey Rudy, I'm Roger Burns, Sausalito Police Department. I'll be helping you with your investigation." They shook hands.

"Nice to meet you, Roger. Listen, congratulations on a good piece of detective work, seeing the similarities in these crimes. Most guys never look at those flyers, there are just too many. With a little luck we might solve something here. Tell you what, I'm ready to go if you are, this is the only bag I brought." Rudy had a medium-sized carry-on bag, with a few days of clothing.

They walked down the concourse toward the arrival exit. "This looks like it could be my guy, this son-of-a-bitch that has been killing beautiful women for no apparent reason for ten years. Do you have any clue about his whereabouts now?" Rudy asked.

"We are not exactly sure, he left a trail of blood down the main street toward his hotel. But after a while the trail vanished into thin air. Bridgeway is the main drag in Sausalito; it goes along the beach, and through the middle of downtown. He could easily have slipped over the rocks along the street every time he saw headlights, and worked his way up the hill to his hotel."

Rudy had been tracking this murderer for almost ten years. "Whoever he is, he always seems to get away, but this time he made a bunch of mistakes." Although he had only visited two crime scenes, those being New York and Sausalito, he knew in his heart they were all connected. "These crimes are planned, you can be sure of that. He has a motive, a weapon, he seduces, he murders and he has an escape plan. These are very clever, intricate crimes. He does not just allow things to happen on the spur of the moment. I think he is very calculating. His actions seem to be scripted, almost as if he were possessed, and directed by someone. It was movie like. He actually takes the time to enjoy, and seduce his victims. As far as we can tell, he has never made love to any of them, at least not on the night of the murder. He seems to seduce them to a point, and not complete the act. None of the victims had had intercourse; maybe he has a problem with completing the act. He has a diverse profile; people who have come in contact with him and the victims have stated how perfect a man he seemed to be. He has been able to masquerade as a perfect gentleman, and then strike out of nowhere and disappear just as quickly."

"Well now that he wasn't successful, maybe we'll be able to find him. This way to the car." Burns felt much more at ease after that short discussion. *This guy is okay,* he thought as they headed for the car. *He didn't have to thank me for the help. I would have expected a big time detective to be a little more condescending,* he thought

As they drove away, Burns handed Rudy a portable tape player, a folder with notes, and a few pictures of the crime scene, and the stairs. "I began the interview early this morning and taped it, but she got tired, I don't blame her. It was quite a struggle and she needed stitches in her foot. It was a pretty healthy gash."

"Did this happen in her home?" Rudy had a few logistical things on his mind that needed clearing up.

"Yes, the guy lived in a hotel in Sausalito call the Alta Mira, which is maybe half a mile from her house."

"How'd she manage to fight this guy off?"

"Well, she's a real athletic type. Her neighbor said she worked out all the time, had done karate or something like that as a teenager. She was able to grab the portable phone receiver, and hit him in the head. She managed to cut something badly, probably on his head; there was a lot of blood in her apartment. She thinks she broke his nose. I think that was the key to her overpowering him; he lost a lot of blood. He was probably weaker than normal, gave her an edge."

"No kidding."

"Then, after he chased her down the steps, he fell, and she got away, and then flipped him over the railing. Had the guts to drive her head into his stomach, and stand up and throw him over. He must have been one surprised son-of-a-bitch as he was flying through the air," Burns said.

"He just underestimated this woman, and he'll be caught because of it. The other killings were easy; he was able to slip in and out. Only one was close, in Daytona Beach, he was only an hour or so ahead of them. The dead girl's friend found her right after he murdered her. They tried to find him at the airport, but Orlando International is so big. He just slipped through the network. But, this slip-up will lead us to him, if he has made one mistake, there will be others. As soon as we get there, I want to walk through the whole scenario before I talk to her, I'd like to get a real clear picture of what happened, before I talk to her. The more I know, the easier it will be to understand how the whole thing went down," Rudy said.

"No problem, we can park on Bridgeway Street, I'll show you where she last saw him, rather his body, and walk up the steps to the apartment. She is at a friend's house, and expecting us," Burns confirmed.

"What have you done to try to find him?" Rudy wanted to make sure these small town guys did their job.

"All the major airports, and car rental agencies have already been checked, but so far nothing has turned up. We have crime lab personnel from San Francisco looking at her place, and the hotel room. Our guys don't have enough firsthand experience to know exactly what to look for, so we asked the San Francisco guys to come in." Burns wanted Auggur to know that small town ego would not get in the way.

"That's a good idea, glad you asked for help." Rudy was impressed.

Rudy spent the next twenty minutes listening to the tape, and viewing the notes and pictures. Some questions were on his mind. How was this guy connected to the others? How the hell was he going to get away if he actually murdered her? Why the hell did he want to kill these beautiful women? What a waste! What was the purpose, his motive? For most murders, find the motive and you would find the killer. But, this guy seemed to have no motive. He just met them, seduced them, and killed them. These girls had no past, no problems, no bad guy boyfriends, and no enemies. The first murder was ten years earlier in New York. Same M.O! These girls were not box office greats, but all had very recognizable faces, and were on track for stardom. According to friends of the dead girls, they had all met the perfect man with no past, only a present. The first one was a whirlwind affair; all her friends seemed to think she would marry the guy. Then, they found her smothered in a hotel bed, and the lover disappeared without a clue. The second girl was found about two years later, the same thing happened in Evergreen, Co., New Orleans, and then Daytona Beach, Fl. They were each found exactly the same way. One was in her own bed, the others were in hotel rooms. All of them were smothered in bed. They were almost exactly two years apart. Except for the first one, the women were found in their hometowns. All had the same physical characteristics, parallel career circumstance, and all were hardworking, honest types. One thing was different, though. Each time the man was described as a little older, which made sense. But, all witnesses described him as handsome, articulate, well mannered, and intelligent; the perfect man. Rudy had come across the number two and three murders the same way Burns had come across this case, by fliers sent out, and the rest had come to him when he had circulated fliers all over the country.

"We are almost there, have you ever been to San Francisco before? How about this Bridge?" The entrance to the Golden Gate meant they were just a few minutes away from Sausalito. "We'll be there in five minutes, Rudy."

"No, I haven't. What a beautiful view! He turned around to his right to see Alcatraz and the city skyline. "That is incredible, almost as beautiful as the view of the Statue, and the waterfront in New York City. This has got to be one of the ten most beautiful skylines in the world." Rudy was looking back at San Francisco from the Bridge as he spoke.

Burns turned onto Alexander Avenue, and headed down the winding road; the road changing names as they made each turn. Sharp left, South Street, sharp right, Second street, sharp right-left-Bridgeway, "Just a couple of hundred yards on your left is the entrance to the step, see it?" Burns made a U-turn, and parked at the curb near the base of the steps. There was a police car, and a uniformed officer waiting.

The area had been taped off with the same type of orange plastic tape that construction crews use to warn of danger. Burns parked the car, and the two detectives got out and headed for the cordoned off area.

Based on Jeanna's description of what she saw lying on the ground the night before, the officers had sketched the outline on the flagstone. Rudy and Burns lifted the tape, and slipped into the zone. "This is approximately where he landed, there is plenty of blood around." Rudy stood next to the body outline and looked up. Burns spoke, "She flipped him up and over just on the other side of the light pole. It appears the fall was broken when he bounced off the side of this wall. Look up at the sides of the wall you can see the broken greenery and moss that had been peeled back from the stones. Otherwise he should have been killed if not seriously injured."

Rudy tried to picture the movement of the body in air; his hands and arms mocked the movement as if he was turning a basketball over and over. He walked up the first section of steps, and looked over the railing. "Pretty good fall over the edge there, isn't it? Let's go up one more flight."

Burns stayed back and watched him, thinking him through the steps as he moved up. "Yes, it could be a serious injury fall from that ledge, but he actually went over the next one, up there." He pointed up at the next railing, where the walkway made a quick turn to the left as the steps wound their way down the hillside.

Rudy arrived at the top of the second flight of steps, and stopped just as he passed the old cement light pole. He turned and looked. "I guess this guy must have one helluva hard head, this fall should have killed him. It is a good twenty-five or thirty feet, and then the large rock." He leaned over the railing, and took a look down at Burns. "Let's go over to her apartment. It's already five-thirty." He started down to meet Roger, but was halted by his new partner's ascent.

"Just wait there, she lives at the top of the stairs, we can walk up." Burns quickly caught up to him, and they walked in single file. "Can you believe this, the neighbors say that she runs four or five times a week and finishes her run by running up these steps?" Burns was already panting heavily, and out of breath.

"According to your notes from Mrs. Bonnelli 's interview, this Jeanna Vitelli is one hell of an athlete." Rudy was still trying to put the pieces of the evening together.

"Yeah, she studied dance and karate, and grew up with a bunch of brothers, kind of a tomboy who grew up to be a beautiful woman. I guess that explains her being able to fight this guy off." Mrs. Bonnelli had been interviewed the night of the attack. Most of the neighborhood had come out during the commotion, although the only person who really knew much about her was Mrs. Bonnelli. She had befriended her fifteen or sixteen years ago, when she was still a student at The American Conservatory Theater in San Francisco. Two or three times a year, Jeanna returned for R & R in Sausalito. The two of them would spend almost every Tuesday morning together for breakfast and also spend some evenings doing some shopping, dining or an occasional trip to a department store.

"How many steps are there here, a million?" Rudy was panting.

"They are so steep, it seems like it, but there are only one hundred twenty-one of them. One of the officers counted them last night."

They reached the top and looked up at the house where Jeanna lived, it was the first thing one would see after walking up the steps. The last few steps were steep, and you would find yourself looking down at the last three or four, get to the top, gasp for air and look up. The house was huge; it had about fifteen rooms. There were four apartments, and hers was the bottom unit, a large studio apartment.

Burns gave directions. "Walk up the street about fifty feet and turn right up the stairs in front of the house." The bushes had grown in to form a tunnel narrower than the steps themselves. The two detectives made their way up to the top.

As Rudy reached the redwood-stained deck, he looked back at a magnificent view of San Francisco, and the Bay. "My God, isn't this impressive, I can see why she kept this place for so long. I wouldn't want to let it go either, not if I could wake up to this every morning. It must be even more spectacular early in the morning. It faces east isn't it?" Burns nodded so Rudy could see. "You can probably see the stars and moon from here, not much city light." They stood on the deck for a few moments taking in one of the most beautiful views in the world. The water of the San Francisco Bay, the City, the Bay Bridge, Alcatraz and a couple hundred sailboats.

Jeanna appeared behind them, "Unbelievable isn't it?" She interrupted their moment. "For fifteen years I have had to stop and look before I could leave, and when I come home I have to look again- I mean I really have to stop and take a good look; it still takes my breath away. Hello Detective Burns, and you must be Detective Auggur? Hello, I'm Jeanna Vitelli." She extended her hand to Rudy.

Rudy shook her hand. "It's a pleasure to meet you, I recognize you from some movies I've seen, you are very good. The camera really does make people look bigger. You are smaller than I thought."

"You mean I'm too small in person?"

"No, no, I just mean that you look like a taller person on film." Rudy fumbled for the correct thing to say. He was caught off guard by her beauty, and her abruptness.

Jeanna was still one of those actresses everybody remembered by sight, but not always by name. But it was only a matter of time. She had beauty and talent, and she knew it. "Did you catch him yet?" She changed the subject.

"No, he seems to have gotten away." Burns was disappointed.

"He seems to have been able to get back to the hotel, and get just enough clothes, money, etc to get either to the airport, or on the highway. He could not have been more than a fifteen or twenty-minute drive ahead of us, but there are three major airports within one hour's drive. We checked every flight that left within thirty minutes of our arrival, and checked every plane on the ground. Nothing! Hopefully, his rental car will show up and then we will have something to go on. Once the car showed up they could check all the flights, but if he was well disguised and used an alias, he might get away again, in fact, there's a very good chance he is already gone. It's happened five times before, with no clues to his identity, he seems to have a perfect getaway plan."

"You mean he's done this before? I'm not the only one."

"I thought someone had told you," Burns said. "There have been four others murders; all of them have been the same type of seduction and murder except they have all been in different cities. The only thing in common is that all of you have spent time working in New York, all of the murders took place a few months after returning home from there. There are real no clues to suggest the same person did the job, yet all the similarities suggest a serial killer. We just can't find any motives yet. You are a very lucky woman that he didn't succeed this time."

"I guess I am," Jeanna looked out toward the Bay with a blank stare.

"I listened to the taped interview from last night. You said you met him while you were fishing?" Rudy inquired.

"Yes, he just showed up from out of nowhere."

"Are you sure you don't remember seeing him before?"

"Well, I'd only been in town one day, and fishing is the first place I went where there were other people around, except for the early morning run. There was no one watching me hit golf balls."

"Try this, close your eyes, visualize your run, your golf practice, look around and see if you can see this man anywhere." Rudy was trying to get some idea of the killer's thought process. Did he stalk them, how did he pick them? How did he know where they live? He had to follow them, stalk them, there had to be an investigation by him. There were too many similarities. Maybe he knew these girls from New York; they all had stage and school backgrounds in New York in common. "Look in the audience at your last performance. Look backstage! Look at your neighbors! He's got to be there."

Jeanna tried to imagine seeing him in other surroundings, but she couldn't. "I can only see him here in Sausalito with me. I wish I could help more, but I am sure I only know him from here, and I am sure the first time I met him was down by the water."

"So he helped you land a fish, a shark, right, then what?"

"Well, it was kind of fun, working together, it was if he sensed what I liked in a man. He helped me, without telling me what to do. The fish, somehow got out of the net, and started wriggling around, and snapping at us, kind of like a lizard. Actually it got a hold of his pant leg, he had to kick it, and it came toward me, I jumped out of the way, and we started laughing. I just worked so hard to catch this thing and now I was afraid to do anything with it. Finally, when it couldn't breathe anymore it just died."

"Then what happened?"

"While we were waiting for the shark to die, we just made some small talk, you know, the weather, where we were from, that kind of stuff. He made me laugh, I felt really comfortable around him. I remember that I liked his clothes. He dressed sort of like a model from Timberland."

"Timberland?" Rudy was not familiar with the place.

"Timberland is a line of clothes, kind of like, LL Bean."

Now, Rudy was really confused.

Jeanna sensed his confusion; "They are rugged, natural, outdoorsy kinds of clothes. You know, heavy cotton pants, hiking boots, loose fitting natural stuff. They are my favorite clothes. I mean, I am attracted to men who dress like that."

Rudy got the picture. "Keep going."

"I have a friend who is a chef at Delmonicos restaurant, and when I catch fish he filets them for me. I said goodbye to Albion, and took the fish to Franco, and he told me to come back in a couple of hours. While I waited, I went to a cafe and had a latte and a croissant, read the paper, then went to the drug store to get a few things. I ran into Albion again, and we talked. I invited him to share a shark dinner out on the deck with me. He was so nice, so handsome, and so polite; I was really attracted to him. He seemed so easy to get along with."

"The feeling continued that evening?"

"Yes, it was really easy to be with him. That evening, he didn't even try to kiss me, we just got along well. I don't know how to explain it. He showed up with a dozen yellow roses, my favorite color, they were even pale yellow, I don't like the real yellow ones as much."

"Keep going." Rudy and Burns were listening intently.

"We had a wonderful time that night, and he asked me if I wanted to go for a run in the morning. We did. Then he asked me to go see Man of La Mancha with Raoul Julia. I had worked with Raoul in New York, and had promised him I would come visit. Albion already had the best tickets in the house. I then went home and called Raoul, so we could get together for a drink after the performance. Even that went perfectly, he was a perfect gentleman. I started thinking marriage right away."

"Did you ever have a feeling that you were being sucked into something that was too good to be true?"

"Yes, and no. I mean, I always questioned the immediate attraction, the perfect choices of flowers, perfume, restaurants, and cars. He even showed up with a '65 Mustang convertible, I had one in high school. I was in love with that car. But he was so nice to me. He was so polite. We just clicked. I just couldn't see anything wrong. I even decided not to sleep with him for as long as I could hold out. He never even mentioned it. We would make out, you know, get passionate, but he never pressed me to sleep with him. He told me that it would happen when we were both ready."

"How long did this go on?"

"Well, last night was twenty-five days. It was the night I was ready for. We had had dinner at Delmonicos, walked down to the Trieste."

"Trieste?"

"Yes, the Cafe Trieste, a little cafe on the north end of downtown, has deserts and pizza, cappuccinos, lattes, that kind of thing. We had lattes and desert, then a beautiful walk along the boardwalk, then along the waterfront on Bridgeway, and up the steps to the deck at Alta

Mira for a Courvoissier, then we started to talk, kiss, one thing led to another... this is not easy to talk about." Tears welled up in her eyes.

Rudy was genuinely concerned, "Take your time, just relax and think of exactly what you want to say, then how you want to say it."

Jeanna thought for a moment, "We were just about to go all the way, I was really passionate, I really felt this was the real thing, I was in love," she broke down and started to cry blurting it out- "He tried... to... smother... me with a pillow." Her voiced shrieked out the last few words as she gasped and cried as the same time. "He tried to kill me."

"It will all be over soon, we'll find him." Burns handed her his clean handkerchief, and searched for the words to comfort her. He put his arm around her shoulder, and pulled her near him in a fatherly gesture. He did have a son and daughter, and understood how she felt.

"I'm sorry, I guess I didn't realize how much I hurt. I feel lost; there is a tremendous emptiness inside me. I'll try to stay focused, and give you as much help as I can, but I can't let my guard down, he may be waiting to try again. Do you think he has left town yet?"

Rudy broke in, "Jeanna, the local police are checking every way to get out of town, but, I think he got out of town before you even got to the hospital. I don't think he'll be back. It would be too hard to get away again, too small a town. Too many people are watching."

"So how do you think you will catch him?"

"It is a long process of tracing people and things down. We start by going over to the hotel. What is the name of it? The Alta Mira, right?" Jeanna nodded yes. "We will run his prints through the FBI, check out the hometown information he left with the hotel. Although, it's probably fake. We also have to see what the lab boys have turned up in his room. Hopefully he has left some piece of evidence of his real identity. We also have to trace his rental car. We don't think Albion Gant is Albion Gant."

Jeanna finally got the idea. "You mean that this guy was a complete fake?"

"I'm sorry to tell you this, but I believe he stalked you, and knew exactly what he was going to do to you from the day he arrived here; he knew from the day you arrived from New York. I have a feeling he was here in Sausalito before you were, casing things out."

Jeanna shivered. "My God, I'm lucky to be alive! But what if he hasn't left?"

"We are going to leave a twenty-four hour guard under the street light on the corner below the house, or on the porch if you like."

Jeanna felt more secure. "Which ever you think is best."

"We are leaving for the hotel now, please just don't go anywhere alone. Always be with someone, and let us know where you are at all times. I know this is going to be an inconvenience, but it is for your safety. I'm sure this guy has left, but just in case."

The trip to The Alta Mira was only a few minutes. In fact, they could have walked there faster than hiking down the hundred twenty-one steps and driving. The old hotel sat on a ridge about two hundred feet above the center of the Sausalito business district. The police car turned left on Princess Street. The city of San Francisco reflected in the rear view mirror, as Burns and Auggur drove up the steep winding incline into the hotel. They parked the car under the canopy, and walked up another twenty or thirty steps.

"A guy has to be in great shape to live in this city, I saw another bunch of steps just on the left as we drove up." Rudy was beginning to see the charm of this city on the Bay.

The pair approached the front desk. "Roger Burns with the Sausalito police, and this is Rudy Auggur with the New York Police Department." Burns and Auggur produced their appropriate identification to the front desk clerk.

"Good afternoon, gentlemen, I'm Tom Golick, let me show you to Mr. Gant's room. This way, please." He walked them up the steps, and turned left down the hallway to room fourteen. "This is the best room in the house, he was paying four hundred dollars a night. He had already paid over six thousand. I've got the bill right here." As they stood in the doorway, the lab boys were busy dusting for fingerprints and looking for anything that may have been left.

Rudy asked, "You mean he had paid for his room in advance?"

"Yes, he paid every four or five days, in cash. He said he was on call, and never knew when he was going to have to leave in a hurry."

"How about phone bills?"

Golick looked over the bill, "Let's see, no, no phone calls. He never used the room phone, except for local calls."

"When did he check in?" Rudy was starting to see a pattern.

The clerk looked at the first entry. "Let's see, the twenty-eighth of June was his first night in the hotel."

Burns blurted out, "You were right, Rudy, he was here more than a week before she was. He never used the phone, and he paid cash for everything. It was all mapped out, he did everything he could to keep from being traced."

Rudy let him think aloud without interrupting. "Keep going."

"He was waiting for her to arrive, he stalked her, didn't he? He planned the whole thing, waiting for the right moment, so he could get away. He must have been very serious, I mean he was in Sausalito more than a month." Burns was obviously enjoying the deduction of the crime, and Rudy appreciated his enthusiasm.

Rudy added. "You got it, Roger, everything was planned, the meeting, the seduction, the attempted murder, and the getaway, all of it. Now, all we have to do is find the motive. If we find out how he was going to escape, and follow the plan backwards, he's got to leave a trail to somewhere. Realize that his plans changed so abruptly, she was supposed to die. He had been successful before, so my guess is that he really did not have an alternate plan. I mean, so far he had always been successful. If we assume he had no backup plan, then he most likely has made a mistake. When we find it, we'll find him."

"Now, let's take a look at his room. Maybe we can figure out what we are looking for.

"Anybody got anything exciting that they want to show me?" He yelled into the room.

"He left everything, sir. There are sport coats, shirts and slacks in the closet," said one of the investigators. "He also took a shower, and changed before he left. Look at all the blood on this towel."

"Bag the towel, and get it over to the lab. When we find this guy, I want to be able to match his blood." Burns directed the other officers.

"Yes sir, right away," he answered.

"In each of the previous murders, he also left all his clothing. But, let's hope he made a mistake, and left something he didn't want to leave. Is there anything good in the dresser?" Rudy walked across the room toward the investigator.

The lab man opened the dresser, and laid it all on the bed. "Take a look for yourself. I haven't had time to go through all of it yet. But it looks like he took a quick shower, changed clothes, took a few things, and hightailed it out of here within a few minutes."

"Burns, he must have driven his car, and parked it somewhere or maybe he left it here at the hotel, and picked it up after he tried to kill her." The logistics of his getaway didn't make sense to Rudy. "Get anything from the car rental agencies?"

"I'll call the office and see what they found out." Burns went to the phone on the bedside table, and dialed.

The dresser drawers contained eight pairs of under shorts, eight pairs of dress socks of various design and color, six ties- expensive silk, six handkerchiefs, running shorts, t-shirt, 1 pair of 1/2 sox, two watches, a gold ring with no markings, and a nail file kit. There was nothing in the case that suggested a place. Rudy talked to one of the investigators, "Write down the names of the labels on these clothes, and see if we can pinpoint an area of the country where they may have been purchased. Also let's get the room and all the jewelry fingerprinted. He always leaves everything, but we never get a match on the fingerprints, except that the fingerprints at each murder match."

"I'm going to look through the clothes in the closet." Rudy started to walk across the room.

"Hey, Rudy, they found the rental agency that rented him the car. They let him pay cash because he left a $1500 deposit. My guys found out that he left the car at the airport, and didn't even get his deposit back. A team from the San Francisco police headed over there to look at the car. They will let us know what they find as soon as they're done." Burns had gotten the information from his office.

"Thanks, Burns, keep up on the car angle. Let's hope something turns up, and send a team out to the airport and see if we can get some prints."

One of the investigators began looking through, and writing down the brand names of each of the items while Rudy worked his way through the closet.

"This guy is pretty gutsy, he came back here, showered, changed, grabbed a few things for the trip, and assuming he left the car near the scene, came back to her neighborhood, got in his car, and headed out. You guys probably were within fifty feet of the guy when he left. That's what it looks like. On top of that, he was bleeding to death."

Rudy held a sports coat. "This guy has good taste in clothes, these sports jackets are all from Nordstroms department store, except for this one, a men's store, Fletchers in Atlanta."

Rudy held up a camel cashmere blazer. "Too bad it's not my size." Rudy slipped the jacket on his stocky body, "Too small in the middle, the jacket's not me. What else we got?" Rudy was mulling over the similarities. "This is the only thing that is not the same as the other murders. All of the other clothes found in his hotel rooms were local to each city. Roger, let's get the number of Fletchers in Atlanta, and give them a call, this jacket is pretty new, maybe we'll get lucky."

* * * * *

The Getaway

The fall from the ledge had hurt. Albion Gant was briefly stunned after his fall, although he never lost consciousness. After about a minute, he opened his eyes, turned his head and glanced up. He could see no one. Jeanna was not at the railing. He figured she must have run back to the house. He knew he had to get out of there. He slowly began to get up. No broken bones, but his arms and right knee really ached, although he felt he could move okay. He got to his feet, and realized he was at the street level. The water was just across the street, so he headed for it. He started to run toward downtown. He had gone about two blocks. My car, my car is on the ramp above her house, he thought. "I've got to get the car, what should I do first?" He stopped for a moment to collect his thoughts. "I have to get the car or I have no way out." He quickly turned around, and headed in the opposite direction of downtown toward the grocery store, he ran. He could hear no sirens, but was sure it would not be long before the police arrived. There were steps on the other side of the house to the street above. He could go up from the grocery store, then up more steps a couple of houses west of Jeanna's apartment. Then he could slip down the street in the dark to the ramp, and his car. He could hear sirens now, but they were still a long way away. He ran up the first set of steps. He got to the top of the steps in a few seconds and looked down the street. There were a few people gathered near where he had chased Jeanna at the entrance to the steps. They were all looking down, and talking amongst themselves. He crossed the street in the shadows. He walked up the second set of steps, which were hidden by bushes on the east side. He worked his way alongside the bushes that skirted the home next to Jeanna's, and walked slowly in the shadows until he reached the parking ramp. He opened the car door, started the engine and slowly backed off the ramp. He put the car in drive, and slowly proceeded up the hill in the opposite direction of the house. Once reaching the top, he turned the wrong way down the one-way street, and headed in the direction of the hotel. He saw the police car lights in his rear view mirror as he turned the wrong way; they were just arriving at Jeanna's house. Everything seemed to be happening in slow motion. He wanted the whole thing to go faster. He thought to himself, "I have to get cleaned up, and slip out of town, get to the airport, and not act flustered. I must relax and act as natural as I can." He drove up behind the hotel, and parked near the back entrance. Not much longer now, he thought. He slowly walked down the hallway to his room, opened the door, and closed it behind him. He took a heavy sigh of relief. Ok, now let's get going, he thought. He quickly undressed, and headed for the shower. "God, this shower feels good," he said aloud to himself. As he lathered his body, and shaved in the shower mirror he thought. "I can't believe this happened, it was always so easy before. But, now I have to get out of here." He turned off the water, and grabbed a towel.

He pulled his duffel bag from the closet and opened it, placing his traveling clothes on the bed. He quickly changed into his jeans, shirt and loafers, took out the I.D. he needed, and headed for the door. He hustled down the hallway and out to the parking lot, took a quick look around, and made a beeline for the car. No one had seen him yet. Not one person had been around. He knew the back way out of Sausalito, and drove up the hill to the expressway. So far, so good, he thought, as he drove south along Highway 101. "At this time of night, it's only about an hour to the airport." He made sure to drive the speed limit. He crossed the Golden Gate Bridge, down the hill and winding road to Lombard, and south to the 101, and the airport. He glanced at his watch. It had only taken him a little over forty-five minutes. So far, so good, he thought.

This time of morning, there was so little traffic. He reached the airport, and headed for short-term parking. It was 5:00 a.m. He wasn't worried about the rental car; he was just going to park the car and go, leave the deposit and get the hell out of there. Once he was parked, he looked in the bag for his ticket. His ticket to Las Vegas was in the name of Peter Hampton. Maybe I can find a different flight, and get out of here earlier, he thought. He had fifty minutes to get to his flight. He felt the pressure to move faster. He looked up at the departure screen; the first leg of the trip should be a very short one. He could switch planes and get on his way with another set of I.D. Las Vegas was still the best choice. He decided not to change. But the fifty minutes seemed much to long to wait. He headed to the Las Vegas gate.

Once at the gate, he placed his ticket on the counter. "Hi! Is the flight to Vegas on time?"

"Yes sir, it sure is." She said while glancing at the ticket. "Good morning Mr. Hampton." The young lady at the counter looked up in shock, and stared at Gant's face, which was scratched in more than one place, with one eye blackened and a swollen nose.

"Oh, this? Nice look huh? Those windshields don't move very far when you hit them at fifty miles per hour. I didn't think it looked that bad, but I guess the look on your face tells me it does." Randy was quick to give the excuse he had thought of while driving to the airport. "Window seat, 34F Mr. Hampton, have a nice flight. We are boarding, as we speak."

The young lady tore the correct page from the ticket, and handed Peter the folder with his boarding pass. He was glad he had made the plan to fly a short flight to Las Vegas. If he were on a longer flight, he would have given the police more time to track him down. This way, he could switch identities, and planes before they had any clues.

"Thank you very much. How long is the flight?" He was looking at his watch.

"It will take about forty-five minutes. You should be on the ground by six-ten." She smiled, and looked at him for a moment. "Heal up fast, Mr. Hampton and take care of yourself."

"Thank you, I will." Randy headed down the loading ramp, entered the plane, and found his seat. He put his travel bag into the overhead storage, seated himself, and buckled up. He only realized how tired he was as he put his head back, and closed his eyes. He hurt like hell.

"Please put your seats in the upright position," was the last thing he heard. The plane touched down at six-twelve, right on schedule.

The passenger, known as Peter Hampton left the plane and headed down the tunnel. He thought for a moment. "What if they are waiting for me when I get off?" He became a little worried. "Surely, if they are, they will know me by my cuts and bruises. Too late now, I will just have to take my chances." He knew there was no getting away if they were waiting, and he was resigned to the fact that this could be the end of it all, but he kept walking. As he approached the exit into the concourse he took a deep breath. He walked into the concourse. There were no police. He looked around again. He saw no one.

"Thank you for flying American Airlines." The attendant was greeting everyone as they entered the concourse.

"You're, welcome, very, very welcome." Peter was happy and dumbfounded to be there, and even happier that there were no police. He immediately headed for the men's room to get another I.D., and then he would look for a flight to somewhere that left as soon as possible. When he left the bathroom, he went directly to the monitors and checked the flight information. He found a flight to Seattle that was only a few gates away. He had thirty-five minutes to get onto the plane.

His new I.D. in hand, he laid it down with three hundred dollars in cash. "Yes, Mr. Pederson, we do have room on this flight, however, I am afraid I cannot take cash here. I can take a credit card, otherwise you will have to go to the main concourse and purchase your ticket there." Jon Pederson had taken cash out to pay for the ticket.

"I am so sorry, Miss, but is there anyway you can help me? I have been in a car accident. My leg is so bad I can hardly walk. I am afraid I can't walk very fast; I don't think I can get there, and back in time. Maybe you can find a way to help." He decided to appeal to her sympathetic side.

"Well, I don't know, let me make a call? She added.

"Yeah, and it really hurts to move my jaw when I talk, and my leg is throbbing." He just wanted his seat on the plane, and to get the hell out of there fast.

It worked. It worked well and she took pity on him. She put the phone receiver back. "Tell you what, I can issue you a ticket, you can board the plane a little early, and I will have someone from the front counter bring the change up here. How is that? I am so sorry; I hope your injuries are not too serious. I am sure we can take care of this right here, and I will be able to fix that for you, sir." She knew there was enough time, and she was treating him as a disabled person, and wanted to help as much as possible.

"This is my lucky day, thank you so very much. You don't know how much that helps me." He wanted to say help me get away, but said nothing. He tried to smile, but even that hurt. He got on the plane and sat impatiently. He felt the plane being backed out of its stall; it turned and aimed toward a runway. He felt the engines kick in, and the plane moved forward. A few more turns and it was in line to take off, with only a few planes ahead of it. A few minutes went by and the turbines became loud and the jet started to gain speed. It was airborne. He had made it. He had made his getaway. In an hour or so he would be landing in Seattle. He would change identification, rent a car in Seattle, and drive down to Portland, Oregon. Once there he would be ready to fly as a different person, and begin his usual pattern of escape. In a couple of days he would be in Atlanta as Randy Curtis. Once in Atlanta he would make an all-important phone call to the good Dr. Bright.

* * * * *

Tuesday, August 4, 1998-This Old Gal

"Roger, do you think you can get Angela Bonnelli ready for an interview this afternoon? I would like to talk to her, and get her perspective on Jeanna and her movements before this wacko attacked her."

"Yeah, Rudy, that shouldn't be too hard, she doesn't work and spends most of her time in her neighborhood. I will call her and see if we can do this right away." It had been two days since the attack, and there were no real clues yet, but both Rudy and Roger were optimistic; Rudy finally had some evidence.

"Hello, yes, this in Angela Bonnelli. Oh, hi detective, yes, sure, I would be glad to talk to you. When is good for you? About lunchtime, yes, noon is fine. I'll see you at my house then."

Angela Bonnelli answered the door with her usual friendliness. "Good afternoon, gentlemen, this is a lovely day, isn't it? Come in, come in. "You must be Detective Auggur, I have known Roger for years, please sit down, and make yourselves at home. Would you like some coffee?" Mrs. Bonnelli had furniture that had been around for some time. They were elegant pieces that were at least thirty years old. "Yes, please, black is fine. Rudy, how about you?"

"Thank you, just black for me too."

Mrs. Bonnelli walked into the kitchen, and returned with a tray with three cups and saucers, and a pot of coffee. She placed the tray on the table in front of the men. She poured the coffee, and they helped themselves. "There we go, gentlemen. Now, what can I do for you?"

"Well, Mrs. Bonnelli, we are trying to find out as much as possible about Albion Gant. This is not the first time he has done this. We believe he has killed four other women in four different cities. He has used a different name in each murder, but they were all seduced and killed the same way. The only difference is that Jeanna lived through the ordeal. She is a tough young woman," Rudy added.

"Oh, she sure is, I can agree with that. She is always exercising and keeping herself in good shape. I wish I had done that when I was young."

Rudy began. "So Jeanna and you had breakfast on Tuesday morning. Is that right?"

"Yes, that's right, almost every Tuesday morning when she's in town," Mrs. Bonnelli agreed.

"Did she tell you about this guy?" Rudy asked.

"Yes, she did, she told me all about him. How wonderful, how smart, how handsome he was, how he seemed to know exactly what to do to make her happy. She told me that it seemed like she had known him all her life. It was such a shame for something like this to happen to her. And the other girls, were they all good girls too?" Mrs. Bonnelli shook her head.

"Yes, Mrs. Bonnelli, the other girls were just like her, young, beautiful, successful and independent," Rudy confirmed her thought. "Did you talk about anything else or just Albion Gant?" Rudy asked.

"Well, I don't know if I should tell you about this. I mean to say that I don't know if this is important, but she had a thing happen with her psychiatrist."

"What do you mean, a thing?" Asked Rudy.

"Well, you see, she had made some kind of deal with this doctor, that he would help her for free, and she would allow him to use her in his research. He was writing a book and needed volunteers. I am not exactly certain what happened."

"Could you just tell us what you think happened or what you do know?"

"Well, Mr. Auggur, he gave her a special number SP6 or something like that. I think she was the seventh person. I guessed there were other ones with numbers like SP4 and 5. But, that is just what I guessed. She told me she could get into his office through the back door so no one would notice so they could have private meetings."

"Why did they want private meetings?" asked Roger.

"He didn't want anyone to know what he was doing. She told me that this was supposed to be top secret. He was going to use her story in a book."

"I don't mean to rush you, ma'am, but what else did she tell you?" Rudy just wanted to know as much as he could about Jeanna.

Roger interrupted. "Mrs. Bonnelli, may I use your phone to call the office? My beeper just went off." He had set it on vibrate so as not to interfere with the conversation.

"Oh, yes, that would be fine. There is a phone in the kitchen," she answered.

Roger excused himself, and made his way into the kitchen and found the phone. He dialed his office number. "This is Burns, you beeped me. What have you got?"

"Well, Roger, we got a match on the sports jacket found in Gant's hotel room. Fletcher clothing store is still there, it's pretty exclusive, they do a lot of tailoring, and make a lot of custom-fitted clothes. He says that if he saw the jacket he might be able to match it with a customer. If it is one they make, the lining is different than an off-the-rack piece. They custom make the linings to the customer's designs, so it is easier to keep track of his customers."

"Great, Jack, that's great, thanks. I will get back to you after I talk to Rudy." Roger hung up the phone. Excuse me Rudy, Mrs. Bonnelli. Rudy, they have a match on the jacket. There is a good chance the owner of the store can figure out who he sold it to. What do you want to do?"

"That's good news, Roger, I'm almost finished here. Mrs. Bonnelli, if you remember anything else from your discussion with Jeanna you call me at this number." Rudy was now in a hurry to get to Atlanta, and handed her his business card.

"Well, I know we talked about other things, but I am afraid I don't remember much. My memory is not what it used to be. We just talked about what she had been doing, her work, that kind of stuff. I wish I could help you, but I just don't recall much about the conversation."

"Mrs. Bonnelli, we have to go now, you have my card and of course you can always call Roger. I put his number on the back. If anything, and I mean anything, comes to mind, you call one of us. I am leaving for Atlanta as soon as I can get on a plane. Take care of yourself, okay?"

"I will, detective. I promise to call if I remember anything." Mrs. Bonnelli started to get up from her chair.

"Don't get up, ma'am, we can let ourselves out," Roger said politely. "And thank you for your time, and your help."

* * * * *

Wednesday August 5th, 1998-Southern Peach

Rudy and Roger left Mrs. Bonnelli's home. It was 4:00 p.m., and the high western sun was beating down on them as they walked across the street to their car. "So fill me in on the sports coat, Roger."

"Well, Rudy, Fletchers Men's store is very exclusive. Apparently, when they custom tailor clothing, especially jackets, they give each customer an individual lining to identify their clothes. They sell both tailored and off-the-rack camel blazers. If the jacket has an individual lining, he can match it with a name."

"I told you this killer make a mistake, they always do." As they reached the car, Rudy became excited. He noticed the lining in the blazer was unusual. Most of the time jacket linings were single colored, and silk. This one had drafting tools and pencils on it; it was different. "Get that store owner on the phone, see if he can identify this guy over the phone, and I want to talk with Jeanna before we go back to the office."

Roger picked up the handset in the car, and called the office. "Burns here, Jack, can you get the owner of Fletcher's on the phone again, Rudy wants to talk to him?"

"Yeah, Roger, I can try, but it's after seven there, he may be closed."

"Try anyway, right away." Roger was adamant.

"Ten-Four." Came the response.

Roger turned to Rudy. "It might be tomorrow before we can talk to the store owner. Jack is calling the Fletchers clothing store in Atlanta, but it may be after hours though."

"Yeah, that's right, I forgot about the time difference. It doesn't matter Roger, have your guy get me a flight to Atlanta tomorrow morning. What day is it by the way?" Rudy had only been there a few days, and he had already lost track of time.

"Tomorrow is Thursday the 6th. Hard to believe this thing is almost a week old!" Roger shook his head in disbelief. At the same time, the radio blurted out. "Unit forty-three, come in, forty-three, come in."

"This is Burns, what have you got Jack?" Burns was at the microphone immediately.

"There was no answer in Atlanta, over, the store must be closed."

"Ten-four, Jack. Can you get a flight for Auggur tomorrow morning to Atlanta, over?"

"Will do, Burns, out."

"Ok, Rudy, no answer in Atlanta. Jack is getting you plane reservations for the morning."

"Hey Burns, I would like to talk to Jeanna again before I leave, let's head over to her house right now." They headed across the street, and up the steps to her front door. Rudy knocked. "Anybody home?" He bellowed through the screen door.

"Hello, hello, I'm here, who is it?" Jeanna had been relaxing in her easy chair, taking a catnap. "Oh, detectives how are you, have you found out anything yet?"

"Yes, we have, we found the store Mr. Gant bought his blazer in. There is a chance the tailor can match up the coat to a customer; this may lead us to the real man. I am leaving for Atlanta tomorrow morning. How are you feeling?"

"Oh Mr. Auggur, that's great, I just want you to find him. I keep rolling the whole month over and over in my mind, and it makes no sense. Why would he take all that time to murder someone? It just doesn't make any sense. Why not just murder them? Why go to all that planning? She looked at the floor, and her eyes began to tear up.

"Look at it this way, Jeanna, with all that planning he has been able to elude us for ten years, that is why he takes all that time. He obviously doesn't want to be caught; he's very cautious, and waits for just the right time. Basically, he's a serial killer, but he does not completely fit the profile of a serial killer. What I mean is that he kills the same type of person the same way, but he does not take anything, that we know of, from his victims. Most serial killers take trophies from their victims. Also, he does not kill them in the same city, but they all are connected to New York City. They are all done in their hometowns, places where they feel safe. These murders are meticulously thought out, and committed. He has, up until now not made any mistakes. Because of you, he finally has made what we hope to be his one big mistake. The jacket could be our break, and we'll know within the next twelve hours who this guy is."

"Oh, God, I hope you catch him." Jeanna was worried that he may come back. "Do you think that he would come after me again?"

"I really don't think so. There is something about this guy that tells me this was not a onetime deal. I just get the feeling that he is not acting alone. My gut feeling is that there is more to this story." Rudy paused for a breath. "Think about it; he takes as long as a month before he attempts to kill, he knows the girls' likes and dislikes, he learns their habits. He has done his research. Or, he has an accomplice do the research for him. His work is so detailed and well planned. Like I said, he has been impossible to trace, until now."

"Well, Jeanna, you have my cell phone number, check in every day, and let me know how things are and what you are doing. Burns is going to have a uniform watching your every move for your protection, but please call me every day to let me know how things are, and at the same time I can fill you in on our investigation. I am leaving for Atlanta in the morning." Rudy assumed he had a flight reserved in his name.

"One thing, I cannot exercise, as my foot is still a little tender, but the doctor said it would probably be better by Sunday. He wants to look at it in the morning though, and he'll probably take the stitches out. The skin has grown back together, but it feels a little sore still, although I should be back to normal in a few days. Maybe not running five miles a day, but able to walk without a limp."

* * * * *

Thursday, August 6, 1998-The Getaway

Albion Gant had made his way back to Atlanta; it had taken three full days and four flights. He had taken his time, used the time to think things through. Now, he was worried. What if they figured out who he was? He needed to talk to Dr. Bright right away. He had to get home and pack. He had so many things rolling around inside his skull.

He must be extremely careful when he got back to his neighborhood, he had to make sure that he had not been found out, and there were no police watching his home. He had to go the doctor's office, and get some money. He had to find a way to hide and change his life again. He was scared; he had never really wanted to hurt anyone. He just wanted to help Dr. Bright, and to be part of a family.

It was only Thursday morning. He had to get home and think. What would Dr. Bright think of what had happened? He had to make a plan and get away.

"Where do you want me to let you out mister?" The cabdriver broke his chain of thought.

"Just pull around the corner and stop, I'll get out there." He motioned to a spot in front of the first house on the street. "This is just fine, I'll walk the rest of the way." He handed the driver thirty dollars for the twenty-three dollar fare. "Keep the change." He grabbed his small carry-on bag, got out of the cab, and walked to the sidewalk. Slowly, he started down the street toward home. He was looking for police cars, but saw nothing. He crossed the street to get a better view of the driveway. There were no cars on the street, or parked in the driveway. Everything appeared normal, and with a sigh of relief he started across the street to his home. As he walked across the street, a car made a turn, and started toward him. He became frightened; his palms began to sweat. He feared it would be the police. It was a neighbor. The car turned into a driveway.

As Randy Curtis approached the front door he began to wonder. "Maybe they won't find me. Maybe they have no clues." He thought again, "But what if they had clues, what if they figured out how to find me? I must talk to Daddy, and get a plan to leave. I have to assume that the police have found me, and are on the way. I have to act as if they have found me. What should I do?" He decided to clean up, and rest, then pack some clothes, and drive to New York. But first, he must call Daddy. He will help me with a plan. He felt like a child again; felt like he needed something from his family, felt like he needed protection. He had not felt like this for a long time, not since he was a child, and he was confused.

Randy stepped out of his long, hot shower, and stared at his face in the mirror. The black eye was fading fast, and his knee was not so sore anymore. His nose was slightly crooked, with a lump about halfway up from the tip. He had some sore spots. "If I drive to New York, it will give me a few days to heal some more. By that time the swelling should go down, and the black eye should be completely gone. I can take some clothes with me. I have to leave as soon as possible. In case they trace me here, I will be on the road as Jon Pederson. I still have the fake ID's and some cash." Daddy had taught him well. His five experiences gave him the tools to get lost in the crowd. "If they trace me here, I can't use my car. If I took my car they would have a way to trace me. They would be looking for my car. Maybe, I should buy a used car as Jon Pederson; I can always dump it later. Daddy will have some cash for me, and he'll help me get a new identity. I'll be okay." He was thinking survival; he had not felt this desperate since he was ten or twelve years old.

Randy Curtis put three days worth of clothes into another duffel bag, and grabbed a sport coat. "Oh my God!" His mind raced. "I left my jacket in California, I left my sport coat in the hotel room." he said out aloud. "I know I left it there, I didn't wear it back here. I left the damn coat. What a dope! I really screwed up. I always wore it when I helped the doctor; the jacket had always been part of my disguise, but, I forgot it." He beat his palm against his forehead. He had this sickening feeling that they would find him, he knew there were no other coats like that one, it was very special. He instinctively knew that he had to get out of the house soon. He reached for the phone, picked up the handset, and called a cab.

"Pick me up at the Tasty Freeze on 34th and Taylor Street, I will be waiting in front." The Tasty Freeze was about a ten-minute walk; he wanted to get away from the house in case the police figured it out. He didn't want anyone to connect him with the cab. He grabbed his bag, and headed out the door, and toward freedom.

He thought for a moment as he jumped into the cab. "Take me to the bus station." He figured if the cabby took him to the bus station, he would change cabs and take another to a used car dealer. Then he would buy a cheap car in cash as Jon Pederson. Once in New York, he would decide what to do with the car. Even if they found him as Randy Curtis in Atlanta, they would never find a way to follow him. They would be checking cab companies, busses and airlines. They would never think to look at one individual car lot in a city as large as Atlanta. Once in New York, he would just be careful when he got to the doctor's office. He could watch the office, and time things correctly. See the doctor, get some money, and leave forever.

"I think I'd like to buy the dark gray, Ford Thunderbird." he told the salesman. Randy noticed the price at four thousand seven hundred dollars. The car looked pretty clean and the tires were new. "How many miles on it?"

"It has about ninety thousand, why don't you get in and take it for a test drive?" asked the salesman.

"No, I am in a hurry. I have about two thousand miles to drive. Think that car will make it?" he asked.

"Yeah, that car is pretty sound. Some old guy owned it from new and took good care of it." the salesman said. "Lots of miles, but well kept."

With the paper work taken care of, Jon Pederson got in, and headed for the highway. He would take Highway 85 through Raleigh, and catch the 95 to New York City. "I have to take my time though, I need to think this thing through, I want to get there by Sunday or maybe Monday morning. I have to call Dr. Bright and get my plan set." He would wait until he was on the road and after getting gas, he would call him.

* * * * *

Thursday, August 6th, 1998, San Francisco Airport

Rudy and Roger sat in the car at the airport in front of the airline entrance. "Well, Rudy, it has been great working with you these past few days. If I can ever help you with anything, don't hesitate to call." Roger and Rudy shook hands.

"Roger, the pleasure has been mine, you are one hell of a good detective, and the main reason I am going to catch this guy. Thanks again." Rudy turned, walked into the double doors, and headed up the escalator and toward the main ticket counter to pick up his tickets. His reservations had been made by the Atlanta Police Department.

"Rudy Auggur, I am here to pick up my tickets on flight 344 to Atlanta." he said to the flight attendant, and presented his credit card.

Quickly pushing the buttons on the keyboard, she answered him. "Yes, sir, here we go." The machine printed them out, and she tore them off the printer and placed them on top of the counter. She then ran his credit card, and asked him to sign the form. "Thank you very much, Mr. Auggur, here is your receipt. Your plane leaves in forty-five minutes from Concourse D, Gate twenty-one. Enjoy your flight."

Rudy took his tickets in hand, and headed down the concourse toward the gate. As he walked, he thought. "God, I hope this guy has let his guard down. I hope the jacket is traceable. Finally we got a break." Rudy was happier about this case than he had ever been about any other. He had been working this thing for ten years. As he found his seat and waited for the flight to lift off, he thought. "Ten years and this could be it, it could finally come to an end. How did he get away all these years? Does our guy live two separate lives? Is he a serious down to earth guy with a second life? Is he a wacko who can put on a great act? Who the hell is this guy?"

Four hours later the plane set down safely in Atlanta. It was 3:00 p.m. Roger's office in Sausalito had made arrangements for Rudy to meet with the owner of Fletcher's at 5:00 p.m. that afternoon. He grabbed his bag from the overhead storage, and worked his way down the aisle toward the exit. Once off the plane, he only needed to find a cab to take him to the store. He found a pay phone in the airport lobby, pulled the Fletcher's information from his jacket pocket, and called the store.

"Fletchers Menswear, may I help you?" came the response.

"Yes, you may, may I speak with Mr. Fletcher?" Rudy asked.

"Could you hold for a moment, I'll see if he is available. Who shall I say is calling?"

"Rudy Auggur with the New York City Police, he is expecting me." Rudy answered.

The salesman pushed the hold button, and pressed the intercom button. "Mr. Fletcher, there is a cop from New York on the phone, a Mr. Auggur, I think he said."

"Thanks Jack, I'll take it." He pressed the line one button and answered. "Mr. Auggur, hello, this is Paul Fletcher."

"Hello, Mr. Fletcher, Detective Rudy Auggur here, I have just arrived in Atlanta. I am at the airport. I would like to see you this afternoon if I can. I can get a cab and be there in a little while." Rudy was getting anxious.

"That will be fine Detective Auggur, I will be waiting. I won't leave until I meet with you." Mr. Fletcher replaced the phone onto its cradle.

"Great, Mr. Fletcher, great, see you in a few." Rudy hung up the phone simultaneously.

He headed toward the curb, and hailed a taxi.

"Where to buddy?" The cab driver asked.

"Take me to…" Rudy fumbled for the address in his pocket, missing the pocket with his hand the first time. "Take me to one sixty-seven Peachtree Blvd in the Peachtree Vine Shopping center. The store is called Fletchers. It's a men's clothing store." Rudy added.

"Yeah, I know that one, it's been there for a long time. We will be there in about thirty minutes." The cabby responded.

"Here on business Mr.?" The cabby asked.

"Yes I am." Rudy answered.

"What kind of business you in?" Apparently the cabby had not been eavesdropping in on his phone conversation.

"New York City Cop." Rudy answered.

"Whoa, what you doing here, investigating some murder or something?"

"As a matter of fact I am. Four of them, and one attempted, " he responded.

"Which one was here?"

"Actually, none of them were in Atlanta, but the clues have lead me here."

"Well, I hope you catch the guy. Is it a guy? Hey, we're here, just a few minutes." The cabby turned into the mall, and worked his way along the front of the stores to Fletchers, and pulled to a stop.

"Yes, it is a guy and I think there is a good chance we will." Rudy glanced at the cabby's meter which read twenty-five seventy-five. Rudy handed him thirty dollars. "Thanks, keep it, can you give me a receipt?"

"Yeah, no problem." He grabbed his tablet from the front seat, and wrote out a receipt.

"Here you go, good luck catching this guy." He handed him the receipt.

"Thanks a lot, it won't be long." Rudy said confidently.

Rudy grabbed his small bag, left the cab, and headed for the front door of the store. Once in, he walked up to the counter. "Mr. Fletcher is expecting me, I am Detective Auggur of the NYPD." He presented his badge.

"Yes, sir, he is in his office, follow me." The salesman led Rudy to the back of the store.

He knocked on the door. "Mr. Fletcher, Mr. Fletcher, the cop is here."

Fletcher opened the door. "Come on in, I'm Paul Fletcher." He extended his hand.

"Rudy Auggur, very nice to meet you, Mr. Fletcher." The two men shook hands. "I want to get right down to business, Mr. Fletcher." Rudy opened his travel bag, and pulled out the camel blazer. "This is the coat we called you about."

"Randy Curtis." He replied almost immediately. "That blazer is Randy Curtis' blazer, I would recognize it anywhere. He is a young successful architect in the Atlanta area." The man was positive.

"You are sure, can you check your records to make sure?" Rudy was dumbfounded; it was so easy.

"Oh, yes, I am sure. This is a one of a kind. He wanted the lining to match his profession, like I said, he is an architect." Mr. Fletcher was absolutely positive.

"Okay, then, do you have his address? I need to call the local police." Rudy was jumpy. He was excited. He couldn't believe it. "Can I use your phone?"

"Yes, I can give you his address, it is here in my customer information catalog. You can use this phone right here." He pushed the phone toward the edge of the counter, and handed Rudy the address almost at the same time.

Rudy used Fletcher's phone to call the police. "…Yes sir, that's right, a murder suspect. I need your help. A warrant. Yes, the evidence is strong. We connected the suspect's clothing directly to the victim." Rudy gave them the pertinent information of name, address, and his own whereabouts. "Yeah, that's good, can you send me a detective and call me at this number?" He gave them the number at the store. "No problem, I will be waiting here at Fletchers Men's Store."

Rudy and an Atlanta detective pulled up two houses away from Randy Curtis' home almost an hour later. "Well, Auggur, from what you tell me this guy has been tough to find, if he is here, he won't get away today." Detective Benefield of the Atlanta police department had brought two cars as backup; he and Auggur would approach from the front, two others would stay just one house down, and another two would be in the back. The six of them would be enough to corral Randy Curtis.

"Is everyone in place?" Benefield talked over the handset.

"In place, in place, let's go." The other two sets of cops responded over the airways. Benefield and Auggur had exited the car, and were slowly walking up to the front door. "Doesn't look like anyone is home." Auggur said. "I think you're right." echoed Benefield.

They stepped up onto the front porch, and Benefield grabbed the doorknob and turned it, it was open. "Careful, Auggur. I am going to open the door, you go high, and I'll go low." Rudy nodded yes, pushed the door open and they burst in. The room was empty.

Thirty minutes later, after a thorough search, they discovered that he had been there shortly before them, and then left, the place was empty now. Benefield got on the horn to the office. "I want a team of men out here right away, go over this place with a fine toothcomb. I also need a check with the cab companies for a pickup at this address. While you guys are searching, see if you can find a picture of this guy, and get me some duplicates made as soon as possible." There was a car in the garage; he had seen it during their initial search. "Then check the airports and busses for a ticket in the name of Randy Curtis. I want you to get each unit on this investigation to get copies of the picture of this guy."

During the next couple of hours, nothing turned up. Rudy himself was looking through everything. "There has got to be something here." Midnight came fast, and there were still no answers, no clues. "This guy has a way of disappearing. I won't be surprised if he does it again, but I know we will find a clue here, this is his home; his guard will be down."

"Hey, Benefield, I found some pictures over here. I think this is the guy." One of the investigators was looking at some pictures of Curtis and friends at a picnic.

"Let me see. Yeah, I think this is probably the guy. He is thirty-ish, good looking, clean cut and athletic. What do you think, Rudy?"

"Yeah, my guess is, this is our man. Let's use this picture here, nice face shot. How fast can we get copies made of this?" Rudy was anxious to get the picture to the cab companies and airlines; he was even more excited about the find.

"Rudy, we can have that ready by 5:00 a.m., and I will make sure that photo is with all the investigating teams first thing in the morning."

"Thanks, Benefield, that's great. I think we have a good chance of finding this guy." Rudy felt good now; first he had the jacket, and now the picture. "I think we have enough to call it a night, what do you say we wrap it up?"

"Okay guys, let's call it a night. We can come back first thing tomorrow morning and start over again." Benefield and his men had had enough.

"That's fine, Benefield, we can start tomorrow morning, what day is it anyway?" Rudy had lost track of time.

"Thursday!" came the response.

"Benefield, can you find me a hotel for the night? Something nearby." Rudy just noticed he was tired and hungry. He also had to check in with his office, and get his messages. Also, he still needed to find Jeanna, and talk to Mrs. Bonnelli.

"I will check my messages when I get to the hotel." he said out loud to himself.

"Yeah, Rudy, there are a bunch of motels not too far from here. I'll take you as soon as we pack up here." They headed for the front door, and out to the car.

They spoke as Benefield drove. "Tomorrow morning we should get the information back from the cab companies, and airlines, not much more we can do now." Benefield found a Best Western Hotel only a few miles from Curtis' home. "How is this, Rudy?"

"Great, Jimmy, close by and cheap. What time should I expect you in the morning?"

"How about eight?" Benefield answered .

"That will be perfect, I want to thank you for your help, I've been chasing this guy for ten years, but today I have a good feeling about this, we are finally going to get this guy." Rudy had great confidence in his voice.

Rudy checked into the hotel, and found his room. He thought to himself. "I need a shower, a drink, some food and a nap." He called the front desk. "Do you have someone who can get me a six pack of Heineken in a bucket of ice, and a burger? There is a ten-dollar tip in it for them. Great, thanks." He took his clothes off, and jumped into the shower. He knew he had about thirty minutes before the beer would arrive. "God, this feels good, nothing like a good hot shower." he thought, as he lathered up and let the hot water run down over his head and face. "Jesus, I hope we find this guy, it's been a long ten years."

He stepped out of the shower, and took a fresh golf shirt, fresh socks and fresh underwear out of his bag. He was wearing shirts for two days each. This was his last shirt, but he did remember to bring some shorts to relax in. There was a knock on the door. "Just a minute." He slipped on his shorts and shirt, and walked over to the door. "Who is it?"

"Heineken man." came the response.

Rudy opened the door. "Is thirty bucks enough?" He handed him the bills.

"Are you kidding? Thanks!" The young guy handed Rudy the bucket stuffed with beer and ice. He walked off snapping the two bills by grabbing each end and pulling the ends quickly away from the middle.

Rudy found an old coke bottle-style wall mounted opener on the end of the sink counter. He popped the cap, and took one long swig. "God, does that taste good, I really needed one."

New Paragraph

He plopped down in front of the TV. It was 1:15 a.m., and he remembered he had to call in for his messages. He called his office He had two messages. He punched in the numbers to retrieve them.

"Hey, Rudy, this is Mrs. Bonnelli. Something I meant to tell you but we were interrupted, and I lost track of our conversation. There is more about that doctor and Jeanna I need to tell you. If you want to call me, I'll be home." Rudy saved the message and waited for the second one. "Hey, Rudy, this is Jeanna Vitelli, call me when you can, thanks."

Rudy decided to call Jeanna, and not Mrs. Bonnelli; he could get the whole story from the horse's mouth. He looked through his notes for Jeanna's phone number. He dialed the number and waited. There was no answer. After four rings the answering machine turned on. "This is Jeanna, please leave a message."

"Hey, Jeanna, this is Rudy, returning your call. Please call me anytime you get this message. I need to talk to you about your doctor, thanks, it's 2:00 a.m., Friday morning." He decided not to call Mrs. Bonnelli; it was nearly midnight in California. He could call her in the morning. It was two-twenty in the morning. He had to get some sleep, and be ready by 8:00 a.m.

The 6:30 a.m. alarm came soon enough; Rudy wanted to shower, dress and get some breakfast before Benefield picked him up at 8:00 a.m. He had to remember to call both Jeanna and Mrs. Bonnelli about 9:00 a.m. He knew they both got up very early in the morning, so he wasn't worried about bothering them. He showered, shaved and did all the other men morning stuff, then put on a fresh shirt, and decided to look for breakfast. He stepped out of the door and headed toward the front desk. He still had an hour before his ride would show up. He felt pretty good, even though he had gotten only four hours sleep; he was used to short nights of sleep. He saw a Burger King across the street and headed in that direction for a sandwich and coffee. "May I have one of those croissant things with potatoes and coffee?" He pointed to the sign. "And do you happen to have the morning paper?"

"That will be two dollars and sixty-cents sir, and I think I have a Journal here somewhere. Yeah here it is." She reached down behind the counter, and produced a newspaper and gave him forty cents change almost simultaneously.

"It's not the Journal, is this okay?" She produced another paper. "Thank you very much." Rudy said.

For the first time in about a week, Rudy actually relaxed. He sat back and had a leisurely breakfast, and browsed the USA Today.

It was 7:50 a.m. when he finished, and he headed across the street back to the hotel. He decided to check the hotel phone for messages and then wait in the parking lot outside for Benefield. He found no messages.

Benefield drove up a few minutes after 8:00 a.m. "Good morning, Rudy, get a good night's rest?" Jimmy had a smile on his face, knowing all too well that the life of a detective didn't allow for such luxuries as a good night's sleep. Most times while working on a tough case, days turned into nights, and back into days. It was very easy to forget the sleepless nights, and remember only the long, hard days.

"Actually, Jimmy, I feel pretty damn good. I think I was so tired that I took more of a power nap. It wasn't long enough to be a good night's sleep. I feel very rested though. How about you?"

"Same for me." Benefield answered. "Same great power nap. Well, lets' get going over to Curtis' house, I will call my boys about the cab and airlines, and see if anything has popped up." He picked up the hand mike from the dashboard. "Dispatch, this is Benefield, over." He turned to Rudy. "You need some food?"

Rudy shook his head from side to side. "No thanks! I had something."

"This is dispatch, go ahead, over." came the response almost immediately.

"This is Benefield, let me have Detective Johnson, over."

"Hey, Jimmy, I am going to have to patch you through to him, he is at the bus station, over."

"Hey Jimmy, Johnson here, over."

"This is Benefield. What did you find out at the cab and airlines about this Curtis guy, over?"

"Jimmy, we got a cabby who says he picked him up at a Tasty Freeze near his house, and dropped him off at the bus station. I checked with the bus ticket sales. No one recognizes the pictures. The morning shift workers are here from 7:00 a.m. to 3:30 p.m. The guys I talked to were all here yesterday. I am going to check with the airlines now, and get back to the bus station at 3:30 p.m., over."

"Okay, Ralph, sounds good, find me immediately if you run into anything, over." Jimmy glanced at his watch. It was 8:30 a.m."

"Well, you heard him, Rudy. What do you want to do?" Jimmy briefly glanced in Rudy's direction, as he drove toward Randy Curtis' house. "The house is just right at the next intersection."

"As soon as we get there, I have to make a couple of calls to California. The girl involved in the attempted murder, and her neighbor both called me last night. I called but there was no reply from either of them."

Benefield handed his cell phone to Rudy. "Will this help?" he asked.

"Perfect, I am going to call as soon as we get to the house, thanks."

A quick right hand turn, and down the block, and Jimmy pulled up in front of Curtis' house. "Here we go Rudy. The crew is already here; I am going in to check with those guys, see if they found anything new this morning." Benefield got out of the car, and headed up the sidewalk.

Rudy looked at his watch; it was 8:50 a.m. He reached inside jacket pocket, and took out his day planner, thumbing to August 7th. He had written the phone numbers to call. First he would call Mrs. Bonnelli. He dialed.

She answered on the second ring. "Good morning." she said in her normal cheery voice.

"Mrs. Bonnelli, good morning, this is Rudy Auggur. Sorry to bother you so early, but I wanted to make sure and talk to you as soon as I could. You left a message saying that you had something else to tell me."

"Yes, yes, detective, I do. When we were talking, we got sidetracked and you seemed in a hurry and well, you know. I had an attack of old-timer's disease, and forgot what I was going to tell you. But Jeanna had told me this story about her doctor." Her voice seemed very excited and anxious.

"Go right ahead, Mrs. Bonnelli, what is it?" Rudy wanted to know what she had remembered.

"While we were talking about her good life, she told me that the doctor had acted very strangely. She told me he…he…well, he had hypnotized her, taken her clothes off, and was playing with himself in front of her. She woke up from her hypnotic state, and couldn't believe her eyes. He had his penis in his hand. Isn't that against the law or something? Do you think this is important? What a dirty old fart, if you'll excuse my language."

"Yes, it is Mrs. Bonnelli. You are right, this kind of thing is a serious breach of medical ethics, and you bet it is important, but I need to talk with Jeanna. Do you happen to know the doctor's name?"

"I wish I knew, detective, but you are going to have to talk to Jeanna about that."

"Actually ma'am, she was my next call anyway. Have you seen her today? She didn't answer her phone last night, but I left her a message." Rudy was concerned. "She was supposed to keep in touch, she was supposed to let me know what she was doing, and where she was going." Rudy sounded a little frustrated.

Mrs. Bonnelli answered quickly. "She went to her family's home in Fresno; she wanted to spend a few days with her mom and dad, before going back to New York on Saturday. She was complaining that her plane had to make too many stops and was thinking about leaving Fresno early in the morning. I know her plans were up in the air about returning to New York."

"Do you have her family's phone number in Fresno, Mrs. Bonnelli?" Rudy asked.

"Yes, I do, just give me a minute to find it; it's in my bedroom." She put the phone down on the table, and went into the bedroom. Then she picked up the extension, and gave Rudy the number.

"Thanks for your help, Mrs. Bonnelli. I'll call you again if I need you." Rudy flipped the phone shut, then immediately opened it, and dialed the number in Fresno. It rang. "Come on, answer the phone." It rang again and again, then for a fourth time. It kept ringing. "Come on, come on. It's 6:00 a.m.; someone should be up and at 'em by now." He was getting impatient. "Don't these people have an answering machine?" It rang ten times, but there was no answer. I'll just have to try again, he thought.

Rudy got out of the car, walked up to the house, and entered. "We got anything yet, boys?"

"We haven't found anything unusual, Rudy. Just the kind of stuff you might have if you went through anybody's home. Nothing strange! What did your phone calls turn up?" Benefield asked.

"Turns out Jeanna's doctor is a pervert. He hypnotized her, and she woke up to find her clothes off, and him playing with himself. He whacks the monkey, wakes her up, and acts like nothing happened, except she woke up in the middle of the whole thing. I can't find Jeanna to get the whole story, though. She's visiting her family in Fresno, and there is no answer there. I am going to try again a little later. Right now, I want to concentrate on this house. According to the old gal, she is spending some time with her family. She should be safe there. I say we go through this house again. This time, we have to rip up the floor, take everything off the walls, and move the furniture. Hell, tear down the walls if you have to."

* * * * *

Rest in Fresno

"God, please let them catch Albion or whatever his name is." Jeanna thought as she watched Rudy Auggur, and Roger Burns get in their car and drive off. She waved as the entire incident flashed in her mind, and her eyes teared up. "How could I have been so stupid?" She turned and walked into her apartment, picked out a Beethoven CD, and put it in the player. She plopped down in her easy chair, and closed her eyes. Jeanna mulled over the last thirty days but nothing made sense. She had always chosen her men, at least her serious men, so carefully. How could she have been fooled? She fell into a light trance as she listened to the music. An hour went by quickly, and then she got up to put on some new music. As she leafed though her CD collection she came across her mother's favorite, but decided not to listen to Willie Nelson. Oh my God, my parents, she thought. She immediately felt guilty that she had not called them. She grabbed the phone, and dialed quickly. The phone rang four times.

"Hello."

"Mom, mom, hi mom. How are youuuu?" She tried to hide her guilt with the sweet voice. "Okay, what's wrong honey?" Mom's intuition alerted her immediately that something had happened. The tone of Jeanna's voice was all telling. "I can always tell when something is off beam."

"Mom, you always know when I am about to tell you about a small problem. Are you sitting down?"

"No dear, I am not, should I be?" Now her mom was worried, Jeanna's voice seemed very serious. While Jeanna grew up, she had a trouble-free child. Her beautiful daughter's life had been mostly straightforward and fun loving. This tone of voice was not normal for Jeanna. "Okay honey, I am sitting down now."

"Well, last month I met a wonderful man, or at least I thought he was wonderful. He didn't turn out so wonderful. I had quite a surprise last night."

"Oh my God, what happened? Are you ok? Are you in the hospital? Oh my God!!!!!" Her mother's voice went to a shrill high pitch, the one that makes the cat jump straight up in the air.

"No, No mom, I'm okay. I'm fine. It was just so scary, but I'm fine." Jeanna tried to calm her down. "Before you get all worried, sit back and relax for a minute and let me tell you what happened. We had been spending a lot of time together. All of our days but we never spent a night together. But on Friday night after dinner, he…he…tried to smother me and kill me."

"Oh, my God." She screeched again.

"Really, I'm okay, mom. I just have a few cuts and bruises. You know all that time I spent with the guys at home growing up? All the tomboy jokes and all the karate training paid off. I fought him off, and he ran. He got away before the police arrived. They are sure he left town and they are tracking him now. They put a guard on my house and watch me just in case he is still here, but they are one hundred percent sure he left Sausalito, and I think they're right."

"Oh, Jeanna, are you sure you're not hurt? I know how you used to try to act so tough when you played ball with the boys." Jeanna would never tell when she was hurt; she always hid her sore muscles and small bruises. She put on a great act. But, she really did learn to tough it out.

"No mom, really, I had a cut on my foot, and a few bruises. The stitches will come out tomorrow, and I can already walk on it. I will be running again in a few days. Really, I'm fine."

"Jeanna, I am going to come there as soon as I get off the phone. I'm getting in the car and heading to Sausalito with your father." She was mad, worried and wanted to be with her daughter.

"No, no, no! Mom, I have a better idea. I'm tired of lying around here. I'm coming there to spend a few days with you, before go back to New York. I have already called the airport and I can be there by ten tonight. The last flight leaves at nine. How is that?"

"Oh, honey, I'm so worried. You hurry up and get here. I am so worried about you. This is best. Your father and I will pick you up at the airport." Her mother was very relieved and happy.

"Ok, then it's settled. I love you mom, I'll see you in a few hours."

As always she had to clean some things up, throw out some food, then do some laundry and pack. She had a habit of not leaving her house without getting it ready for her next visit. She called Angela, and thought about calling Rudy again. Naw, I will call him from mom and dad's house before I leave for New York, she thought. This is going to be great; I can really rest for the next two days. She called a cab, and decided to tell the police guard when the cab got there.

She packed a few essentials. She grabbed her bag. She locked her door and looked for the guard, but he wasn't there. He's probably taking a break, she thought.

The United Flight landed in Fresno about ten after ten. Jeanna's mother met her at the base of the stairway on the tarmac. "Oh baby, it's so good to see you." Both mom and daughter broke into tears. "Are you sure you're all right?"

"Yes, mom, I'm fine really. My heart is broken, and I am so confused, but physically I will be okay in a few days. But the rest of it, I don't know how long it will take until I am back to normal. I just don't get it. Let's talk about it later. I am so tired. How about you? It's so good to see you. Where's daddy?" She glanced toward the ticket office.

"He's in the building looking for luggage, where is your luggage, honey?"

"Traveling light, mom, just this carry-on bag." Jeanna kept both apartments stocked with clothes. It was so much easier to travel with only a carry-on, and a few favorite pieces. "Let's get daddy and go back to the ranch. I just want a hot shower, and a beer with you and dad.

How does that sound? I will tell you all about everything after I get out of a hot, hot shower."

"There's your father." She pointed to the doorway.

"Oh, daddy, daddy, it's so good to see you again. I know it has only been six weeks, but I really missed you this past weekend. Don't say it Dad, I know I should have called you earlier. But, really, nothing serious happened and I wanted to get things straight in my head and come visit. If it had been more serious, I would have had Angela call. I am okay, really. I'm just fine." She hugged and kissed him both. She worked herself in between them, and started toward the front door and the parking lot. She felt great all of a sudden; her foot didn't hurt and she was happy.

"Honey, sometimes I wish you would tell us more of what's going on. Your mother and I were so worried, we were both so jumpy until you got off the plane." Her father was as worried as her mom, but didn't show it as much on the outside.

Thursday and Friday were spent with her mother and father on the farm. Jeanna and Anne took some long walks around the farm in the hot, summer sun. Freddie and Jeanna sat on the porch and drank lemonade, then switched to beer early in the evening. She told them both many of the details of the attempted murder, but she didn't tell them about Dr. Bright. They didn't need to know what he had done. She wanted to get back to New York, see him, tell him that she no longer wanted his services, and that she would file charges. If she told them about the doctor, she would never get out of Fresno. She had been violated, and was deeply hurt. Jeanna wondered how many other victims there had been. The one thing that bothered her the most was that she had really loved Albion; he was so perfect. He was the man she wanted in her life. What would she do if she ever met him again?

Jeanna called the airlines and made arrangements to leave for New York late on Friday afternoon. She had difficulty finding the right time for the flight and the only one that really worked was to Las Vegas first. She called Catherine, and made plans to stop off in Las Vegas for a day. She had not seen her in a long time and thought it may be a good place to start her rest.

The trip to Fresno had helped with the healing process; she was able to be with her parents without interruption. They were on the ranch all by themselves. Her brothers had all left the Fresno area for the high tech valleys north of San Jose. Mom would call the boys, and tell them what had happened and assure them that Jeanna would call them when she got back to New York.

The trip to the airport was ten minutes. She, mom and dad made the drive. She arrived at the Fresno airport at about 5:00 p.m. It was still over one hundred degrees and unbearable for most. She had grown up in the heat of the San Joaquin Valley and even though she only made short occasional visits, she maintained a tolerance to the stifling temperatures.

Her plane left Fresno in the late afternoon on Friday, August 7th. She would fly to Las Vegas, and spend the night with her old college friend, and then leave for New York late Saturday afternoon. She still had to call Rudy, but decided to make that call the next morning from Las Vegas. She needed a few days rest with diversions, and knew that her friend Catherine would be just the person to help her relax and loosen up. Las Vegas was just the right place. The big decision she had made was that she must confront Dr. Bright on Monday night.

* * * * *

Lost Time–Friday Night–August 7, 1998

Randy Curtis, traveling as Jon Pederson, pulled into the Radisson Hotel parking lot on Friday night. He had efficiently made his way to Mansfield, New Jersey. The used car ran perfectly. He had planned to take the New Jersey Turnpike into the City when he left. The turnpike was only a few miles from his hotel. He had taken his time to get this far. He wanted his cuts, bruises and broken nose to heal before he met with Dr. Bright. He needed to be able to blend in with the crowd. The soreness of everything, even the broken nose was almost gone. The black and blue was gone from his eyes. He decided to stay Friday and Saturday night, and try to meet with him on Sunday night. He knew that Daddy would figure out a plan to get him away safely. He had protected him since he was young, and Randy trusted the doctor with his life.

It was 9:00 p.m. He was so tired, exhausted. What a life he had led. My God, he thought. I am a murderer. It finally dawned on him. "I have murdered women for ten years. I have been protecting my family by murdering women."

He had only wanted a normal life, maybe even a wife and children of his own. The first few years with the doctor had been tough, but once he reached his teenage years, life began to get easier. After college, life was nice. Then came the first murder. It seemed easy. He had always done exactly what Daddy had told him. He was even able to put the first murders out of his mind. In real life he was asked to just do what the doctor said, follow some rules, study, and be nice to people. Life was good. Now, as he thought about the murders, life seemed undisciplined again. He felt like he was with his mother. "Why did adults do this to their children?" He would ask himself over and over. He felt he must get to the doctor and ask for help. He wanted some explanations; needed some explanations. "Would the doctor help him? What was next?"

Randy unpacked his travel bag, and lay back on the bed to watch some television. He glanced at the bedside clock. It was 11:00 p.m. He set the alarm for 6:00 a.m. He muted the television, and let the screen flicker. "I'll get a good night's sleep and call the doctor in the morning." He thought as he let his eyelids droop.

Brrrieeeenngg! What a terrible sound, he thought. He had forgotten to set it to music, and instead the alarm shocked him awake. He sat up on the edge of the bed, and glanced around the room. Saturday morning cartoons flashed across the television. A two-cup coffee machine took up space on the counter above the mini bar. "Coffee first, shower then call the doctor," he planned aloud.

Coffee cup in hand he dialed. "This is Dr. Eric Bright's special project answering machine, please leave a message, and a phone number. I will return your call within two hours." Bright kept a separate phone number in his back office. His secretary was aware of the office, but not of what was he was doing or who his clients were. He had kept everything back there a secret. Even his records were locked in a safe. Other than the doctor, Randy was the only person with access to the safe. Each time the doctor needed his help; he would go into the safe to get a file on the girl to be eliminated. Randy would also get the money and alternate identification. Upon returning from each assignment, the first thing he did was return to New York. He would go to Daddy's office, put his travel bag, money and I.D. back in the safe. He didn't need the doctor to get into the office or the safe. He would then call the doctor in the front office, and wait for him. He would spend a few hours with the doctor, mostly under his trance. He used meditation to cleanse his mind of the terrible things he had done. Strangely enough, after each job, he was convinced he would never need the bag again. He was sure that he was finished eliminating people. But, he was always mistaken. Nearly every two years, Bright asked again and each time Randy had obliged. This had to be the last time. This was the first time the plan had not worked, and he was scared, very scared.

"Daddy, this is Randy. I have registered at a motel in New Jersey as Jon Pederson. I need your help. Things got crazy in Sausalito and didn't turn out as planned. I need to see you Sunday. Please call me at 973-555-6523, room 135. He hung up the phone, and drank his coffee. Physically, he felt surprisingly good, considering what he had been through. Now, all he had to do was wait for Bright to call back. It was Saturday morning, and Bright may not get back to him right away. He would only check the message machine about every two hours. Randy waited in his hotel room.

Lunch came and went without any food. Randy began to worry about his relationship with the doctor. He wondered. Did the doctor know what had happened? He called again. There was still no answer. He was hungry, and headed out for lunch. But, first he would leave a message at the front desk just in case.

"Front desk, this is Barbara, may I help you?" the clerk answered.

"This is Jon Pederson, room 135. I am expecting a very important message. I will be leaving for a few minutes to get something to eat. Would you mind telling the caller I will get back to them as soon as I return?" Randy was scared and worried. He was not sure what to do, but he knew the doctor was the only place he could go for help.

He found a fast food Mexican place just a block down the street. It wasn't his favorite, but he had not eaten in quite a few hours, and biting into a spicy taco actually tasted good to him for a change.

He opened the door, and immediately saw the flashing message light. "This is Jon Pederson, room 135, I have a message?" he asked the front desk clerk.

"Yes sir, a Dr. Bright said he was returning your call, and asked that you call him back. He said he would wait."

Randy had only been gone for about half an hour. He would call as soon as he got off the phone. "Thank you, I will. Thank you, very much. I will call him right now."

* * * * *

Saturday-Secrets Revealed in Atlanta

"Hey Rudy, Jimmy, get down here, look at this." One of the investigators had found a room hidden behind an old bookcase in the basement. The old bookcase was used to store paint and other canisters. It had been fastened to the wall with hinges. The hidden room was about fifteen-foot square. The team had spent most of Friday scouring the home of Randy Curtis with no leads. Finally, first thing Saturday morning, it looked like they had gotten a break.

"What have you got, Hendricks?" Benefield called out, as he walked down the basement steps to meet him.

Rudy was right on his heels. "What is it, man?" He called out as he reached the bottom step.

"Well, it looks like an office. He's got a computer, a phone line, files, and closed circuit television. It's on; you can see the front door. Nice little deal. I need something like this at home." The investigator was smiling as he looked at Jimmy and Rudy. "This guy must have liked privacy for his work." He looked around the room. "Wonder if he was a good architect?"

Benefield looked around the room. "All right guys, let's take this room apart," he said. "Look into everything, every file, every note and wastebasket. All of it." Benefield took control of the investigation on his home turf.

It was almost 11:00 a.m. One of the officers called downstairs. "Rudy, you have a message from your office. They want you to call right away."

Rudy decided to use the phone on Randy Curtis' desk. "This is Rudy Auggur, I have a message?"

"Yeah, Rudy. Some girl named Jeanna. She asked us to find you and she also left a message on your machine. I'll put you through."

They transferred him. "Hey Rudy, this is Jeanna, I'm just checking in with you. I'm in Vegas with a girlfriend, and I'm going back to New York later today. I will call your office when I get there. Talk to you soon."

Damn her, she didn't leave a number, why did I forget my cell phone? He thought. Then the number would be in my missed numbers log in the phone. I'll just have to wait, and I could stop using pay phones.

Rudy turned his attention to the hidden office. "First, Jimmy, let's get that computer down to some experts, and have them look through it and see if anything shows up."

"My computer guy has already looked at this thing. All he can find is architectural stuff. There are business letters, drawings, that kind of thing. It appears to be all business. There are about a hundred discs though. He is in the process of taking it apart, and will take it to the lab and sift though everything. It will take till late tonight." Benefield had been through this kind of thing before; he had an idea based on past experience.

"That's fine, Jimmy, we've a lot to go through here. I'm sure your guys will do it right. Let's get back to work."

One investigator carried the computer keyboard and mouse past Rudy and Jimmy, and up the stairs while another walked past them with a box of diskettes. "God, I hope they find something, Rudy."

"Yeah, me too. By the way, Jimmy, how long before your captain wants you back? I mean it's not your case."

"Our captain is on vacation, and his assistant is in charge. He's an old partner of mine. He gave me the weekend to help as long as he doesn't need the forensics team on another site, so we are good to go." Benefield was happy to work on this case with Rudy. He had looked through all the newspaper articles that were in the file Rudy had brought; he felt privileged to help him.

Rudy walked over to the desk, and sat down. He swiveled around in the chair, and pulled open the top drawer in the file cabinet. "Here we go, Jimmy, you want a few of these files?" Rudy reached over the bottom file cabinet drawer, pulled out a stack of files, and slammed them down on the desk. "I'm going to call Jeanna's parents in Fresno. It's 11:30 a.m. thirty. I should be able to raise someone by now." Rudy sat at the desk and dialed the number again.

He put the phone to his ear, let it ring seven or eight times, but there was still no answer.

"Hey, Rudy, I thought you said she was in Vegas and didn't leave a number?" Benefield remembered the last call.

"Yeah, Jimmy, that's right, but I'm hoping her mother knows how to get a hold of her so I'm calling her family's home in Fresno. I need to talk to Jeanna about this doctor. Maybe there is a connection. Guess all I can do is keep trying." Rudy glanced at his watch again. It was now 11:45 a.m. "Why does five minutes seem like three hours when you need something to happen?" He smiled, and shook his head from side to side. Benefield agreed with a chuckle.

"You want some lunch, Rudy?" It was 1:30 p.m., and they had gone over a third of the files, yet had found nothing.

"Yeah, Jimmy, let's get some pizza, okay with you?" Rudy wanted something easy and fast with flavor.

"Great, Rudy. Let's get some air." Their noses had been in the file folders for four hours without a break.

They stood up simultaneously. Benefield headed for the steps first, and Rudy followed. Benefield spoke, "There's a pizza place a few blocks from here; one of those chain restaurants. You like thick crust Rudy?"

"Any crust is fine, I know I can't get my New York style here, so I'll take what I can get. They all advertise New York Style, but only in the City is it really New York Style. Probably the water." Rudy laughed.

"Yeah, Rudy, I think maybe this Randy Curtis guy has been into the wrong water too."

Glancing at the menus, Jimmy spoke up, "Anything you don't want from the deluxe list, Rudy?"

After a few seconds, Rudy answered. "Anything you want is good with me."

"Miss, we will have a large deluxe, and a couple of draft beers. Okay with you Rudy? Even though it was only 3:00 p.m., it seemed later.

"Beer actually sounds good to me, Jimmy." He glanced at his watch. "God, it feels like midnight, and it is only halfway through the afternoon."

Rudy felt like talking about the case. "This Curtis guy is slippery, he must have help. I mean that he seems to know what to do. Imagine this; he manages to seduce five women. All these women are beautiful, and unattached. All are actresses and/or models. All hang out in New York, and all were killed almost exactly two years apart. All visited their permanent homes, and got murdered. All of them were killed at home, except the first girl."

"Except the first girl?" Benefield asked.

"Yes, she was murdered in a hotel in New York. But it turns out that she spent most of her time in New York. The others kept homes or apartments in their hometowns or near their hometowns. But the first one, Julia Phillips, spent ninety percent of her time in New York. She had pretty much moved there."

"Did the girls ever come in contact with each other? Like, work together, or anything?"

Rudy shook his head no and confirmed. "We can't find a connection, but I am betting my ass that if we do, we find the killer. What do you think Jimmy?"

"I would bet my ass too, Rudy. This pizza is pretty good, didn't realize how hungry I was. Want another beer?"

"No, not for me, Jimmy. One of these big ones is enough for me." Rudy glanced down at his watch "I'm ready to get back to work. Do you mind?"

"Naw, I can live without the beer. I'll drop you off at the house and go back to the office for a few hours, then be back about seven thirty to pick you up. I have a lot of paperwork to catch up on. I almost forgot I have a job here in Atlanta. I got so caught up in your investigation." Benefield knew he had things he had to catch up on.

"Listen, Jimmy. You've done more than I could ask for. I am going to keep working at the house, and when I am ready for dinner or quitting, whichever comes first, I will call a cab." Rudy knew that he had taken enough of Benefield's time but he also knew that there must be something there; there must be a lead in that little basement office in a normal Atlanta suburb.

It was still early evening as Rudy walked up to Randy Curtis' home. He took a deep breath, and sighed heavily as he opened the door and headed across the living room, into the kitchen and to the basement entrance. He walked down the steps and once at the desk, settled in with more manila folders of records. He began pulling papers from each folder, and glancing down at the words. Three hours went by quickly and he had found nothing. In frustration he began pulling out the drawers of the desk. Nothing, nothing, nothing he thought and tried to slam the right hand drawer shut. It stuck. He pulled it out and tried again. It was stuck on something. He pulled the drawer completely out of the desk and turned it over. There was a small leather notebook taped to the bottom of the drawer. He ripped it off and thought to himself… what do we have here? He opened the booklet to the center page and read, "I am not so sure I did the right thing by protecting Daddy, and Debra seemed so nice. She didn't seem like the kind of girl that would hurt Daddy. I know I eliminated her, but I don't think I should have. I don't know if I can do this again."

"He started to feel guilty after the second girl." Rudy thought.

Rudy thumbed though the book, and read another passage. "Daddy has given me everything I need to know about Brandy. She likes yellow roses, beef filets, big salads with blue cheese, mixed with sweet vinaigrette. She also likes convertibles and old movies," Curtis had written. The list went on. Rudy thumbed quickly through the book, who the hell is Daddy? He saw reference to the other girls and their likes and dislikes. He turned to the front of the book, and glanced at his watch at the same time. It was 9:30 p.m. on Saturday evening.

There has to be a reference to Daddy somewhere in this book. He began reading from the first page. "Daddy has given me a number SP1001. He says I am his number one Special Project, and he wants me to eliminate SP1002. He says that she is ruining our lives and if she talks, then we will lose each other. I must help him. I will have to eliminate Julia." Rudy put the book down for a moment and thought. SP1002, this sounds familiar. Yeah, Mrs. Bonnelli told me about Jeanna's doctor and SP…where the hell is my notebook? He fumbled through his pockets, and finally retrieved the small spiral bound tab from his right inside jacket pocket.

Rudy flipped through the pages of his notebook glancing at a few words on each page. "I found it! Here it is, he thought, SP6! Close enough! Mrs. Bonnelli had said that Jeanna had a SP number, he thought to himself. I found it. I've got the connection. Daddy and the doctor is the same guy. God, why didn't Jeanna leave me her phone number? I have to get to New York. I have to get to this doctor."

Rudy looked for a phone; he found it on the desk. He fumbled for Benefield's phone number, and dialed. It rang only once and someone answered. He thought for a moment sarcastically. "Yeah, just like New York. Rings once. Don't I wish?"

"Atlanta PD, Homicide, Officer Melbourne speaking!"

"I would like to speak with Officer Benefield please. This is Rudy Auggur from the NYPD."

"Yeah, hold on a minute, he's around here somewhere." The Atlanta officer scanned the room for him.

"Hey, Benefield, pick up line eight, got NYPD on the line."

"I found him, be just a minute." Rudy was put on hold.

"This is Benefield." Jimmy had found his way to his desk and phone.

"Hey Jimmy, this is Rudy; I hit pay dirt. Right after you left I found this small journal taped to the bottom of a desk drawer. It's like a diary. He wrote it all down. The doctor in New York is the guy; he's been pulling the strings. I was right. This Curtis guy hasn't been doing it all alone. He had help."

"No kidding, that's great. What's next? Do you want me to pick you up?"

"That would be great. Could you have someone in your office get me a ticket on the first thing smokin' going north? I need to get to the City as soon as possible. Make the reservation to La Guardia. Can you pick me up, run me by my motel, and get me to the Airport?"

"Not a problem. I'll have you there in less than an hour. You will be in New York by 8:00 p.m. tonight."

"Thanks Jimmy, I just wish it could be faster." Rudy decided to call his office.

"Homicide, NYPD, this is Officer Edwards, how can I help?" came the answer from New York.

"Hey Joe, this is Rudy, I need someone to help me with that serial murder case; the young actress thing."

"Where the hell are you, Rudy? We haven't seen you for a couple of weeks." Edwards wasn't completely in touch with the case.

"I'd love to fill you in Joe, but I'm in a bind; I need your help real fast. Three things I need you to do. First, if a woman by the name of Jeanna Vitelli calls, send a squad car for her. Go get her immediately and don't let her out of your sight. She is in danger. I am in Atlanta. I am about to leave for New York. Second, I need you to help me track somebody down. I don't have much to go on. The guy is a New York psychiatrist. He treats a lot of actresses. He also does a lot of research in the area of self-improvement. I know it is not much to go on, but it is the best I can do. I will be in New York in about three hours. The Atlanta police will call and tell you which flight. Third, have somebody pick me up. I don't have much confidence you will find this guy's office, but give it a shot. Once I get there I have another person that can help. I am going to call her as soon as I get off the phone. If I get the information from her, I will call back. Otherwise, I'll see you when I get to New York."

Rudy knew that his only chance was to get to New York and find her. He had to get to her before she got to the doctor. He still had her family's number in Fresno; surely they must know the name of her doctor? The leads were pretty slim, but it was his only hope.

* * * * *

Everybody In The Same Direction At The Same Time- Saturday, August 8, 1998?

Dr. Bright walked into his back office, and noticed the message light was blinking on his answering machine. He pushed a button, and listened. "Daddy, this is Randy. I have registered at a motel in New Jersey as Jon Pederson. I need your help. Things got crazy in Sausalito and didn't turn out as planned. I need to see you Sunday. Please call me at 973-555-6523, room 135. " Dr. Bright pushed the button again and again, listening to the message each time carefully. He sat back in the chair at the desk and thought, jotting the information on his notepad. The tape ran further and a second message from Randy came up. "It's Randy, I must speak with you." Then a click, there were no other messages.

Eric Bright's mind began to race. What had happened? Had Randy botched the job? He must call him right away. Bright picked up the phone and dialed.

"Radisson in the Park, how may I help you? May I speak with Jon Pederson in room 135 please?"

"Just a moment, sir, I will connect you." The phone rang seven or eight times with no answer. The desk clerk broke in. "I'm sorry sir, there's no answer. Would you like to leave a message?"

"Yes, I would. Do you have a message center?"

"No sir, we don't, but I will be glad to pass the message on as soon as he returns."

"That's fine. My name is Dr. Bright, and I would like Mr. Pederson to call me as soon as he gets back. He has my number. Please tell him

I will wait by the phone until he calls me. Thank you." Bright hung up. He sat back in the chair, spun around, and looked outward toward the New York skyline. "Oh my God, what has happened?" He too was concerned about the future.

He waited impatiently, staring at the phone for what seemed like hours although only forty minutes passed when the phone rang again. "Hello, Dr. Eric Bright here."

"Daddy, it's Randy. We've got real trouble; she's not dead. She got away, and the police came. And, and…" Randy Curtis was frantic.

"Calm down, Randy. Tell me the whole story, and we'll work this out. Just calm down, and tell me what happened."

Randy went into the whole ordeal. How he had seduced her, and gotten her in position to eliminate her, but she had fought back and broken his nose. How he fled when he heard the police sirens. He told Dr. Bright how he had worked his way to Atlanta, and then to New Jersey.

"Did the police see you? Did they get your name or anything?"

"No, I used my other names, and flew back the same way I always did. But I left the jacket. I left my jacket, the one I always wore with the architectural lining."

Eric Bright knew that the police could trace that jacket. He knew that they were most likely already on the way with Randy's identity. Bright had designed the lining; he had helped Randy design the lining. It was so unusual. It would be easy to trace. Randy had moved to Atlanta for his first job after graduation. Bright knew that Randy's life was about to unfold in front of him. It may soon be over for both of them. Bright needed time to formulate a plan. He needed some time to think.

"Listen Randy, sit tight for the rest of today. I'm going to put a plan together for your escape, but I need a couple of hours. I'll call you back later today, and tell you what to do; just sit tight and try not to worry. Things will be okay, I'll fix it, I promise."

Randy was still worried, but agreed. "Okay, but please hurry. I am really worried they will find me. I am really afraid." Even though

Randy had no reason to believe they knew who he was, he had a sense that they would find him. He just knew. He also knew that Daddy had always had a good plan. Daddy had always figured things out for him, and he was always right.

"Don't worry, Randy, just give me some time, and I will figure this thing out. Just relax and do not leave the hotel. Promise me you will not leave the hotel."

"I promise, just hurry." Randy reluctantly put the phone receiver down.

Eric Bright knew that Randy would be found out, as he sat back in his chair he realized that there was really only one solution if he expected to remain free. He thought about it for a couple of hours, but could only find one solution to the problem; he must kill Randy, and make it look like Randy was a lunatic, and that he had used his familiarity with the doctor's office to track these women down. He must make Randy look guilty, and make it look like Randy had killed Jeanna. It was the only way.

* * * * *

Now, Jeanna's Turn

Jeanna hugged Catherine. She made her way down the gangplank to the jet and found her seat. She and Catherine had mostly talked. They made a nice Italian dinner the night before. They shared a bottle of California red grape and caught up on time lost. Jeanna shared the details of Dr. Bright's assault during her session in the office. She shared the attempted murder by her new lover. She shared her sadness.

Catherine had her short stories but nothing as scary as what Jeanna had been through. Together, they decided that Jeanna would expose Dr. Bright as the hypocrite he was, and set the record straight so other women would not have to put up with his lies.

She had called Rudy, but had not spoken with him since August 3ʳᵈ the day after the attack. She had left him a message just before she left for Fresno, and decided to call him again before she went back to New York.

Once in her seat she began thinking about the previous few weeks. What a month, she thought. He seemed so right. How could I have made such a mistake? This thought had gone round and round in her mind a thousand times. Would she continue thinking this way for the rest of her life? Maybe once he was caught… but what if he didn't get caught? Would he come back? So confusing to put it all in one picture. Jeanna closed her eyes, and lay back on the headrest as the plane took off. She would be home in three hours. Tomorrow, she thought, tomorrow I will contact Dr. Bright. I need to set the record straight; I need to tell that dirty son-of-a-bitch what I am going to do to him. She knew he would be in his office on Sunday. He was always in his office. She could leave him a message, and make arrangements to see him on Monday. She was very tired. Sleep came easily.

The plane set down on La Guardia Airport at about 10:00 p.m. Saturday, August 8th. Jeanna grabbed her bag, and left the airplane as quickly as possible. She ran down the concourse, and leapt down the escalator. She hailed a cab and was on her way home minutes after the plane stopped rolling. She felt pretty good. She had made some serious life decisions, and had her plan. Now she had to find Dr. Bright.

Once home, she took another long, hot shower. Physically, it was about the only thing that she did that felt good. She was washing Albion Gant away, one shower at a time. Her head hit the pillow. She hadn't realized how exhausted she was. She didn't remember a thing about that night when she awoke; she had literally passed out. She slept right through the phone calls and messages left by Rudy and her mother. Her hand hit the sleep bar on the radio over and over again until she finally pulled herself out of bed at 9:40 a.m. on Sunday morning.

Strong coffee was the first order of the day. She ground those espresso beans like always, and put them into the coffee maker. Adding water, she pushed the 'on' button, and headed for the shower. The washing off of the dirt of one week ago seemed to be the only thing on her mind. Once out of the shower, coffee cleared her thought process. She started a list, and spoke it out loud as she wrote it down. "First, I am going to get a hold of that bastard and see him tomorrow. Second, I am going to let him know what an asshole he is. Third, I am going to organize my lawsuit."

It was already 10:00 a.m., and she was ready to call the good Dr. Bright. She picked up the phone and dialed. She glanced at the message machine and saw the blinking light, and told herself to check the messages after the call.

"This is Dr. Bright." He answered immediately.

She was stunned and stuttered out her question. "D.D…D..Dr. Bright, this is Jeanna Vitelli, I'm back in New York. Can I see you tomorrow?" Although she had it all planned out in her head, she felt extremely nervous when he had answered the phone. As tough as she was, he still intimidated her.

"Well, actually Jeanna, I am going out of town tomorrow. In fact I am getting ready this afternoon. How about you come by the office today? Furthermore, I could meet you in a couple of hours, let's say at noon." The doctor had caught her off guard, but he needed to get her to his office to keep her away from the police. Obviously, the original plan had failed. He needed to put his new plan into effect and quickly.

Even though Jeanna's plan was for Monday, she agreed. "Yes, Dr. Bright, I can meet you at 12:00 p.m. today at your office. I'll be there." She was tense. She had no reason why she was this nervous, she just was.

"Okay, then, I'll see you in a little while." Jeanna hung up the phone. Now, it was done. Her hand was trembling. She was going to get her chance to tell him what she felt.

Wow, that wasn't so hard, it was almost easy. Now I get to put this jerk in his place, she thought. She sat back, and stared at the wall. Soon, she would be in the doctor's office. She would put the record straight. She felt very uneasy. So uneasy, so thrown off guard she had forgotten to check her messages.

* * * * *

Lucky Dr. Bright

Everything was working in his favor; Jeanna had put herself in the right spot at the wrong time. She was going to be there at noon. He would sedate her, then bind her first with gauze, and tape over the gauze. Once she was asleep, he would smother her. There would be no bruises on her wrists, and if a toxicology report was done, he could tell them that she was so upset he had given her a sedative. He would then catch Randy by surprise and shoot him, telling the police that he was ranting and raving like a madman and that he had no choice. Dr. Bright could see the plan unfolding, and it was perfect. Now it was his own survival; he must eliminate them both. He would look like the hero, by killing the man who had tracked Jeanna from California to New York to finish what he started. Now he had to call Randy, and ask him to be there at 1:00 p.m. That gave him time to get Jeanna ready.

* * * * *

Smokin' Goin' North

While on his flight north, Rudy devoured the journal left by Randy Curtis. He read and reread every page, every sentence. He put the pieces of the puzzle together for each murder. He took up two seats, and their food trays. His papers were spread all over. He now understood how everything was done. He understood how Randy Curtis found his victims. How he was able to seduce them. It was all there. He found it all except one thing. Why had Randy Curtis never mentioned the name of his Daddy in this journal? Did he do this on purpose, or by accident?

The flight would only last a few hours, and the plane would probably spend more time trying to get on the ground in New York than it would in the air between cities. Once down, he had two phone calls to make. The plane finally landed at 8:35 p.m.

When the plane's door opened, Rudy was off and running. He had his small bag in hand, and made a beeline for the concourse.

Joe Edwards met him at the gangway exit. "Hey Rudy." he yelled. "Over here." Joe waved his arms, and walked toward him.

"Joe, how are you doing?" Rudy shook hands with Officer Edwards.

"Any luck finding the doctor?" Rudy asked almost immediately.

"Nothing, Rudy, there wasn't much to go on." Edwards assured him.

"Yeah, I know, but it was all I had. I need to get to a phone immediately. I have to try to find Jeanna." Rudy made a beeline to the phone in the concourse. "Can you believe the NYPD wouldn't get us a contract with the cell phone company that would let me call long distance when I traveled? I guess they never thought we might be outside of New York working on a case." Rudy shook his head form left to right.

"Listen, Rudy, why don't you use my phone? This is important." Joe handed him his personal cell phone.

"Thanks, Joe." Rudy reached inside his jacket pocket, and pulled out his notebook. He quickly dialed the number for Jeanna's parents in Fresno.

"Hello." came the response on the second ring. It was Jeanna's mother.

"Mrs. Vitelli, my name is Rudy Auggur. I am a detective with the NYPD, and I'm working on your daughter's case. We are trying to locate her. I haven't heard from her for three or four days. She calls but hasn't left me a phone number where I can contact her. Can you help me?"

"How do I know you are a detective Mr. Auggur? You might be the guy who is after her." Jeanna's mom was being extra cautious.

"You're right ma'am. Here is what we do. You call the NYPD Homicide branch, and ask for Detective Edward's cell phone number, and then call me back. I am using his phone. Will that be okay?" Rudy did not want to frighten her and went along with her questions.

"Yes, that will be fine. What's the number?" she asked.

"Got a pen?" Rudy asked. "The number is 212-445-9659." He repeated the number, thanked her, and hung up.

Five minutes lapsed and the cell phone rang. "Detective Rudy Auggur, NYPD." he answered.

"Hello, Detective Auggur, this is Mrs. Vitelli. Jeanna went to Las Vegas to visit a girlfriend. She was only going to stay one day. Then go back to New York." Mrs. Vitelli sounded very sure of Jeanna's plans.

"Mrs. Vitelli, I have some very important questions, I want you to think very hard. Firstly, Mrs. Vitelli, do you know the name of Jeanna's doctor? Secondly, do you have Jeanna's phone number here in New York? And, thirdly, do you have the number of her friend in Vegas?" He asked.

"Gee, I don't know his name. She only referred to him as her doctor, but I don't recall her ever mentioning his name. I do have the other numbers though." She gave him the numbers. "Is anything wrong detective? Is Jeanna alright?" She was worried about her daughter.

"No, no, no! Everything is fine. I just haven't heard from her except for a few messages at my answering service. I just need to ask her some questions. Everything is fine." He reiterated. "If she calls you, will you please tell her to call on this phone?" Rudy tried to make his voice sound reassuring. He didn't want to unduly alarm Jeanna's mom.

"Mrs. Vitelli, thanks for your help. As soon as Jeanna checks in, I will have her call you."

New Paragraph

Rudy made sure not to worry Mrs. Vitelli, and let the police know they cared about the family as well. "Thanks again, take care of yourself." Rudy closed the cell phone.

"Thank you detective, take care of my little girl, will you?"

Rudy immediately dialed the New York number. The phone rang six times, and the answering machine came on. "Jeanna here, leave a message."

Rudy spoke. "Jeanna, this is Rudy Auggur, please get in touch with me as soon as possible. It's about 9:30 p.m. on Saturday. It's very important that I talk to you." He left the cell number, and hung up.

He immediately dialed the Vegas number. After four rings the message machine came on. "Hi, you have reached Catherine, I am out, please leave a message."

"This is Detective Rudy Auggur, NYPD. I am trying to find Jeanna Vitelli. Could you please call me at this number." He left the cell phone number again.

"God dammit. I can't find her anywhere Joe, and her friend isn't home either. I only hope she hasn't gone to the doctor yet. She doesn't have a clue that he is the guy behind Albion Gant or Randy Curtis, whatever name he uses. We can't be sure that one of those guys isn't still looking for her. Drop me off at my house. Do you mind staying at my place tonight? You have the phone. If one of them calls, I need to get moving right away. " He dialed Jeanna's number again but there was still no answer. It didn't dawn on him to go over to her apartment and bang on the door. He assumed she was not there.

"No problem, Rudy, anything you need. Let me call the Mrs. and tell her what's what."

It was now 10:30 p.m. Saturday night, and Rudy did still not know where Jeanna was or how to find the doctor. His gut feeling was that he was running out of time although he was not sure why he had this thought. He just knew there were too many unanswered questions, and someone had tried to kill Jeanna Vitelli.

By the time Rudy and Joe arrived at Rudy's walk up, it was 11:30 p.m. "I can't believe these girls aren't home. How about a beer Joe?"

"That sounds great, Rudy, got any snacks? I got some crunchitis when I have a late beer. You know, cheetos, chips that sort of thing?"

Rudy answered, "Yeah, I'm sure I have something like that, maybe even some cashews. "

"That would be great. Thanks."

Rudy put the beers on the table, and went to the cupboard for snacks. "This will take care of your crunch Jones." Rudy pushed the cashews in front of Joe, and took a swig of beer. Putting it down he spoke, "This has been one hell of a chase, I have been after this bastard for ten years, and it turns out that he was under my nose all the time. Can you believe that this doctor could talk this poor schnook into killing these girls? After reading his journal on the plane, I almost felt sorry for him. I mean it reads like this. If the doctor, whoever he is, hadn't called him, he would never have killed anyone. Poor bastard was completely controlled by this doctor; I wonder what kind of guy he is. You know, I wonder if he really still wants to kill her, or he just wants to get away?"

"Good point, Rudy. From what you have said, he is controlled by this guy who calls every two years and says, "Kill this girl." And he does. Then he goes back to Atlanta, and leads a pretty normal life. Kinda like a spy or hit man, isn't he?"

Rudy didn't speak for a few moments. "Boy, now that we sit here and talk about it, he was like a hit man; I wonder though if he is a real killer at heart or just doing what the doctor wants? You know, the guy's journal read like a book, like a perspective of someone's life. I read it, and it gave me a lot to think about. My brain is worn out from trying to figure this Randy guy out. It's time for bed. I need some sleep. See you in the morning Joe." Rudy finished his beer, and got up from the table. "The couch is all yours, turn the volume up on that phone just in case, okay, Joe? The bathroom is down the hall; towels are in the hallway closet. Anything you need, just use it." Rudy pointed in the direction of his bedroom, and headed for the hallway. "I'll see you in the morning."

"Thanks, Rudy, see you in the morning." Joe took his beer, and headed for the living room couch. Both of them settled in with only one thing on their minds; hoping that Jeanna would call.

Joe was awakened by a shake of his shoulder Sunday morning. It was 7:30 a.m. "Hey buddy, coffee is on, shower is open. Do you take anything in your coffee?"

"Wow, can't believe that night was so short. Where's the coffee?"

"Cups are in the cupboard next to the fridge; coffee is almost done. If you need anything in it, look in the drawers or yell." Rudy headed to his bedroom to finish getting ready.

Joe helped himself. "What's the chance of an extra razor and toothbrush?"

"I put that stuff out for you in the bathroom, Joe. Help yourself." Rudy had a new travel pack of toiletries he had put out for Joe. "You didn't sleep through the phone ring did you?"

"Not a chance, Rudy."

Rudy decided to call Jeanna again. This time he used his own phone. He let it ring until the machine answered and hung up. "Man, I can't believe this girl has not come home yet. I'm calling Vegas." He dialed the girlfriend's number and waited. There was no answer. "Don't these girls sleep?"

Rudy glanced at the clock as Joe walked into the room. "8:15 a.m., let's head for the office. Ready to go?"

"All ready, Rudy." Joe tucked his shirt in, grabbed his phone, and slipped his jacket on.

New Paragraph

"Let's go."

The two headed out the door and down the steps. They walked down the street to Joe's car. "What's next, Rudy?"

"I'm not sure, Joe, we both know we have to find this doctor. We don't know where Curtis is. It is Sunday morning. It's not going to be easy to find someone to talk to about this. I guess we just go back to the office, get the yellow pages out, and look for psychiatrists and wait for the phone to ring."

They walked into the NYPD precinct at 9:30 a.m. on Sunday August 9th. They still had not heard from Catherine in Las Vegas nor Jeanna, wherever she was. Rudy was really worried. He called Jeanna. There was no answer. He called Las Vegas again. He let the phone ring. The machine picked up. "This is Detective Rudy Auggur of the New York Police Department, please call me." Rudy gave the number and hung up. He left the message again, just in case Jeanna's friend had somehow accidentally erased it. "Not knowing anything is driving me nuts." He glanced at his watch. It was 10:00 a.m.

Another hour passed and nothing happened. Rudy was getting impatient. He had begun to pace the office floor; Joe was working on paperwork from another case. Rudy made another pot of coffee, and decided to read the journal he found in Curtis' house. Maybe there was something I missed, he thought. Maybe the name is in there and I just failed to notice it.

He sat down with the book and read very carefully. Page after page but there was no mention of the doctor's name. Randy Curtis only mentioned the girl's names, and how he had gotten all of his directions and information from the doctor. Something about the way it was written suggested that after each murder he became less and less agreeable to killing the girls. The first murder was perfect; but each killing after that something would go wrong. Each murder seemed a little more difficult by the way Randy Curtis described them. It was as if he became disenchanted with the idea until he was almost caught in Sausalito. "I am going for a walk down to the deli, you want something to eat?"

Joe answered right away. "That would be great, Rudy, get me one of those bagel breakfast sandwiches with sausage and cheese."

"You got it, Joe, I'll be back in a couple of minutes. Let me take your phone, in case one of the girls calls while I am gone."

"Yeah, Rudy, here you go." Joe handed him the phone.

It was 11:50 a.m. when Rudy walked back into the precinct. He went directly to Joe's desk, and put the sandwich down. "Here's your breakfast, Joe."

Just as Rudy sat down the cell phone rang. "This is Rudy Auggur." he answered.

"Mr. Auggur, this is Catherine Dobson in Las Vegas."

Rudy sat up. Hey waved at Joe. "It's Las Vegas." He turned his attention back to the phone. "Man, is it great to hear from you." Relief was the only thing he felt. "Ms. Dobson, I am the detective working on Jeanna Vitelli's attempted murder case. I need your help." Rudy sounded desperate.

"Sure, Mr. Auggur. I will do anything I can to help."

"Ma'am, just call me Rudy. When was the last time you saw Jeanna?"

"Well, Rudy, I put her on a plane for New York yesterday afternoon. Then I went to a friend's house and spent the night."

"Did she say where she was going, and what she had planned to do when she got there?"

"Yes, she was going to see that slimy doctor, and set him straight. Then she was going to get an attorney and have the son-of-a-bitch put in jail. Why, what's up?"

"We found out the doctor is behind the attempted murder, and all the other murders. He controlled the boyfriend. I assume she told you the whole story."

"Yeah, yeah, she told me everything. What can I do to help?"

"We can't find her, and we have reason to believe that she might be with the doctor. Do you know his name?"

"God, I can't remember if she said his name. Let me think." There was a pause.

"Dammit, I don't remember, I don't remember. I think it was something like 'Light' or 'Sunshine' or something like that. Let me think."

"Joe, get the yellow pages, and look under psychiatrists. We a looking for a psychiatrist's name that is something like 'Light' or 'Sunshine'"

"What, are you nuts, Dr. Sunshine? " Joe began searching through the names in the phone book.

"Here you go, Rudy, got two 'Lights,' a 'Sundial' and a 'Bright' " Joe wrote down the phone numbers and addresses.

"Thanks, Ms. Dobson. Would you mind staying home by the phone for the next four hours or so, until we find Jeanna?"

"That's no problem, I have the day off, and I want to do anything I can for Jeanna. But let me know as soon as you find her, okay?"

"You bet, I will call you as soon as something develops, thanks for you help. If you remember anything else, call me."

"Sure will Rudy, thanks." Catherine hung up the phone.

"First call the offices. Then get the white pages out and cross check these Dr.'s for a residence. Call them at home and verify if they know Jeanna." Rudy took Sundial and Bright, and began to look in the white pages while Joe checked the other two. It was 11:58 a.m. (it couldn't have been 11:50 a.m. because it was that time when he arrived back with the breakfast.) He called Jeanna's apartment again. There was no answer.

They both finished making their calls by 12:50 p.m. "What did you get Joe? I've got Sundial at home, never heard of her. There was no answer at Dr. Bright's home."

"The two Lights were home, Rudy. Neither one of them had heard of Jeanna. What do you want to do next?"

"There is only one thing we can do. Three of the four check out. Let's follow the only lead we have, and go to Bright's office. Maybe he is there working on something. If not, we have either found the right guy or we are back where we started."

* * * * *

Jeanna sat in the chair across from Eric Bright. He heard the faint ring of a phone in the outer office, but ignored it. She was ready to tell him her plans. She spoke. "Dr. Bright, I am disappointed and hurt, I have been doing a lot of thinking about it and I have decided that you are a pervert and a sicko, and don't deserve the trust of anyone else. You should have your license revoked, and tomorrow morning I am going to a lawyer to press charges. You had my trust, and you insulted and degraded me, and for that you are going to pay. I have nothing else to say."

"Jeanna, I know that we have had a misunderstanding. Please allow me to explain myself. Please try to understand this type of therapy; you just don't understand." The doctor stood up, walked around the desk, and into the middle of the room.

"Sorry, doctor. There is no explanation for what you did except that you are sick and need to be exposed and locked up." Jeanna began to stand up.

"Well, I guess there is no other way then. He lunged toward her, and stuck a hypodermic needle in her shoulder blade while pushing the plunger. "You will be asleep in a few minutes, Jeanna. You will never know what has happened. Too bad it has to be this way, but it must."

Jeanna grabbed for the needle, and Dr. Bright. She fell woozy within a few seconds. She felt weak. Sat down in the chair. Her eyelids started to close. She tried to talk. "What have you done? What is that? What the hell is going ......" She fell asleep.

Bright walked around his desk, and pulled heavy gauze and adhesive tape from the deep bottom drawer, and a small handgun from the top drawer. He put the gun in his front right pocket. He went back to Jeanna, and first sat her up in the chair. This sedative should keep her out for an hour or so, but just in case it doesn't this will keep her still, he thought. He wound the gauze around her wrists and ankles, and covered it with a few strands of tape. He then put a couple of winds of tape around her middle, and taped her to the chair. The clock showed 12:40 p.m. Randy would be there in twenty minutes, and it would all be over quickly. He stood back, and admired her from a few feet while facing the desk from the middle of the room. He spoke aloud directly to her and the empty room. "My God, I didn't mean for any of this to happen when it started. I just had this deep-rooted need to be with a beautiful woman. I couldn't help myself. I just had to look." His voice was filled with sadness.

Randy used his passkey to gain entry to the private elevators. He carried his small leather travel bag. He boarded the car, and pushed the penthouse button. The quiet elevator took him slowly to the top of the building. He thought. "I'm a little early, I'll just take a little rest. Daddy will help me. He always has the answers. I will get away." He had a childlike look on his face. He felt helpless, but he also felt betrayed. "Why did it have to be this way?" he said aloud. "All my life, all I wanted was a simple life, I just wanted a family." The silent doors opened, and Randy heard Bright's voice just around the corner.

Eric Bright was still talking to Jeanna as she sat in the chair. "Poor Randy, he will never know what hit him when I pull the trigger. Understand Jeanna, I don't want to kill either one of you. But I must protect myself. You put yourself here to help me get away. He is the only real link between myself and the other girls. After I kill Randy, I can blame it all on him. He would be called a madman. The police will think that everything he did was an incredible fantasy. That he had read my files, and imagined himself with these women. They will never suspect that I was behind it. Never! Now I must kill you, Jeanna." I must untie her, he thought, and set the stage. He reached over to the couch for a pillow. He spoke again. "The proof that Randy had killed her will be the pillow. He always used a pillow."

Randy listened patiently; he didn't know what to think. He was dumbfounded; thoughts raced through his mind. "Daddy is just as bad as my mom; he just used me." He stepped into the room behind Dr. Bright.

The Doctor still had his back to Randy, but felt his presence as he glanced toward the pillow.

"Daddy, how could you do this to me?" Tears filled his eyes. "How could you?" He looked at Jeanna tied so peacefully in the chair. "How could you do this to me?"

Bright was caught completely off guard; Randy had shown up fifteen minutes early. He had heard the Doctor talk about him as if he were nothing more than a puppet. He began to sob. "It's not fair, my mom, my step dad and now you! Everybody treats me like shit. I am nothing more than a little pawn for you guys to move around when you feel like it."

He reached out and with both hands grabbed the Doctor by the neck, and began to choke him.

Eric Bright began to fight back, trying to pull Randy's hands from his neck. Randy was too strong. Bright reached for the gun in his pocket, but he was only able to get it halfway out before Randy grabbed his wrist. Bright put his finger on the trigger, and tried to aim it Randy's direction.

One shot rang out and the gun hit the floor. Bright's limp body slumped downward. Randy held him under the armpits. "Why did you want to hurt me?" He cried. "Why?"

He let the body fall to the floor. Standing over Dr. Eric Bright, in tears. He looked around the room. There was Jeanna. He walked over to the chair and knelt down in front of her looking into her serene face. She was in a deep sleep. Randy was now totally confused. He began to think. "You are so beautiful, such a wonderful person. I wish my life was different."

"I must go someplace. What should I do? What can I do?" He looked back at the Doctor lying on the floor. He thought. "I have money. I have identification. I have a car. I have an education. I have everything I need to go. I don't need anybody."

He thought. "There is more money in the safe." He stood up, went over to the picture on the wall, and opened it like a door. He turned the knob and cranked the handle down; pulling the door open. There were stacks of money. He filled his travel bag without counting. He knew from experience there was probably $75, 000. He looked back at Jeanna. Her head moved.

Jeanna's eyes opened. She looked straight at Randy. Her eyes widened with fear. She tried to speak, but the tape only allowed her to make muffled sounds. She tried to squirm away, but was stuck in the chair. She looked down at the ground and saw Bright's body. Randy spoke.

"There is no need to be afraid of me." She looked at the dead body again. "He was going to kill both of us; he pulled a gun on me but ended up shooting himself. You are safe now. I am not going to harm you. I never wanted to harm anyone. He made me do it." He glanced at the body. "He had control over me since I was very young. He made me do some very terrible things. I only wanted a real life. I will take the tape off your mouth if you promise me you won't scream." She agreed. He pulled the tape back.

For some reason, Jeanna believed him. She actually felt safe and secure. "Thank you, Albion, thank you, but I don't understand, I have so many questions." Small tears built up in her eyes.

Randy heard voices in the outer office. "I must go, forgive me, please." He walked around the corner, and into the elevator, and pushed the button labeled one. The elevator silently started downward. The ride was very fast. It was on the ground in about thirty seconds. The doors opened, and Randy confidently walked into the alley and headed toward his car. He had parked it a few blocks away.

"Oh, thank God you are here. I was sure I heard a gunshot in the back office." Rudy had shown her his badge as he got off the elevator. The cleaning woman had gone back into the hallway from the outer office five minutes before they got off the elevator, because she was frightened and was waiting for the elevator.

"Stay right here. Is the office open? Is the back office open? Where is the door to the back office?" Rudy asked.

"The front office is open, but I don't have keys to the back office. The door is through his main consulting room. There is another door behind his desk." She explained.

Rudy and Joe entered carefully, listening as they slowly walked into the office. They took turns moving toward the back office. They looked cautiously behind every chair and checked the two closets. They entered the front office. "Anybody there?" They yelled. There was no answer. Again they yelled. "Anybody there?" There was no answer.

"Joe, get ready to break the door down." They moved closer to the door and stood on either side. "NYPD, anyone there?" They knocked on the door.

"Help me, help me!" she cried. Jeanna had finally heard them. Randy had left the first time he heard them call. By the time they broke the door in, the elevator was on the ground floor. Randy was already in his Thunderbird heading for the turnpike.

As Randy approached the turnpike out of the City, he daydreamed. "I have money. I have knowledge. I have identification. I have everything I need. My only hope is that I can find peace in my life." He adjusted the radio to a classical music station. And while Beethoven's Bagatelle in G Minor began, he thought to himself. "I wonder what Seattle is like?" He gazed at the open highway on that wonderful Sunday morning and contentedly anticipated his future. "It looked great from the airplane."

THE END